THE KING'S RANSOM

The Bewildering Adventures
of King Bewilliam
Book Two

DEVORAH FOX

Mike Byrnes and Associates, Inc.
355 Keewaydin Lane
Port Aransas, Texas 78373

Also in *The Bewildering Adventures of King Bewilliam* series:
The Lost King, Book One

http://devorahfox.com
ISBN: 0-9778245-3-5
ISBN-13: 978-0-9778245-3-3

DEDICATION

to Gabrielle Rico. I will always treasure the time I spent in her workshops, the most fun I ever had writing

and to everyone who read *The Lost King* and asked for more.

AUTHOR'S NOTE

.

THANKS TO

Mike Byrnes and Barbara Sanchez who always did and still do support my noveling efforts.

Jerry Bateman for his wisdom which continues to guide me. Miss you, Jerry.

Mike Green, my longtime secret weapon.

John Rojas who indulges me.

Chip Cooper, a knight in shining armor.

The members of the Rockport Writers Group, Port A Pens, and South Texas Scribes who never fail to inspire and teach. Special thanks to Kay Butzin, Alice Marks, Gloria Vasquez, and all the officers for all the time and effort that they put into these groups so that the rest of us can benefit.

Alesha Escobar, Samantha LaFantasie, Francene Stanley, and Cecelia Robert, for their advice and tips.

The Office of Letters and Light for National Novel Writing Month and Camp NaNoWriMo without which I probably never would have started *The Lost King* or *The King's Ransom,* and to Getrude Matshe of How to Write a Book in 40 Hours for leading the charge to the finish line.

Ian Ridout for engineering expertise, brainstorming, cheerleading, and greeting me at the end of a long writing day with a NaNoWriMoTini.

King Bewilliam's knights and ladies who encourage me. Special thanks to Diana Fabrie, Alan White, Kenneth Scott, Joyce Walters, DeeDee Shields, Andrea Dobson, John Howell, Phyllis Sayre, the Parrot Heads of Port Aransas, and Mike Daigle.

and The Lost King for continued inspiration.

CHAPTER ONE

Robin's stomach cramped, folded in on itself from emptiness. His mouth was so dry he thought that his tongue might have shriveled. His body demanded food and drink but he had no appetite. Though he could picture the groaning board feasts that he had enjoyed as King of Bell Castle the memories did not rouse any yearning.

He put one increasingly reluctant foot before the other. Like the morning mist, Robin's enthusiasm for the journey had burned off hours ago. The sunlight hurt. Dust rising from the road irritated his nose. Shortening days told of the approaching autumn although the temperature here was still summer-hot. The air was heavy with moisture and the sky an uneasy gray as though threatening rain yet it was cloudless.

Where was he bound? Nowhere. Robin envied the travelers he passed, all with destinations. Somewhere to go and a reason to go there. People who would miss them when they left, rejoice when they arrived. Robin wondered why he even bothered to take another step. Why not simply stop, right here? Stripped of his title "king" even "husband" and "father" Robin felt hollow, light. With nothing to anchor him to this world it was as though he could easily turn to dust and vanish into the air.

Who would care? Who would miss him, a royal failure? Not his apparently faithless wife. His sons? Where were his sons? He could only assume that the Queen had taken them with her.

He paid little attention to the trees, shrubs, and grasses lining the way. Their odd spindly spiky appearance had long since ceased to startle him. Their color was naturally more anemic yellow or sage than blue-green, very different from the foliage of his home kingdom.

Kingdom. Though he was King no longer the Chalklands would always be his home. Should he go there? And do what? Work the fields, pull a plow alongside those who had once served him? Able-bodied and in the prime of life, Robin did not lack for talents and skills, many of them quite practical, but he had been a king, a husband, a father. What could he be if not that?

He glanced at the aged mount walking beside him, head hanging. Usually willing but not always able, the chestnut nag was almost too swaybacked to ride. As if aware that he had Robin's attention, Thief looked up with mournful eyes. Robin realized that the horse must be hungry, thirsty, and no doubt tired as well. Robin might not want to eat but he ought to at least water his horse. They had wandered a long distance today.

Robin's cat, Meeyoo, whined from deep in a rucksack hung from Thief's saddle casting her vote for getting some respite. As a kitten she had demonstrated her willingness to carry her own weight by trotting beside him until Robin decided that they could make better time if he carried her in the sack. Now when they traveled Meeyoo rode like a queen in a sedan chair. At night she curled up on his chest and purred him to sleep.

Robin said, "I hear you two. I'll look for a place to stop." He thought he remembered there being a public house on this road. Sweet Water served food and wine as well as ale. He had stopped there on more than one occasion.

The short scraggly trees here cast little shade. Their blade-shaped leaves had dropped revealing gnarly branches studded with needle-sharp thorns as long as fingers. Through the trees' leafless screen he spied a structure set back a bit from the road.

The three-story, half-timbered building along a creek was indeed Sweet Water, home to Eian, maker and purveyor of a particularly robust blend of fortified wine.

Robin watered Thief and entered the house. The warm smell of cooked food and the tangy sweet aromas of wine and ale greeted his nose. The dimly-lit interior was not much cooler than the outside even though the wooden shutters stood wide open but at least it afforded some respite from the sun.

A slender man with salt-and-pepper hair, neatly trimmed beard, and sparkling eyes, Eian greeted Robin warmly and invited him to sit at one of the long wooden tables where other wayfarers enjoyed ale or a plate of food and exchanged tales of their travels. He poured Robin some ale from a jug and took a seat on the opposite bench. "I must say, it's been some time since you were last here."

Indeed, in many ways it had been a lifetime. Robin was a man greatly changed from the one who had last broken bread at Sweet Water. He told Eian of his travails, of the struggles he had faced trying to make a new life for himself after being displaced from the only one he had ever known. It was a story that he had been telling often lately, of life-changing loss, though recounting it grew no easier with repetition nor did he gain any new insights.

Robin sighed. "I would imagine this is not the first time you have heard a tale like that."

Eian smiled gently. "Nor will it be the last."

"I'm sorry, I must have bored you terribly."

"Not at all," said Eian. "True, I do hear many tales of loss. While the stories may be familiar to me I try to remember that for the teller the pain is very fresh." He refilled Robin's cup. "If it's been so hard to start anew why not go back to being who you were, do what you know how to do?"

Robin tried not to laugh. One simply could not stride into a village square, declare himself king, and expect everyone to kneel. He would need proof of his claim and supporters to help defend it but the deeds and titles to his lands were gone, his vassals scattered. He hung his head. "Impossible."

"We can't really know what's possible and what isn't until we try, wouldn't you agree? Have you tried?"

Robin raised his head. He hadn't. He had just assumed . . .

Eian shrugged. "Perhaps you lack the courage."

Robin nearly rose from his seat. "I am not a coward!" The others at the table glanced at him with startled expressions. He had faced and bested multi-headed dragons, stared down angry sword-wielding men bent on beheading him, and lived to tell of it but Eian wouldn't know any of that. Robin lowered himself to his seat.

Eian gave him another knowing smile. "Where are you headed now then?"

Robin had no ready answer. "I don't know. I find myself . . ."

"Yes?"

Robin shook his head. "No, it's a foolish idea."

Eian said, "You can speak of it if you wish. No extra charge and I won't tell a soul."

Robin chuckled. "I find myself thinking about my sons. I would like to know how they fare."

"Of course you do. Tell me about them," said Eian.

Robin sipped his ale and pictured the boys as he had last seen them: not quite yet men, but definitely no longer children. "Conrad is the eldest, smart, quick yet he seemed to have little interest in his training."

The first born son, Conrad would be heir to the throne and so would need to master the kingly arts and sciences. Nevertheless Conrad's masters would report to Robin that the boy would leave assignments half completed, would disappear from the training grounds only to be found later under a tree reading a book.

"His younger brother, Zachary, on the other hand was always smiling, playful, full of energy. He liked to invent different roles for himself. He would pretend that he was a bird, a monk, the sister that he didn't have." That particular persona had earned Zachary a serious scolding from his baffled parents. "Dale, he called her Dale. He would behave as if he were Dale for days. Sometimes it would be difficult to get him to stop and be

4

Zachary." Zachary would turn sullen when forced to drop his latest character.

Eian said, "All children are like that, trying on different identities before they settle down to who they need to be. Surely you remember being a boy and play-acting that you were a knight, a prince, a king?"

Robin shrugged. He did not mention that he had been a prince destined to be king and no play-acting had been required.

"And you mean to find them?"

Perhaps on some unspoken level that had been his intent when he set out. He knew not where they were, only where they were not, making it hard to set an itinerary. He would not go back from whence he had just come and there was no point in going to the Chalklands. Nothing for him there any longer. King Bewilliam was truly as dead as people believed him to be. Now he was just Robin. His kingdom was gone, his lands, wealth, his title, his role—everything that had defined him. No longer did a crown rest on his red curls. Instead he wore the coif of a rough tunic.

Gone too was his family. The whereabouts of his wife, the Queen, were a mystery. Perhaps she ruled in another realm at some other king's side. The thought of it left Robin baffled, angry, and hurt.

He couldn't think of his two sons without a stabbing pain. Where were they? What had become of them? Did they think of him at all and if so was it just to curse him? Or did they wish he were with them, to teach them, to answer questions, questions they would have aplenty now that they were coming into their majority? He should be with them preparing Conrad to be king someday and establishing Zachary as the prior of an abbey, a fitting position for a king's second son. Tramping around the countryside doing hard labor was no life for a man of Robin's breeding and years.

Eian excused himself to serve a new customer who had taken a seat at the table beside Robin, a young man whose deeply shadowed eyes and hunched shoulders made him look older than his years. The long fingers that wrapped around his cup were stained black at the tips. He introduced himself as Terrowin, an advocate who traveled from town to town, representing plaintiffs and defendants in legal disputes.

"Litigations become more complex and time-consuming. A single case can easily take a year. I just completed one that took longer than that. The defendant wasn't the only one who was tested and tried. I'm expected to know the finest points of law and believe me, there's a lot to know. Changes every day, it seems."

Terrowin said he had studied for many years, "three of them in silence because our masters felt it more important for us to listen than to speak. Then years of practical experience. I served as a notary public while still at the University of Wellington."

"Ambitious," Robin said.

A fond smile softened Terrowin's weary face. "My parents labored long hours and denied themselves much to send me to school. Not just any school, the best school."

That's what loving parents did, Robin found himself thinking.

"I couldn't let them bear the entire burden of my training. I am proud to say, though, that their investment in me was justified. I have done well and can provide for them as well as myself."

"You've worked hard, then."

"I did, but I think I've also always had something of a natural bent for the practice. I was an argumentative child and liked nothing better than to stop childhood battles by getting the parties to compromise." He chuckled. "I also took to writing quickly, which serves me well."

Many documents got generated in the course of a proceeding and it was rare that the litigants could read or write. Terrowin waggled his blackened fingers. "So I make the necessary records. Keeps me busy, I can tell you. Courts want written accountings of all who attended, everything that was said, all the evidence presented, for their archives."

Robin nodded. Indeed there were circumstances that demanded more than simply an avowal or pronouncement. Were that not so Robin could simply appear at the Chalklands and declare that he was the King. Without the supporting titles and deeds, those would be empty words.

A notion fluttered to the forefront of his brain like a moth approaching a flame. "Wait," he said, clutching the young man's arm. "You said that you record agreements. What happens to them, to the documents?"

"I give them to whoever pays for my services, of course," said Terrowin.

"You didn't keep copies?"

Terrowin sighed. "For myself, no. I don't need a copy. The court always wants one for its archives should anyone ever have a question about what transpired."

"Archives?"

"Yes, of course. The abbey keeps records of births, death, marriages, divorces, debts, deeds—"

Terrowin continued to talk but Robin no longer listened. The moth of an idea had grown to the size of an eagle and the flapping of its huge wings demanded all of Robin's attention.

CHAPTER TWO

Could it be possible, Robin wondered? Could Mathus Abbey have records of his family's history and holdings?

So devastated had Robin been to witness the ruin of Bell Castle he had wandered as if in a trance far from the Chalklands. He could go back now, visit the abbey. Supported by deeds, titles, records of his lineage, Robin could assert his claim.

The flapping of the eagle's wings had scattered the fog that had clouded his mind, his spirit. He would restore his kingdom. It wouldn't be easy, might be the hardest thing he ever attempted but Eian was right. Robin could not declare it impossible until he had tried and failed.

He stood, collected his cup, and scooped up the remains of his meal to share with Meeyoo. He stepped outside to find that while the sun was as strong as ever it no longer hurt. Energized by its golden glow he took to the road once again, now with a spring in his step. As if he shared Robin's revitalized spirit even Thief carried himself taller.

The road had little traffic on this sultry afternoon. A well-used packhorse track it had earlier this morning been crowded and Robin had exchanged pleasantries with other wayfarers. Now alone with his thoughts he realized that as important as official records were his plan would require more than documents. Even after he had reaffirmed his claim to the land he would need money, much more of it than the coins he had in his purse. His steps slowed as he considered how he might along the way to the Chalklands raise a king's ransom.

As a prince he had been a curious fellow and had mastered not only hunting, riding, and fighting but many useful skills. He could play a musical instrument, milk a cow, repair rent fabrics. Now he could also fashion and sharpen a blade and knew quite a bit about the smelting of metals, new expertise he had acquired in his recent tribulations. While practical, none of those talents would bring him the necessary bounty.

Lost in thought, he ambled on until Thief tugged at the reins. They must have been traveling longer than Robin realized. Thief was hungry and thirsty. Robin looked about. There was little grass in the roadside verge, only parched shrubs and stubby leafless trees.

"Stay here a minute," he told Thief and stepped off the path. Perhaps deeper into the foliage he'd find water and green plants. He plucked a tiny round leaf from a shrub. Its dusty sage-green color made it appear dry but to the touch it was springy and fresh. Robin rubbed it between his fingers and found it moist. It gave off a light herbal aroma. He returned to the road and held the leaf under the horse's nose. Thief's nostrils twitched. Robin led the horse to the shrub and Thief stripped off mouthfuls of leaves with his big teeth. Ah hah, Robin thought, I've learned something new. Those sage-green bushes were aplenty. With any luck they would sustain Thief until they reached the Chalklands.

Meeyoo left the confines of the rucksack to stretch her legs. An efficient huntress she pounced on the undergrowth and quickly snagged a small lizard. Robin remembered with bittersweet clarity a bleak and desperate time when she had hunted for him and brought him her kill, a starling.

The animals somewhat refreshed, Robin returned to the road and resumed walking. Finally, in the distance he spied a crossing. As they neared the intersection Robin saw a road marker, a stone block. Numerals carved into the stone indicated the distance to the next settlements. Robin chose the shorter one. It lay east not north, the direction of the Chalklands, but it wouldn't be too much of a detour. Robin hoped the settlement would be large enough that he would find some work. He tugged on the reins and led the horse onto the new path.

They hadn't traveled far when the first hint of their destination came into view. A veritable manmade mountain, a motte stood thirty feet tall. Stone walls with crenellations terraced the motte and a cylindrical stone keep pierced the sky. Red pennants fluttered in the breeze. No simple settlement, what lay ahead was a fortress.

The closer Robin drew to it, the more intimidating the fortress appeared, so completely did it dominate the landscape. The woods gave way to a clearing empty of trees and shrubs, foliage having been removed to make room for peasants' huts and farmland. However Robin saw no habitations of any kind, no struggling family plots eked out of the rough country, no small pens for pigs or fowl. The remains of such dotted the land but they had crumbled and fallen to ruin, overtaken by grasses and vines.

Unfamiliar with the area, he knew nothing of its history. Why was the acreage vacant? Was it an embattled region and all the subjects from the poorest to the wealthiest had taken cover inside the fortifications?

Or had something more sinister driven everyone behind the high walls, something like a curse or a spell? Despite the heat of the day, Robin felt a chill. Magic. Few things frightened him as did magic. He could and had with aplomb faced down the most fearsome human foes, been threatened with the sword that now hung by his side, taken Thief from a highwayman bent on Robin's destruction. He saved a woman from peril, dispatched many a dragon. But if truth be told, he felt helpless against the dark arts.

Scorched timber and blackened brick spoke of a great fire. Given the dryness of the surrounding foliage, a blaze could easily have been sparked by a lightning strike.

Or a dragon.

And Robin felt an idea take shape.

Now doubly eager to enter the fortress, Robin mounted Thief. To be seen riding a horse albeit an old one might grant him a stature that walking would not. At least he would be able to meet a mounted castle guard at eye level.

He guided Thief onto the planked footbridge crossing the moat and leading to a hefty stone archway. To his right and left, a steep escarpment rose from the moat to the base of the tall curtain wall enclosing the inner ward. Should intruders manage to thwart the moat they would have no place to hide. Cleared of trees and bushes, the sloping curtain-wall footing afforded no concealment.

As if the moat and fortifications weren't discouragement enough, stone gargoyles perched on the archway. Snarling dragons, long-toothed lions, and winged demons glared at him from above. Their fresh and unweathered appearance suggested that they had been installed after the calamity that had driven the people behind the fortress walls. Had the stone grotesques already been in place, they had failed to prevent the catastrophe.

Were he King Bewilliam he would appear at the gate riding upon a well-groomed and liveried steed, garbed not in rough leggings and tunic but in fine brocaded garments that while dusty from the road would be of unmistakably luxurious fabric. He would simply present his royal credentials to the gatekeeper. Arriving uninvited, Robin of course would not expect to be granted an immediate audience with the ruler. But for his appearing without an army or even an escort his motives might even be suspect. Likely he would be detained at the gatehouse until his pedigree, truthfulness, and intentions could be confirmed but courtesy would be extended. He would be offered food and drink, his horse's needs seen to by the lord's stable hands.

But he was just Robin, a simple wayfarer. Certainly there was nothing about his appearance that implied royalty. His red curls had grown long and scraggly. His beard needed trimming. He wore a simple muslin tunic and woolen leggings. True, his footwear was somewhat unusual. Sturdier than a turn shoe, his heavy leather boots had been made by his court's shoemaker on a last sized for Robin's foot to accommodate his penchant for long walks about his kingdom. Those same walks had imparted his skin with a golden glow but his many hours out in the sun of late had darkened it even further. There was little chance of him being taken for "blue blood."

A single rider didn't present much of a threat but settlements had homeless, penniless beggars aplenty and did not need any more. Guards would see it as their duty to turn mendicants away, perhaps to a nearby church. The fortress's defenders would be especially wary if the realm had been plagued with evil magic.

Robin made a mental inventory of his possessions: an old horse. A knife and a cup. A sword of his own manufacture. A rucksack with a change of clothing. A cat, who might not be welcomed at all as many regarded felines as familiars, consorts of witches and wizards.

And buried deep in the sack, ermine pelts, all he had left of his kingly cloak. No, he would not try to pass those off as royal credentials although that's what they were. To do so would likely result in him being accused of being a thief.

Robin passed under the archway. Before him stretched the drawbridge leading to the first entry: a portcullis gate flanked by drum towers adjoining the curtain walls. In the distance rose another motte atop which perched the formidable keep, itself enclosed by a wall.

Thief had no sooner set foot on the drawbridge when an armored rider came out to meet them. Robin imagined that he did not present an intimidating figure, a middle-aged man in rough breeches and tunic riding a swaybacked old horse. A few strands of gray streaked Robin's red beard and curly hair at the temples. To his credit Robin could say that owing to his recent travails, he was fitter and stronger than he had been as a pampered king. The challenges he'd lately met had built up his shoulders, arms, and chest. All the walking he had done before he had acquired Thief had strengthened his legs and whittled his waist as had many days with little or no food. Still he doubted that a lone rider on an old horse would be perceived as much of a threat.

"Halt there!" said the guard. He sat tall astride his robust black horse, his red and black tunic in as fine repair as his mount's tack. The guard's chainmail, sword, and helmet gleamed in the late afternoon light. "Who goes there and what business do you have with Lomroddoy Fortress?"

Robin studied the crest on the guard's livery and horse's tack. Like these foreign lands they were unknown to him. The heraldic symbols put him on alert. To be sure the overall message was one of fierce aggression. The red color signified a warrior and the image of the boar bespoke of one who fought to the death. Black told of grief.

Robin pulled up on Thief's reins. "I am Robin. I am a dragon slayer."

CHAPTER THREE

Below his conical helmet, the guard's brow furrowed in a derisive glare and his tone of voice was just as skeptical. "You?" He scoffed. "Your horse is old. You have no armor."

"Armor, I have learned, affords little protection against a dragon," replied Robin, and it was true. "The best defense is a good offense." With a sweep of his arm, Robin indicated the charred surroundings. "Would armor have prevented this?"

The guard's shoulders slumped. "Come with me," he said, and Robin knew he had guessed correctly. The fortress's occupants believed that some unnatural malevolence had laid waste to the land. Robin followed the guard across the drawbridge and through the gate, his pulse quickening. His gamble had paid off. Believing the conflagration to be the work of a dragon, the lord had chosen not to fight but had instead raised fortifications and retreated within.

The guard led through the covered gateway to the inner entryway also defended by a portcullis gate. Leaving Thief in charge of stable hands Robin returned to the gatehouse to confer with the high constable of the fortress's army. Arms crossed over their chest and skeptical expressions told Robin that neither the guard nor the constable truly believed his claim to be an experienced dragon slayer. They didn't need to. Dragon fighting was perilous work with little chance of success while the price of failure was agonizing death. Few volunteered as there were less risky ways to prove one's mettle or demonstrate fealty. Those who went up against a dragon did so under orders and often deserted long before they ever neared the beast.

The constable had required little urging to take on a dragon slayer-for-hire. "It's your hide," he said with a shrug.

In exchange for endangering that hide, Robin negotiated provisions for the quest and a bounty for the dragon, half to be paid now, the other upon successful completion. Robin could hardly wait to tackle and accomplish the mission. The handsome reward would get the restoration of his kingdom off to a strong start.

The fortress's armorer was summoned. He was surprised not only at what weapons Robin requisitioned but also at what he declined. Robin tried not to smile. The armorer could not know that as a prince, Robin had received extensive training in all manner of warfare. As well, experience had sharpened his skills and broadened his knowledge in ways that even the best teacher could not anticipate.

First Robin would have to find the dragon. The most recent attack had left damage that was easy enough to spot. But dragons could fly and leave no tracks pointing the way to their lair.

Robin considered the countryside through which he had just passed. The closer he had gotten to the fortress, the flatter the terrain became. He recalled few hills tall enough to provide a cave in which a dragon could hide. The motte upon which the fortress stood was the highest ground. Behind it stretched the sea.

Could the dragon have come from there? Robin doubted it. He knew there were sea-dwelling behemoths. Every map indicated "here there be monsters" but he never heard of one coming ashore and spitting fire.

Robin put the fortress behind him and set out on the track, his purse heavy with the coins of his advance payment, his blood running hot in his veins. He pictured himself quickly vanquishing the beast. He hadn't met one yet that he couldn't defeat. It was true that in all but one of his previous battles he relied on the support of a troop of brave knights but he was not daunted.

Robin pushed away the fearful disadvantage of fighting a dragon singlehandedly. He had confidence in his sword and his swordsmanship. He did not doubt that if he could get close enough he could deliver a mortal blow. Therein lay the challenge.

Flames had scarred the vegetation more heavily on the right side of the track than the left. Robin guided Thief off the track and into the woods. Fire had consumed leaves and small limbs but many of the shrubs still bristled with thorns that Thief tried to avoid with mincing steps, slowing their progress. Ash rose up in puffs with every one of the horse's footfalls and the smell of burned timber was strong. With a whine, Meeyoo complained of having spent too much time in Robin's sack. She was mollified when he allowed her to ride draped across the saddle between his knees. The woods' mingled scents set her whiskers twitching. As he rode Robin studied his surroundings for clues that they might be nearing their target. Gradually the black and splintered growth gave way to plants that were relatively free of damage.

His animal companions detected the imminent danger before he did. Thief's pace slowed. Meeyoo's fur stood on end and her ears flattened. Her shoulders hunched and a low growl emitted from her throat.

"Yes," Robin said. "This is as far we go today." The light was fading and he didn't want to confront the beast in the dark. They would camp here. He would not even make a fire. If the dragon were near, he could probably smell them. They did not have to provide light and make it even easier for the beast to find them.

By the light of a setting sun, Robin fed and watered Thief from sturdy sacks, part of the fortress's provisions. Meeyoo typically hunted at dusk but Robin was leery of her straying too far afield so he kept her close, tempting her with bites of cheese from his own supper. He bedded down and spent a fitful night only half-sleeping, on guard against any suspicious movement. Every little sound of woodland creatures hunting their own prey startled him to full wakefulness.

A tremor under his back brought him to high alert and he sat upright, his ears attuned to the woods' noises before his eyes adjusted to the dark. Was the dragon on the move? Robin sprang to his feet, his hand on the hilt of his sword. Muscles taut, he stood at attention for many long tense moments. At last, he determined it was safe to lie down but he spent the rest of the night dozing fitfully.

The dawn light filtering through the trees woke him. He saw to it that both animals ate but he skipped breakfast, all the better to be light on his feet in the battle.

"You go no further, Meeyoo." He grasped her by the scruff of the neck, returned her to the rucksack, and hung it from Thief's saddle. "You too, Thief." Being astride a horse would give him the advantage of added height and Thief was sturdy and loyal but he was also slow and not battle trained. "Stay here," he said, "or if it goes badly, run. Save yourself." He patted the horse's flank. "But don't worry. The only one it's going badly for is the dragon."

He tucked his chosen weapon into his belt and slung the heavy sack of ammunition over his shoulder. He strapped the other supplies to his back. Robin hoped that he would not have to walk far with the weighty load. He didn't want to expend all his energy before the battle even started. He set out, attentive to vegetation crushed by a heavy animal stomping about and the beast's dank odor.

At last he spotted the dragon's lair. Set in a rough clearing of trampled plants was a den framed by a fallen tree overrun with vines that had grown unusually long with large fleshy leaves colored a vivid green. Those unfamiliar with the ways of dragons attributed the lush growth around dragons' lairs to magic but Robin knew it was due to fertilization by the beasts' dung. By the den's dimensions, Robin reckoned the dragon it housed would be a juvenile. Their smaller size made younger dragons a less formidable opponent but only by a margin. Unlike their elders, juvenile dragons were impulsive and took unpredictable risks.

Robin unloaded his supplies and set up his defenses. He took the three shields that he had gotten from the armorer and set them standing in the dirt behind him at slight angles. Highly polished, they caught the light in the clearing and when Robin stood before them, reflected back his image. To the dragon it would appear that there were four combatants rather than a single fighter. Robin's weapon-of-choice would give him the advantage of being able to fight from a distance.

Now all he had to do was wait and he didn't have to wait long. His rustling about had gotten the animal's attention. Robin felt the earth shake under his feet, heard the dragon's lumbering, and smelled its fusty odor before it emerged from its shelter so he was ready, his weapon loaded.

A verdant green, lean, and muscled juvenile, the dragon stood and blinked at the blindingly bright vision of four gleaming adversaries. Robin didn't wait for the dragon to get its bearings but with his slingshot let fly the first of several rocks, intending to fell the beast by knocking it unconscious or at least dazing it. The creature would fall to the ground whereupon Robin would rush in and finish it off with his sword.

Robin had aimed for the dragon's forehead but the rock hit the creature in the eye. The dragon opened its mouth to let out a ferocious scream of pain. Smoke billowed from its nostrils signaling the vengeful fire to follow. As the first flames sprouted, Robin's second rock, already in flight, flew into the dragon's mouth and to Robin's amazement, went down the creature's throat where it stuck, choking off the beast's howl. The dragon stamped its feet, shook its head and snorted, trying to dislodge the rock to no avail. Furious, it raised its head. Next, Robin knew, it would bring its fierce head down in a flame-throwing arc. His pulse pounding louder in his ears than the dragon's cries, Robin stepped behind one of his shields ready to launch another rock when the head came into range.

The dragon's throttled roar became more of a strangled gargle. Robin saw the beast's chest heave as it tried to expel the rock. The more the dragon struggled the thinner became the puffs of smoke while its throat pulsed and bulged. The dragon pounded the ground with its feet and flailed its wings. It hunched its shoulders and pulled in its head, then thrust out its neck and with a massive effort tried to cough up the rock. Before Robin's incredulous eyes, the dragon's neck exploded in a burst of flame and smoke, flinging wide the rock, scaly flesh, and blood. The head flew into the air, sailed over the trees, and landed with a crash in the distant brush. The body collapsed where it stood, shaking the ground.

Astonished, Robin too landed with a crash on his rump and sat for a moment in disbelief. In all his dragon-slaying experience he had never seen such a thing nor fought a shorter fight. At last he caught his breath and stood. He gathered up the shields and went in search of the head. He would need the horns as proof of his accomplished mission.

With the shields strapped to his back. Robin trudged back to where he had left Thief and Meeyoo, dragging the dragon's head by a rope lashed around the horns. Though the battle had been brief Robin was exhausted, drained of the energy surge sparked by the threat of death.

He found that Thief had retreated into a covert of brush. Robin set down his load, spoke soothingly to the horse, and released Meeyoo from her cover in the pack. She inched toward the dragon's head and sniffed, curious perhaps as to whether this would be good to eat, and backed away with a growl.

The search for the dragon's lair had been long but the trip back to the fortress took even longer. The dragon's head was too awkward for Thief to carry and had to be towed behind over rough ground where it caught on every stump and fallen branch. At last they reached the track that led to the barbican gate. Robin felt his pulse quicken. Soon he would receive his reward. He would be on his way toward reestablishing his kingdom. He would find the documents, find his sons. Together they would restore and refurnish Bell Castle, reclaim the land and its bound servants.

Lomroddoy Fortress's wall came into view and Robin straightened himself to his full height.

He hadn't even started across the moat when a guard galloped across the footbridge to meet him on the track. Robin recognized him as the guard who had stopped him yesterday.

"Halt there!" he said as he had the day before.

Robin slowed. "It is I, Robin, the dragon slayer. I have been victorious. The dragon has been vanquished. You need fear it no longer."

The guard made a slow circuit around Robin and his cargo but said not a word. Instead, he pulled a red cloth from his sleeve, held his arm high, and waved, then drew his sword and held it pointing at Robin's chest.

Two riders clattered toward them, another guard and the constable. They pulled up and like the first guard the constable examined the dragon's head secured to Thief's saddle. "That is no dragon," he said.

"What?"

"It's too small to be a dragon."

"It's a juvenile, not grown to full size. Look at the horns. Would have you have preferred to allow it to mature?"

"That is the head of an ox."

"Ox? What are you saying? Look at it. Look at the snout, the teeth, the green skin, the scales. Surely you see——"

"That can't be a dragon. You could not have possibly vanquished a dragon singlehandedly." The constable drew his sword as well. "Do not move." He directed the guard to untie the animal's head from Thief's saddle and attach it to his own. "I see that you seek to deceive us, cheat us out of a substantial bounty."

Who was cheating whom, Robin asked himself with a sinking feeling. This couldn't be happening, not again! As if dragon slaying wasn't risky enough——

"How could I possibly have made up an ox's head to look like that?"

The constable exchanged glances with the two guards. "Magic," he said, his tone grave. "That's an ox's head made to look like a dragon or you felled a dragon yourself, which is impossible. Either way, you must be a sorcerer. Take his weapons, his sack," he commanded.

"What!" Robin reached for his sword but was stopped by the prick of a blade against his neck.

One of the guards dismounted, took Robin's sword and knife, and tucked them in his belt. He lifted the rucksack off the pommel of Thief's saddle.

"Check for more weapons," said the constable.

The guard raised the sack's flap. Meeyoo poked her head up over the rucksack's opening.

CHAPTER FOUR

"Saints preserve us!" yelled the guard, dropping the sack.

Meeyoo crawled out. She raced across the footbridge and disappeared in the shadows under the archway.

"My cat!" Robin cried. "Meeyoo!" He tugged on Thief's reins to urge him in the direction Meeyoo had taken.

The guard slapped the flat of his sword's blade against Robin's chest. "Don't you move!"

"But that's my cat! She doesn't know where she is."

"So you admit it. You are no simple wayfarer, but are a sorcerer, and that was your familiar. Your manner, your speech . . ."

Robin cursed himself. His royal blood had betrayed him. The constable was right; a commoner would not have spoken with such authority, would have shown timidity and obeisance. Trying to sound more humble and cowed, he said, "I'm not a sorcerer. I am a wayfarer, a mercenary. I go from town to town, earning my keep by slaying dragons. Meeyoo is just a cat."

"Do you think me a fool? You are a sorcerer and you have unleashed your familiar on our land." He commanded Robin to dismount and ordered the guards to bind his hands.

22

"What should we do with him?" one of the guards asked, stepping back and putting some distance between Robin and himself.

"Shall we kill him?" asked the second guard. He drew his sword and made ready to run Robin through.

No! thought Robin, I can't die today, not now, not when my life is just beginning again.

"Nay, not like that," said the constable. "You can't kill a sorcerer that way. That will destroy only his body. His demonic spirit will simply find another home."

"Like in one of us?" asked the first guard in a whispery voice.

The second guard kept his sword at the ready. "What would you have us do with him then?"

The constable said, "We should take the sorcerer back to the castle. Put him in the dungeon. He will be far removed from anyone else until we can dispose of him safely."

The guards escorted Robin at sword point across the moat to the archway.

Thief neighed and brought up the rear.

"My horse!" Robin said.

The bloodthirsty second guard gave a glance back. "Let's kill him," he said.

"No!" Robin cried. "He's not a magic charm, he's just a horse, a faithful old horse. Please!"

"Take back our provisions and supplies which the sorcerer obtained by treachery," said the constable. "Let the horse go. He is aged and feeble. He will die in the woods, no threat to us."

Robin's pleas fell on deaf ears. The guards prodded him forward. Tears stinging his eyes, he risked a rearward glance to see his horse plodding after him. "Thief! Turn back. Go! I'll return soon, I'll find you!"

Thief stopped, his head low. Then he turned, walked across the footbridge, and down the track from whence they had come.

Under the arch, Robin searched for Meeyoo but she was nowhere in sight.

Sword points at his back nudged Robin along the drawbridge. The guards escorted him between twin stone drum towers and through the covered gateway but this time they did not stop at the gatehouse. The main portcullis gate lifted and Robin found himself inside the fortress's high curtain walls.

On full alert, he took in as many details as possible about the fortress's construction and layout. To his right stood the chapel, a small wooden building whose purpose was revealed by a cross on its arched door. To his left, a single-story rectangular stone structure was the barracks judging from the flight of stairs along its front wall that gave soldiers quick access to the walk along the top of the curtain wall. Tall rectangular watch towers pegged the four corners of the roughly square bailey, the great hall at its center. The guards urged Robin forward past wooden buildings housing kitchens, workshops, stables. Beyond them he spotted the serfs' simple dwellings and small plots.

Ahead another stone archway opened onto a footbridge crossing a second moat. At its terminus, steep steps climbed the motte on which stood the keep. Robin's heart was leaden. He suspected where he was headed. All too soon he learned he guessed right.

The guards escorted him not upstairs to the lord's personal chapel or his private chambers but down, down below the level that housed the food stores, ale vats, and wine casks.

The clammy dungeon smelled of mold, rotted wood, and yes, of despair and death. Its dirt floor was damp and cool under Robin's butt but not as cold as his heart. Lit only by whatever light filtered through a barred opening high above at ground level, the room was dim but his mood was darker. His death was certain. Without anything like a trial or even an inquiry, he had been taken for a sorcerer when he feared magic as much as did the guards.

Did they know who they had in their dungeon? He was a head of state, Bewilliam, King of Bell Castle, ruler of the Chalklands, and their treatment of him was a capital offense. Were it not for exhaustion Robin's anger could have burst into flame. When he got out of here—

Robin looked about. How would he get out of here? There appeared to be no way to leave except to die. The only question was how soon would he die and by what means? How did they deal with witches and sorcerers in this realm? Drowning? Burning?

Or did they mean to leave him here to die slowly of thirst or hunger? He hadn't eaten or drunk since last evening. He noted that his stomach ached and his mouth was drier than dust but the pain he felt most acutely was heartache. Poor Meeyoo! What would become of her? Was she still within the city's walls or had she escaped to the wood beyond? She knew no more about her new surroundings than he did. Would she find food and water? Robin reminded himself that she was a good huntress and reassured himself she would not starve. But what about shelter? Would she find a safe place to hide? And hide she must because now Robin was more certain than ever that this domain was bewitched. Why else would the guards be so quick to assume that he was a sorcerer and that Meeyoo was his familiar? Meeyoo was canny but could she defend herself against magic?

Robin shivered although the temperature of the underground room was actually a comfortable respite from the heat of the outdoors.

And what of Thief? Robin hoped that the horse would find his way back to the last creek that they had found. Would Thief know to nibble on those sage-colored bushes? And what then? Would some journeyer or peasant find Thief and take care of him, an old horse? Robin didn't want think about the alternative.

He propped his elbows on his knees and buried his face in his hands.

He could do nothing for either animal except feel guilty about its predicament. It was his fault that they were in peril. Had he not taken it into his head that he could reclaim his kingdom, he would not have accepted this dragon-slaying mission. Eian of Sweet Water was mistaken. It was wrong of Robin to have tried. He had failed and would die for his presumption, and two innocent lives would be lost.

Meeyoo and Thief trusted him. It was his responsibility to rescue them. Figuring out how to do that was a much more interesting line of thought than pondering his fate.

He studied his prison. Could he chip and tunnel through the masonry walls? With what? He had nary a tool at hand. The guards had taken his knife, and sword, his purse with the money that had been advanced him to kill the dragon. No doubt they had his pack too. Robin wondered what they would make of the ermine pelts buried in the bottom.

Without even a cup or spoon, how could he hope to make even the slightest dent in the bricked walls, especially as he had only one truly free hand with which to work? The other hand was shackled to a chain hanging from a ring bolted to the wall.

The cell had two openings. One was the heavy locked door. The other was the barred window a couple of feet over his head for which he was grateful even if he couldn't reach it. The iron bars were set not in a frame but directly into the wall. Even if he could free himself, somehow reach the window, and remove the bars, the opening was too small. He would not be able to fit through it.

Before he could even attempt any escape he would have to free himself from the shackle. Why the guards had bothered to chain him to the wall was a mystery. Were he truly a sorcerer, chains and locks would not defeat him. But he was merely a human. Chains and locks were formidable impediments.

Robin studied the heavy iron padlock that kept the shackle fastened on his wrist. Now that, that had possibilities. Robin smiled. He knew a little something about locks. As a young prince curious about the working of things, he had spent a rainy afternoon with the castle's locksmith. It had seemed to young Robin that locks were long on intimidating looks but not all that daunting as security devices. He was confident that he could pick the one that held his shackle fast, if he had the right tool.

Or any tool. Would that he had his purse. Maybe he could employ his steel as a tool. Even his belt would have been helpful. He might have been able to use the prong, but the guard had taken his belt as well. There was nothing in the room or on his person that would be of any use. His clothes were all made of soft fabric; nothing stiff or sturdy enough from which to fashion a pick. The instrument had to be rigid but it didn't have to be very big. Something the size of his little finger would do.

His little finger. In the twilight he regarded his hands. If he could get down to the bone, the bone of his little finger might work. The prospect of pain and dismemberment did not discourage him. Animals escaped traps by gnawing off limbs and they survived. He probably wouldn't even feel the pain, Robin thought. He was already numb with despair about the fate that was likely to befall Meeyoo and Thief if he didn't find them.

He poked his little finger into the lock's keyhole. Indeed, absent of flesh the finger bone would be the right size.

Robin slipped his finger into his mouth, tasted salt and dirt. He pressed his teeth against the finger and felt pressure but not pain. He clenched his jaw tighter. His finger throbbed and stung. He bit down harder but before he could break the skin, his finger's weight on the back of his tongue made him gag. He took his finger out and rubbed it, thinking this was proving more difficult than he had expected. He didn't want to bite off the finger, he wanted to skin it. Were his teeth sharp enough?

His desperate ruminations were interrupted by the sound of a voice.

"Me. You."

The hair on the back of Robin's neck rose. He lifted his head and looked around. The gray light cast shadows on the walls and floor but he saw no one and nothing else in the room. Yet he distinctly heard someone speak.

"Me. You," came the voice again. An unusual voice, not quite human yet the words were clear, unmistakable.

Robin shook his head. He must be hallucinating. The hunger, thirst, shock of his arrest, and fear of imminent and painful death must have loosened his mind. All this talk of sorcerers and familiars had planted ideas in his head. Still, he was certain he had heard someone speak.

Robin's mouth twitched in a small smile. "Me, you," had been his cat's first utterances. Then but a tiny kitten, she had camped out one night in his boot. From then on she stayed near him by day in his quarters, sleeping on his chest at night. When he made to go and leave her behind, she told him that she was going with him. "Me. You," she had said in no uncertain terms.

Robin heard it again. He looked up. A movement at the window caught his eye. Silhouetted in the fading light he saw a familiar shape against the bars.

"Oh, Meeyoo!" Robin replied. His heart swelled in his chest. "How did you find me? Are you all right?"

"Me, you! Me, you!" came her excited reply.

Robin took the first deep breath he had breathed since first being approached by the guard. "Oh, my faithful friend, I am indeed in a sorry predicament and I have yet to find a way out."

Aloud, Robin reviewed the escape strategies that he had entertained and rejected. "I think they mean to leave me to starve and wither away from thirst . . ." He stopped in mid-complaint. "I'm going to keep trying, Meeyoo, I haven't given up. I will fight with all the fight that I have left in me. Meanwhile you need to look out for yourself. The people in this fortress are not friendly to cats. You must get yourself outside these walls. Escape. Go find Thief. The two of you, make your way back to Sea Gate Fortress. You were welcome there."

At the window, Robin heard Meeyoo purr followed by a rustling. The shape of the cat vanished from view.

Robin's heart sank in dismay. He had sincerely meant that Meeyoo should go, save herself, only not so soon. He would have liked to have her company until he could see and hear no more.

He slipped into a torpor until a rustling overhead startled him alert. Again he saw Meeyoo's dark shape against the bars. He wondered if it was a dream or if it was an image conjured by wishful thinking, but then the form moved. Meeyoo poked her head between the bars.

"No! Meeyoo, stay out of here," he cried. "Run away!"

An object fell from her mouth, hit the floor, and bounced halfway to the door. He made out a shape the size of a sparrow. A dead bird. Tears stung Robin's eyes. Meeyoo had done it again, had heard of his need for food and had answered his plea. This time he thought that he just might be desperate enough to eat.

He stretched out his hand toward the bird but could not reach it for the chain. He felt his head and shoulders slump and sighed, even this last relief denied him.

No, wait, there might be a way. He stretched out on the floor to the full extent of his arm, torso, and legs. With the toe of his boot, he scooped the bird and dragged it within reach.

Robin sat upright and studied the tiny prize. He tugged at the sparrow's feathers but they would not loosen. He recalled with dismay the time that he had spent satisfying his youthful curiosity in Bell Castle's kitchen. Kitchen maids had dunked fowl in boiling water to loosen the feathers before plucking.

He had seen Meeyoo devour a bird more than once. She ate every part, feathers, feet, beak, and all. He tried to do the same and bit into the bird's side but ended up with only a mouthful of down for his efforts.

He looked up at the windows where Meeyoo lay against the bars. "Thank you, Meeyoo. I'll . . . eat this later," he said. Perhaps later after the kill was not so fresh the feathers would loosen and he could get to the meat. He laid the bird beside him.

The dead sparrow made a dark spot against the gray earthen floor, its eyes dull as coal, its bony feet slightly curled.

Bony feet. Bones. Robin took up the sparrow again and studied the feet and legs. The scaly legs were about the size of the bones of his little finger, the tiny talons curved with sharp tips.

Bird in his right hand, he cradled the padlock in his left, and poked the bird's talon into the keyhole. It appeared that with some modification, the bird's feet and legs had potential as a lock pick. He bent back the smaller toe. The leg made a straight handle while the front and back talons made hooked picks. No serious burglar would ever attempt a hurried break-in with such a clumsy tool but Robin thought he might have the advantage of time. Since his incarceration, not a single guard had come near the cell. Sorcerers apparently didn't merit even token human kindness, or perhaps the guards were simply too afraid to render it.

Robin set to work in the dark, relying on his senses of sound and touch. With deliberation he wiggled the improvised pick slowly, feeling his way through the lock, moving tiny unseen wards aside to their unlocked position. He made several false starts. His improvised tools proved to be frustratingly flexible and the ward kept slipping back onto place. Cursing he kept wiggling the tool until he found just the right size and configuration of bone and claw to keep the repositioned wards in place while he tackled the next.

At last he moved the final ward and slid the bolt that clamped the shackle in the lock's body. The lock opened and he removed the shackle from his wrist.

"Oh, Meeyoo, we did it!" he cried.

From her perch at the window, Meeyoo let out a congratulatory cry.

Now to tackle the iron lock that secured the door. Robin crawled across the room, sat beside the door, and studied the keyhole, outlined by illumination in the corridor. Would that the guard had left the key in the lock. Robin might have found a way to jostle it loose, snag it with a bird-bone hook, and slide it under the door, but no, the keyhole was empty. The lock was large and Robin suspected it was much more complex than the one he had just sprung. His examination was interrupted by a metal-on-metal sound on the other side. The keyhole went dark. Someone had inserted a key into the keyhole and turned the lock.

CHAPTER FIVE

Robin stood and stepped back a few inches.

"Food," announced a voice tinged with menace. It was the bloodthirsty guard who had assisted in his arrest. Robin wondered if the guard's mission held more menace than mercy.

The guard cracked the door open. Driven by an armored toe, a cup slid through on the floor. With his left hand, Robin snatched the cup and with the right, grabbed the door, pulled it fully open, and rammed the guard. As the dazed man staggered, Robin clenched the fingers of his right hand and shoved them into the cup. Its contents squished out as Robin drove his metal-jacketed fist into the guard's jaw. The guard dropped to the ground.

Robin looked about and saw no one else in the dimly lit corridor. He stripped the guard of knife and sword. Robin recognized his blades. The guard had taken Robin's weapons for his own. Robin felt a spark of anger. He would not be so easily deprived of the sword that he had over many long nights made himself.

The guard moaned. Robin unfastened the belt and purse—his belt and purse!—and stripped the guard of his jerkin which Robin tugged over his own tunic. Would that the man still wore his chainmail but Robin took what he could. Had the guard been wearing his helmet, a blow to the head would not have fazed him, but Robin could have used the headgear to complete his disguise. He took the guard's red signal flag and a companion white one. There wasn't much Robin could do about his beard but at least he could use the guard's coif to hide his hair which tonight would be a red flag in its own right. Robin reclaimed his belt and purse and dragged the stunned guard into the cell.

Before leaving the cell, Robin picked up the dead sparrow. He would leave no sign of how he had slipped his bonds. They already thought him a sorcerer. Let them believe that he had used magic. Meanwhile, Meeyoo might want to make a meal of the bird.

Robin locked the cell door, tucked the key in his purse, and hurried down the corridor.

Robin's right fist throbbed. He raised it to his lips and sucked on the bruised knuckles. He smelled a foul sharp odor and his skin tasted bitter from what had been in the cup. With what little saliva he had, he spat. What had been in the cup? Had the guards sought to poison him?

The corridor held doors to two other cells but Robin did not stop to investigate. He knew not who the other prisoners might be or even if the cells were occupied. For all he knew they could be murderers whose first act upon escaping their cell would be to kill him and take his newly-recovered weapons.

The corridor led to a flight of stone steps, dark because the candles in the sconces mounted on the wall were still to be lit. Robin took the stairs one careful step at a time, listening for the presence of others. On the ground floor at the top of the stairs, he would no doubt find a guard room which he needed to avoid at all costs. Opposite the guard room he expected to find stores of wine, ale, and threshed grain, pantries, and storage for household supplies.

At this hour the staff would be busy ferrying food from the keep's stores to the kitchen to prepare a light evening supper. Robin tucked himself into a darkened corner where he could dodge the guard room and monitor the traffic. A kitchen maid and then another passed him on their way but were too busy balancing baskets and trays to give him any notice. To Robin's eye they seemed to be carrying quite a bit more food than was typical for a late day meal. They groused about the untimely arrival of unexpected guests. A late feast would explain all the dishes.

He darted into the stores where a busy staff gave him scant notice, and ducked into the scullery. His eyes also fell upon a pitcher of fresh water for washing and a pile of food scraps and rinds awaiting disposal. In less time than it took to debate the wisdom of his actions he drained the pitcher, bundled the food in a washrag, and tucked it under the guard's jerkin. At a respectable distance he followed the servants out of the keep. They continued down the stairs, across the footbridge, and through the rear archway to the kitchen but Robin stayed behind. He found a dark corner, pressed himself against the cool stone of the keep, and tried to get his bearings.

To get away he would have to descend the motte, traverse the keep's moat, pass through the rear archway, scurry across the bailey, and defeat two portcullis gates and a drawbridge to get beyond the curtain wall, then make it over the footbridge crossing the outer moat. But first he would have to find Meeyoo.

Might she still be keeping watch at his cell window? Where was that window, anyway?

He thought about how his Bell Castle had been arranged. Like this castle, his had below-ground dungeons. The window to the cell from which he had just escaped would be in the base of the keep. He looked down at the building's foundation but saw no openings. In the dark of night they would be hard to detect. The cells would not be lit from within, and this wall was in shadow from the tall defensive wall opposite. He edged further along the keep's wall.

"Meeyoo," he said, loud enough he hoped for her to hear him but not so loud as to draw anyone's attention. He waited but heard no response. "Meeyoo," he tried again and was rewarded with silence.

He felt his way along the wall working his way around the roughly cylindrical keep. The air here dampened his face and smelled of salt. He knew that scent from when he had walked along the shore at Sea Gate Fortress. It meant the sea was nearby. He had reached the rear of the keep, the side that overlooked the water.

He closed his eyes and sighed. He had found no openings to below-ground chambers. The window that opened to the room in which he had been imprisoned must be on the keep's other side. He continued to feel his way around. Lights from the floors above cast some illumination on the top of the curtain wall but threw the corridor he traversed into shadow. He worked his way around. At last he found a section of the keep's wall that had two barred windows, but no Meeyoo. Where was she? Was she somewhere inside the keep or one of the other buildings? Had she already left the fortress's grounds?

Robin edged to his right. He found another shadowed corner from which he could observe the stairs leading away from the keep down the motte to the rear archway and the bailey. He flattened himself against the wall, his pulse racing. For the moment the track was vacant. He decided to chance it and scurried down.

At the bottom he darted to the left and tucked himself into a space between the inner curtain wall and the nearest building. The aromas that flooded his nostrils told him that the building was the kitchen. Straight ahead across the bailey was the main gate. He considered making a mad dash across the grounds but there were far too many people about. Garbed in the guard's jerkin he might escape notice but there was an equal chance someone might try to press him into service.

He could try circumnavigating the entire bailey, ducking into one shadowed corner after the next. Soldiers and guards paraded on the walk atop the walls but their attention was directed toward threats from outside, not from within. Even if they were to look down, it would be hard to spot someone cleaving to the wall.

The route to his left seemed the shortest but after passing the kitchen and great hall he would have to make it past the barracks. The route to his right, past stables, a forge, and workshops was longer but seemed less risky. At this hour there should be few people about. There was no traffic at the postern gate which was secured for the night.

He worked his way around, seeking out shadows and structures to hide behind while keeping an eye on the main gate. The portcullis rose and guards came to attention. Riders entered and were approached by men and women dressed in finery and in work clothes. They must be the castle's lord, ladies, and servants attending to the arrival of guests, Robin decided.

If he could mingle with the crowd at the gate he would have a brief window of opportunity to slip through it while it was still open. He would have to go now. Without Meeyoo. Who had saved him.

The structure in whose shadow he hid was dark and quiet. Only two more buildings lay between him and the gate. One was the armory.

Hoping that tonight all the guards and soldiers had already armed themselves, he walked briskly past it. He got successfully beyond it and had but one more building to bypass to arrive at the gate: the chapel. From behind him came the sound of a door opening and men talking, soldiers leaving the armory no doubt headed for the gate. Robin didn't even risk stopping and turning to see if he was right but pushed the wooden door to the chapel. It opened and he ducked inside. He would hide just until whoever was behind him went past. Then he would rejoin the throng at the gate.

He found himself in a dimly lit room smelling of incense. Ahead, five wooden settles stood one behind the other on the brick floor. They faced a wooden altar upon which stood two stubby candles, their flames reflected in the metal bowl of a chalice.

For the moment he was alone but he wouldn't be for long. The lord would no doubt bring his guests here for a welcoming blessing.

Let there be a closet, a screen, something to hide in or behind, Robin pleaded. Yes! The chapel had two doors. The one to his right was a wooden ambry. Its polished door glowed warmly in the candlelight. He pulled the door open. The small closet was packed full of Bibles, sacramental utensils, and chalices, and left nary a space for a candle much less a man.

He darted across the room to the other door. Of plain rough pine and barely bigger than he was, this closet didn't hold much promise. He opened the door to find the chapel's garderobe— the latrine.

He stepped inside and pulled the door closed, plunging himself into a pungent darkness. The tiny closet wouldn't hide him for long. This was likely to a popular spot, in demand by the travelers just arrived.

So close yet so far. The gate was just beyond the chapel. He would wait, just a bit, Robin decided, then leave the chapel and make a try for the gate.

His eyes accustomed to the dark. A few vestments hung from pegs on the wall, exposing them to the rank pisshole humours thought to protect garments from fleas. At Bell Castle, he hadn't found that to be true.

Something else about the Bell Castle garderobes nagged at his brain. What was it? Would that he could pace but there was no room. He scrunched his eyes closed and clenched his fists, all the better to squeeze out the thought.

Yes, that was it!

A brass holder on the floor next to the seat held the stub of a candle. Robin dug his flint from his purse and lit the wick. He tugged at the wooden plank that served as a seat and was rewarded to find it not nailed down, only wedged into place. He lifted it off, set it aside, peered into the hole, and down the discharge chute. The illumination outside the curtain wall was faint and he could barely make out the opening at the bottom of the chute. He held the candle high over the hole but it didn't cast enough light.

The opening did not appear to be grated. For all their concerns about security, had Lomroddoy Fortress left a gap in its defenses?

Robin sat on the stone next to the hole and tried to picture what he could recall of the fortress's plan. The guards had led him through the gateway into the inner ward. The chapel had been to his right. This garderobe had to be hung on the front curtain wall. Waste discharged onto the sloped escarpment alongside the moat.

He swung his legs into the hole. It would be a tight squeeze but he would probably squirm down the chute. There was a time when his belly would have squelched that plan. Now, however, he was in fighting trim.

And, he vowed, when I'm out of here, when I'm back at Bell Castle, I mean to stay that way.

How long of a drop was it from the discharge opening to the ground at the base of the wall? How far could a man fall without breaking a bone? Robin sighed. This was still his best chance to escape the fortress so he was about to find out.

It probably didn't matter but he wanted to leave as few clues as possible as to how he got away. He blew out the candle and replaced the bench partway. Once he was in the hole, he wouldn't be able to pull it back completely but perhaps no one would give a second thought to a bench that had been joggled slightly ajar.

Though the walls of the discharge chute were slick it was a snug enough fit that Robin didn't have to worry about a sudden drop to a landing an unknown number of feet below but the nauseating fetor of the narrow passageway nearly suffocated him. What if when he reached the bottom he found that it was grated after all? Could he inch back up or would he be stuck in the shaft? He almost sent up a cheer when his feet dangled clear telling him they had reached the bottom of the chute and found it open. Robin felt for the wall with the toe of his boot and somehow gained purchase on the stone. He continued to worm through until his legs, torso, then his head cleared the chute and he could look down.

The ground was too far below for him to jump.

His heart racing with panic, he clung to the wall. Clung? To what was he clinging? He risked a glance down. A series of light and shadow suggested ledges. Years of discharge had eroded the wall's stones, giving him something of a ladder to descend.

He edged his way down, feeling for toeholds and handholds. Another careful foot, and another, and one more, and he would be—

A noise from the parapet walk above startled him. He lost his grip and skidded down the wall, landing with a thump on the damp grass, the sudden impact knocking the breath from him. Before Robin could get purchase he found himself sliding down the escarpment and into the moat.

Chilly water thick with mossy growths, silt, and wastes from the fortress flooded his nose. Thrashing, Robin fought to thrust himself to the surface before hitting the bottom of the moat which was likely to be lined with broken crockery, pointed sticks, and sharpened bits of metal.

His head broke the water and he risked a look back at the curtain wall. So far none of the guards atop it had spotted a man taking a late night bath in the moat. If he could swim across it and gain the other bank, he would be clear of the fortress.

Staying submerged as much as possible, Robin paddled through the water. He scrabbled onto the bank, flattened himself onto the ground, and sucked in air. Coughing, he spewed moat water from his nose and mouth. He stretched his fingers and toes, extended his arms and legs. Every bone in his body jangled, every muscle throbbed, but nothing seemed to be broken. The unplanned dousing had rinsed away most of the stench from the discharge chute but now he reeked of pond scum.

Behind him, the fortress's guests crossed the footbridge to the archway, too intent on crossing the moat without mishap to notice anyone splashing around in it.

When the last rider traversed the footbridge and passed under the arch, Robin rose to a crouch. As soon as the guests were all inside the fortress and the defenders had relaxed their vigilance, he would race for the wood.

He was about to dash for freedom when he heard a voice.

"Me. You."

Robin stopped stock still, his blood frozen in his veins.

"Me. You."

Robin sucked in a deep breath and his blood flowed once more. Again, he pleaded. Say it again.

"Me. You."

The sound seemed to come from above and behind. Robin looked up. Perched on the archway at the end of the footbridge, outlined by moonlight, Meeyoo could easily have been taken for one of the stone gargoyles but for her glittering eyes.

"Meeyoo! Get down from there. Let's get out of here!" he said trying his best to sound commanding while keeping his voice at a whisper. "Don't make me come over there and get you!"

The cat stood and walked from one side of the arch to the other.

"Meeyoo," Robin hissed.

He was about to dash across the footbridge to get her when she jumped down to the ground and nosed around the archway, investigating all the new smells the fortress's guests had introduced.

"Meeyoo," he called again. He wanted to be off this track, under the cover of trees and bushes, and out of sight of the fortress guards.

Apparently finding nothing of lasting interest under the arch, she bounded across the bridge. Robin started toward the woods hoping Meeyoo would follow but she hung back. Then he saw why.

His rucksack lay in the weedy verge alongside the track near where the guard had dropped it. Robin could only assume that the guards had been afraid of what they presumed were malevolent contents and thought it best simply to leave it outside the fortress walls.

Meeyoo nudged the sack open, crawled inside, then poked her head out of the opening as if to say, "I'm ready. Let's go!"

Robin grabbed the pack. From inside the jerkin he drew the dead bird and the bundle of food scraps, all sodden from the dunking in the moat, and stuffed them inside the pack. Then as fast as his weak and wobbly legs could carry him, he ran across the clearing to the woods.

In the moonlight he crashed and stumbled through the underbrush, not stopping until they were deep enough into the woods to be shielded from the fortress's sight. He could barely see the high walls or the pennants for the trees' canopy and felt it was a fairly safe bet that no one could see him.

He set his pack on the ground at the foot of a tree and slid down the trunk. He did not know which he felt more urgently: hungry, thirsty, or tired. What he did feel for the first time since his arrest was a relief so strong it made him lightheaded.

"Meeyoo," he sighed, emptying his lungs of desperation and despair. He took a deep breath. The herbal aroma of the sage-colored bushes took the edge off the odors emanating from his clothes. In a moment, exhaustion would overtake him. He turned back the flap of the rucksack. Meeyoo crawled out and curled up in his lap. He pulled the bundle of food scraps to his side and untied it. He found that he had come away with bread trenchers, apple cores, green bean tips, carrot and sweet potato peels, the ends of celery stalks, and pea shells. Oblivious to the unsavory odor of moat water, he put an apple core to his lips. Too tired to bite it, he held it in his mouth and sucked whatever juice he could from the fibrous core.

The next thing he was aware of was his face burning. Robin opened his eyes only to have them stung by the sunlight slanting between the branches overhead. He blinked. At last his weary eyes adjusted to the bright light of day. He looked around. He sat at the base of an oak tree with his back against the trunk. By his side was the bundle of food scraps or rather what was left of it. Nearly all of it was gone. Ants swarmed over what remained.

Robin shook his head. He didn't remember eating the scraps. His empty stomach and light head confirmed that he hadn't. It had to be the lack of food that caused him to see the apparition to his left. There stood an old horse, reins dangling, snuffling at a pile of carrot peelings.

"Thief?" Robin said, his voice ragged.

The horse turned its head and regarded him. It was Thief!

Robin struggled to get to his feet. Woozy, he braced himself against the tree until the lightheadedness cleared. He picked up his rucksack. It felt bottom heavy. He lifted the flap and was greeted by Meeyoo's furry face.

"Well," he croaked. "Now that we're all together again, let's resume our trip." He hung the sack from the saddle and threw his arms around Thief's neck. With effort Robin pushed and pulled himself up onto the horse's back and into the saddle. Without even the strength to sit upright, he clung to Thief's neck. He gathered up the reins. "Go," he said, leaving the "where" to the horse.

Thief plodded along. The glade grew brighter and warmer as the morning advanced. Only half awake, Robin rode barely cognizant of their surroundings. Now and again Thief would stop to munch on a shrub.

When Robin heard a gurgle, he thought at first that he was dreaming. He lifted heavy eyelids to see that Thief had stopped beside a pond and had lowered his head into the water to drink. Robin slid from the saddle, crawled to the bank, and scooped handfuls of water to his mouth. Would that it was ale. The water was slightly brackish and tasted of rotted vegetable matter but it was wet and drinkable. He knew that he should go easy or risk making himself sick but it was all he could do not to simply stick his head in the pond and drink it dry.

At last he felt that he had his fill. Somewhat refreshed, he took off his purse, boots, and belt, and removed his sword and knife. He stepped into the pond and stretched out on his back in the shallow water, rinsing his hair and clothes. His garments would dry soon enough in the heat of the day.

Dripping, he left the pond and looked about. Around him were oak trees and the sage-colored bushes that Thief liked to eat. Robin also spied a vining plant with flat leaves, some bright green, some yellowing and turning to brown. The plant also bore clusters of berries. The green and purple berries looked for all the world like grapes.

Robin remembered Eian, the winemaker at Sweet Water, saying that the grapes he pressed grew in the area. Robin had been surprised to learn that the fruit managed to grow in an area that so often was terribly hot and dry but the winemaker assured him that it did. Could these be grapes, Robin wondered. Did he dare sample one?

He decided that if he poisoned himself he wasn't much worse off than he would be dying of hunger. He plucked a berry from the vine and popped it into his mouth. The fruit was juicy and tangy sweet. He ate another and another and finally handfuls, then sat back and waited for pain.

When he suffered no ill effects, he plucked whole clusters from the vines and with the washrag that had held the castle's food scraps tied them to Thief's saddle.

Would that he could take water with him as well but he had no flask, only his cup. Pewter, engraved with his family's royal crest, it was such a familiar part of his daily life he had long since ceased truly to see it. All this time he had been carrying a souvenir of his kingly life. Clearly no one had given it much notice or thought but Robin would have to be more aware in the future. It might behoove him to scratch out the design before anyone asked him how he came to possess the item.

Thief shook his head and pawed the ground. Yes, Robin thought, it was time they were on their way. He still wanted to gain the harbor. Sooner or later the castle guards would discover that he had escaped if they hadn't already. They might be grateful to be rid of him or they might intend to hunt him down to annihilate him. He could very well be a wanted fugitive. At the harbor, he could perhaps book passage on a ship, get far away to somewhere that tales of a red-headed sorcerer with feline and equine familiars had not reached.

He considered whether the guard's jerkin would aid him as a disguise and decided that anonymity would be a greater asset. He pulled off the jerkin, folded it, and tucked it into his rucksack.

The water and food had helped to clear his head. Robin still felt weak but at least he could think. Upon fleeing the castle, he had taken off to his left. If he went back the way he came could he come just within sight of the fortress? He could then stay out of view, within the protective screen of the forest but work his way around the area outside the guards' scrutiny until he reached the rear where he was certain that he would find the harbor. He had been able to smell the salt air when he had crept around the back side of the keep.

Resolute, he mounted Thief. It would probably be easier to walk through the forest leading the horse but Robin still felt too feeble. With a tug on the reins, he guided the horse away from the pond.

As they made their way, the foliage became shorter in height and drier in appearance, looking more like the plants that lined the track that they had taken. By midday, Robin reached the edge of the wood. In the distance he once again saw the fortress's red standards bright against the blue sky. He would go no further towards it but would stay screened by what foliage there was. Using the keep as a point of reference, he guided Thief through the undergrowth toward where he believed the harbor lay.

CHAPTER SIX

The burnished light and shortening shadows told Robin that it was afternoon. He had eaten all the grapes and the energy they had bestowed on him this morning had long faded. He was hungry again and thirsty and no doubt Thief was also.

When Robin had first fixed eyes on the keep, he could see the stair that led down the motte to the bailey. He directed Thief forward putting that landmark to his back. Now, hours later, that view of the keep was well behind him. What he could see of the keep was featureless save for the narrow fenestres and he concluded that it was the structure's rear, the side that overlooked the sea. Somewhere at the fortress's base he hoped to find the harbor. But was there a road or track that led to it? He and Thief could spend all day picking their way through the woods only to find their way blocked by another fortress wall.

He spotted a sturdy tree and with effort hauled himself up a couple of branches to get a better view. From the higher vantage point he saw the walls terracing the keep's motte. Below them ran a line of shrubs and below that he thought he saw rooftops that hinted at habitations. Beyond that stretched water as far as the eye could see. To his left a track led toward the settlement. Laden and empty carts drawn by oxen and donkeys and travelers on foot and horseback plied the track going to and fro. Robin decided to risk leaving the shelter of the woods in hopes of reaching the settlement along the water.

As he neared the track, he became uneasy. Although enclosed by many concentric tiers of walls the fortress seemed but a few gallops away. Robin could make out figures on the wall walk and they had a clear view of the people on the road. If he could see them, no doubt that they could see him. The guard's coif would at least disguise Robin's red hair. He hoped that the guards would give little notice to people moving away from the fortress and would concentrate on those who seemed to be headed towards it.

Once he gained the track he felt somewhat reassured. He saw no soldiers, no guards. None of the other travelers bore the fortress's heraldic symbols on their clothing or gear nor any other crests for that matter. For the most part they appeared to be merchants or humble wayfarers and like him wore plain rough but sturdy clothing suited for travel.

Striving to attract as little interest in himself as possible, he gave courteous replies but was neither too inquisitive of nor responsive to his fellow journeyers save to purchase ale and sausage from traveling merchants. The less he said the better lest he be taken for something other than what he wanted to appear to be, a simple wayfarer. Too often he forgot to modify his speech, his language the hallmark of an education and upbringing inconsistent with his apparently humble station. His royal speech had betrayed him more than once, most recently with the fortress's guards.

That should tell me something, Robin thought. I am a king. I was born and bred to be a king. Why struggle to pretend to be anything else?

The track curved around a grove, widened, and at an intersection with a trail running perpendicular to it stopped abruptly as if reaching land's end. To the right the track ran along the edge of a bluff overlooking a rocky shoreline. Arrayed along the bluff lay the settlement's heavier industries: a blacksmith, a baker, a miller. Robin could see the smoke from the forge, smell bread baking, and hear the rumbling of the millwheel.

To his left the track led down a slope. Robin could see the tops of buildings, tall masts, and beyond those only water and sky. His heart stuttered as it had the first time he had been presented with such a vista as if with fear that with his next step he would fall off the very earth.

He guided Thief toward the harbor. At the bottom of the slope a line of two- and three-story structures ran parallel to the water's edge. The brick and half-timbered buildings stood cheek to jowl with hardly a space between them. Washed in white and pale pastel they hugged the foot of the motte like a string of pearls. By contrast the motte with its gray stone walls and keep rose like a malevolent growth and loomed over them.

In front of the waterfront buildings ran a narrow street. Bright white, it appeared to be paved with marble. Beyond it the land truly did drop off into the water held back by a stone embankment. At its farthest end, the street curved and climbed the motte to an archway in the lowest fortification and beyond that to a postern gate in the fortress's high curtain wall.

From his vantage point at the top of the grade Robin could see the protection that the fortress and harbor shared. The water was the fortress's first line of defense. Land fortifications extended onto walled jetties that stretched into the water at the right and left. Tipped with watch towers the jetties appeared to embrace the harbor like sheltering arms with the watch towers forbidding as clubs held in menacing fists. A channel between the two towers was just wide enough to permit ships to enter the harbor. Some were tied to the wharf with rope while others maintained their position at a distance, anchored in place somehow. Ships with sails unfurled waggled slightly in the breeze while those whose sails had been gathered in simply bobbed gently. White pennants dipped and rose above the decks of ships. Robin could see no lines lashing those pennants to the ships and wondered what kept them suspended. He thought it might be some kind of magic until a clutch of pennants went aloft as a mass and flew off, and Robin realized that they were not pennants after all but birds, white gulls with broad wings.

Thief's nostrils twitched and Robin could imagine why. The air was filled not just with the scent of the sea but also the smoke of fires and the aromas of cooked food. Even Meeyoo poked her head out of the rucksack to investigate the new surroundings. Robin urged Thief forward.

He followed the traffic down the grade to the crowded waterfront. The narrow street between the shops and the wharf was not paved with marble as it had appeared from a distance but rather crushed shell. The line of buildings stretched for about a mile. Trunks, crates, barrels, and casks stacked alongside nearly every building or piled along the wharf opposite left little room on the narrow street for horses, donkeys, or oxen. Stray dogs and cats nosed the rubbish piles. Even the large white birds that Robin had taken for pennants seemed interested in the trash.

He came first to food stalls fitted with baskets and trays that earlier in the day would have had vegetables and fruits, breads and baked goods, and meats. Now only a few dried bits and scraps remained. Empty also were the hooks overhead from which would have hung poultry and joints of meat. A few spilled grains marked where sacks of grain had stood. The business day having ended, the merchants were nowhere to be found but would likely return on the morrow.

He passed shops offering goods and services typical of any settlement judging from the shingles that hung above the doors. Next to the food stall was a linen-draper followed by a chandler, a soap- and candlemaker. Shutters covered the street-level windows. Illumination from the floors above suggested that the merchants had retired to their living quarters.

Next came a jeweler, a fortune-teller, a potter, glassmaker, and apothecary that sold lenses and reading stones.

A young woman in a flowing purple robe and a man in a simple tunic and leggings emerged from the fortune-teller's shop beaming. The man took the young woman's hands in his and pumped them with enthusiasm. Clearly he had received a good prediction. Robin found himself thinking that perhaps he should consult this soothsayer. Maybe he could get some hint about the success of his plan.

Or would he? He had had seers and soothsayers at court and had consulted them but never found their pronouncements to be of much help. Looking back on it now, he had to wonder why none of them ever mentioned that he would lose it all, his kingdom, his family, his very place in the world. Why had he been surprised to find himself in a fortress's dungeon fearing for his life? Shouldn't they have foreseen that?

Maybe he had been warned, had heard but simply didn't listen? Robin's steps slowed. He would have to give that some thought, try to recall just what his royal seers' predictions were. Recently and more than once he had been advised to look to his past for answers. Perhaps he should more closely examine the prognostications.

He doubted that this fortune teller would be any more enlightening about his future than his court's carefully vetted seers and yet he felt drawn to the shop as though any information, any guidance would be better than none at all.

Robin dismounted and tied Thief's reins to a bollard. He grasped the rope that was the handle to the door of the fortune teller's shop and pulled. The weather-beaten door opened with a squeal of metal and leather hinges and wraiths of thick, perfumed air embraced him. Aromas of smoke, herbs, flowers, and spices were so varied and so mingled that he could not identify a single one. A distant chime sounded.

Long wax tapers and brass lanterns lit the windowless interior. Silks and wools in bright colors and patterns draped the walls. A case crammed with bound volumes, scrolls, and slates stretched from floor to ceiling against one wall. In front of it stood a tall ladder-backed chair and sturdy table whose thick coat of shiny white paint had yellowed and become waxy in spots with age. Facing the desk sat a red velvet wingback chair, its upholstery worn thin and smooth in spots where many had taken a seat.

Robin heard a creak on the stair leading to the upper floors. He expected the purple-robed young woman he had seen with the beaming man. Instead, an elderly man appeared. Tall and husky with wisps of white hair and a neatly trimmed white beard framing his face, his fair countenance and green eyes gave him a gentle appearance.

"Greetings," he said with a welcoming smile. "My name is Gerald."

"Gerald, I'm—"

"Not from around here," said Gerald.

Robin would have asked how the man knew but realized that if Gerald were a soothsayer worth his weight he would divine that. "No, I'm not. I have—"

"Traveled a long way."

"I have indeed."

"So, sit." Gerald indicated the red velvet chair. "May I offer you something to drink?"

The sausage and ale Robin had had on the road now a distant memory, he was happy to avail himself of hospitality. He produced his cup. Gerald took a cup and a jug from a shelf in the case behind the table and poured out ale for the two of them, then sat in the ladder-backed chair.

"I need my fortune told," said Robin. Uncertain as to what fortune tellers charged, he took two small coins from his purse. "Will this do?" Enriched by the dragon slaying bounty he had coins aplenty now but found the frugal habits that had recently sustained him hard to break.

"A few pennies, eh? Then I will tell you only what will happen in the near future," said Gerald. "You will drink your ale, we will exchange a few pleasantries, and you will leave." He fell silent for a moment.

Robin was searching for a suitable rejoinder when Gerald laughed and said, "Oh, the look on your face! I'm sorry, I was just having a bit of fun at your expense. How rude of me when here you are at a crossroads in your life and know not where to go. You seek direction. Ask away, good fellow, and I will give you my best answers."

Robin felt his cynicism fade and his confidence in this soothsayer grew. How could the man know all this when Robin had barely spoken? What Gerald said was true, Robin realized. He had come to this waterfront not by intention but quite by happenstance. Now that he was here, a hint of what the future had in store would help.

Robin said, "Yes, look into the future. Where do you see me?"

Gerald tipped his head back and closed his eyes. After a moment he said, "Where you want to be."

Hmph, Robin thought. A response just like the ones he had gotten from his court seers. Why did these prognosticators have to phrase their divinations in such cryptic terms? He was about to press Gerald for specific details when the man spoke.

"You have been on a quest and have not yet achieved your goal. What you seek is not easily attained. You have experienced loss but things are not as bad as they seem."

Robin felt again the chill from the dungeon floor against the back of his legs and the hollow feeling of hopelessness. He could at this moment still be in the fortress's dungeon awaiting a torturous execution or worse, be already dead.

Gerald leaned forward. "No, things are not as bad as they seem. When you think you are at your nadir you must remember that when you have reached the bottom, the only other direction in which you can go is upward. You have to make an effort though or at the bottom is where you will remain."

Robin found himself recalling the words of Eian at Sweet Water. Something about nothing being impossible, only untried.

"You have taken the first step. You have chosen life over death. To achieve your goal you will need allies but should use caution in placing your trust. There are resources at your disposal. They will come from unexpected quarters. To avail yourself of them you must change your perspective. You will achieve nothing alone. A commander such as yourself should know that."

Robin felt again how uplifting it had been to see Meeyoo's face at the dungeon window. Yes, there had been times when he would have said he had reached his life's lowest point, yet none of those rivaled the night spent chained to a dungeon wall. Help then had indeed come from an unexpected source. Or had it? Should he have been surprised that Meeyoo would try to help him? Gerald was right; Robin had accomplished nothing alone, not even his rescue from certain death.

"You—"

"Father!" the purple-gowned woman called from the staircase's bottom step. Hands propped on her hips, she said, "Are you boring another poor stranger with your tiresome philosophy?"

Gerald gave her a sheepish smile.

"So you are not a soothsayer," Robin said, trying to hide his annoyance.

Gerald chuckled. "No more than you are a simple traveler. Yet my words rang true, did they not? Shall I continue?"

Robin had to admit that they did and nodded. Gerald waved his daughter off and she stomped up the stairs in a huff.

Gerald leaned back in his chair. "I am an old man who has lived many years, seen many things." He took a sip of ale. "Many people fear old age. I certainly did when I was young, even more so perhaps when I was your age. All I could see were the aches and pains to come. My capabilities to work, to shoulder my responsibilities, to support those whom I loved diminished. I dreaded becoming weak, dependent, being a burden.

"And of course there is the specter of death. At my age, the Reaper is so near I can see the crinkles at the corners of his eyes." Gerald shrugged. "We have become close, he and I. We will never be good friends, as his friendship comes at a high price but I have become resigned to having him as a companion.

"What I didn't anticipate were the gifts of old age. Yes, I have more of my life to look back on than what lies ahead but the view is spectacular. Like from a mountaintop, I can see the whole of it spread out before me, can see where the roads begin and where they lead, the detours and the dead ends, the quagmires as well as the bright oases." He nodded. "Some find my perspective useful.

"No, I'm not cloaked in robes like my daughter. I have no crystal balls or tarot cards, and some trust those more than the advice of an old man." He shrugged. "That's more their problem than mine."

"So if you're not a soothsayer, how did you know all those things about me?" Robin asked.

"That you are not from here? I know all the permanent residents. The rest are travelers. Your clothes are dusty, dirty, smelly, and stained; your hair and beard overgrown. It's been days since you have been able to see to your grooming because you have been on the road, a trip for which clearly you were not prepared. As to your need to know your future, why else would you have called on a fortune teller?"

Robin chuckled. Of course, all those clues would be obvious to someone paying attention. "My stature? You called me a commander."

Gerald said, "Much as you try to hide it, your breeding comes through. It's how you speak, how you hold yourself. You look a man in the eye with the bravado and confidence of one whose leadership is not questioned. Here by the waterfront I might have taken you for a ship's captain but you bear not the signs of a life spent on the sea.

"And then there's your cup, sir. That's no common mug. However you came by it, the circumstances were extraordinary.

"As for your wish not to die . . ." Gerald shrugged. "We are all going to die. We start dying the minute we are born. We just don't want to die too soon, not before we are done with Life. You, good sir, are not done with Life. If you were you wouldn't be here wanting to know what Life has in store for you."

True enough, Robin thought. He did not want to die. If he had he could have easily let the fortress's guards take care of that. Instead, he had fought for life. "You can't tell me that, can you?" he asked.

Gerald shook his head. "Nor with all due respect can my daughter, or anyone. And it matters not. We think we are in control, that we can bend Fate to our will. Yet time and again we are shown that the opposite is true. No matter how carefully we plan, how hard we strive, Fate can block our way, turn us from our chosen path."

Robin sighed. How accurate those words were. One only had to look at the unfamiliar roads he had traveled lately.

"When that happens, we are challenged to look deep within ourselves. How committed were we to that path? How hard do we want to fight to get back on course? Or should we consider taking a new direction? A fortune teller cannot provide answers, only ask good questions. The answers are within you." He handed back Robin's pennies. "It was never my intent to cheat you. If you want, I can call my daughter. She does actually have a gift. No, it's not some sixth sense. Just perceptiveness beyond her years." He chuckled. "Maybe she gets it from her old man. She's smart enough to know that if she dresses up good counsel with the trappings of mysticism, people will be intrigued and minds that would have been closed will open."

Robin slid the pennies back across the table. "As gifted as she may be, I doubt that your daughter could do any better." He drained his ale, collected his cup, stood, and bade Gerald farewell.

Robin stepped out into the street. After the time spent in the candlelit shop, even the waning light of a dying day made him blink. He had taken only a couple of steps when he heard, "Wait, good sir."

CHAPTER SEVEN

He turned to see Gerald framed in the doorway of the fortune teller's shop. Robin doubled back.

Gerald took Robin's hand and into it pressed the two coins. "I think it important that you never be penniless."

Robin smiled. Indeed there had been dire consequences from decisions he made for want of a coin. He untied Thief and continued down the waterfront street.

He next came upon a small thatched roof wooden structure alongside a three-story half-timbered house. Smelling of hay and manure, the stables held six stalls. "Hello," Robin cried. "Anyone home?"

"Who calls?" came a throaty reply.

"My name is Robin. I have traveled a long way. I hoped to find water and food for my horse."

"Do not go. Stay. I will be with you without delay." To Robin's ears the voice had a curious quality: husky yet almost feminine.

The stableman emerged from behind a door midway between the stalls. Tall with an angular face, the stable hand was neither a boy nor young. Robin stood face to face with a woman. Tied back away from her face with a worn and faded red ribbon her blond hair had a few streaks of gray at the temples. Days spent outdoors had warmed her complexion. Her worn muslin blouse, its sleeves rolled to the elbows, was a pale shade of the yellow it once was. Hay clung to her dark woolen skirt, stockings, and shoes.

She gave him a small curtsy and smiled. Little lines crinkled the sides of her mouth. "Robin, you say. I am Gabrielle, pleased to meet you today." She wiped her hand on her skirt and held it out in greeting.

Robin shook it.

"You say you need water and hay? Not to be rude, but can you pay?"

"Yes, I can pay." The words had rolled blithely off his tongue before Robin fully recognized their significance. The bounty on the dragon had been a handsome reward and for the first time in a long time money was not a problem. Robin offered a coin.

"That will nicely do. I will take good care of your horse for you," she said. She invited him inside the stable. Two stalls were occupied. To Robin they appeared neat and clean and the animals seemed content. In her curious singsong way, she explained that she managed the stables for the adjoining inn. "Next door you will find lodging, food, and drink—to your satisfaction, I should think. I'll get your horse squared away. What is his name, by the way?"

"Thief," Robin replied.

The woman Gabrielle took a step back.

"He belonged to a highwayman who meant to do me harm. I convinced him he would be better off walking away. I took charge of his horse. The highwayman had been mistreating him."

Gabrielle chuckled. "So you helped a steed who was in need."

Robin struggled to suppress a chuckle of his own. Was every one of Gabrielle's utterances a little song? Was this a sign of some mental defect or worse, an enchantment? He wondered if it truly was safe to leave Thief in her care. He found the neat appearance of the horses, stalls, and grounds somewhat reassuring. He told himself that he would not be gone long. If when he returned he found anything amiss he would find some other accommodations.

Gabrielle indicated which stall he should use. Robin gave Thief drink from a trough and then led the horse into the stall where Gabrielle had set a bale of fresh hay. When Robin was certain she was out of sight he set the rucksack down and laid the flap back.

As he expected, Meeyoo poked her head out to discover that she was in an unfamiliar place. She quickly retreated back into the pack until just her face showed. She looked at Robin and spied Thief.

Robin said. "You can stay here with Thief while I get myself some supper." He didn't really believe that she understood the words but hoped that she would be reassured if he sounded calm and relaxed.

He found a brush, set about grooming Thief, and out of the corner of his eye watched Meeyoo get acclimated. By inches she crept from the rucksack to reconnoiter the stall. She nosed the straw covering the floor and startled a lizard out of hiding. The little creature didn't have a chance. In seconds Meeyoo had it in her mouth, its tail twitching.

"All right. You both have your meals taken care of. Now it's my turn," he said. He heard the crunch of footsteps on gravel. Meeyoo started and burrowed into the straw but not before Gabrielle spotted her and took a step back.

"Oh, a stray cat. Robin, I apologize for that," said Gabrielle.

"No apologies, necessary," Robin said. "Meeyoo is no stray, she is my cat." He studied Gabrielle's reactions. Would she too take him for a sorcerer? Would he have to grab his cat, his pack, and his horse, and run?

Meeyoo sat on her haunches and regarded Gabrielle with yellow eyes.

"Her name is Meeyoo? Like your horse, did you rescue her too?"

On the contrary, Robin thought. More than once she has rescued me. "No, she chose me but she's good company. Would it be all right if I leave her here? She will keep to herself, won't bother the other animals, and might even rid you of some vermin."

56

"That will be fine. She can stay. Where are you off to today?"

Robin said he would seek food and drink next door.

Gabrielle waved her hand. "Do not dawdle, then. Be on your way. I will get Meeyoo some milk, and Thief more hay."

As strange as the rhyming woman was, her acceptance of Meeyoo made Robin warm to her.

Outside the adjoining inn, two men perched on half-barrels and drank from tankards. Robin acknowledged them with a nod and pushed open a heavy board-and-batten door bleached gray and splintered from years of facing the wind coming off the sea.

The windowless room was warm even though the hearth at the right was cold. The smoke of old fires stained the wall above it. Suspended from the ceiling, a scant number of oil lanterns glowed weakly in a dusty haze that hung like a fog under the beams. The feeble light threw the figures of the occupants into shadow. Clutches of three or four men seated on three-legged wooden stools grouped around the old tree stumps, wooden crates, and half-barrels that served as tables. Robin couldn't tell if their swarthy features and stern expressions were true indicators of fearsome natures or just a trick of the murky illumination. The dark wood of the men's tankards soaked up the dim light and gave none back. The room rang with laughter and the noise of a dozen conversations all held at once.

Robin took a few steps across a stamped earth floor carpeted with rushes. His boot heel crunched on a nutshell. The room's noisy buzz stopped altogether and it seemed that every face turned in his direction. He met their curious hooded stares with a friendly smile but no one smiled in return. The room fell silent but for the clank of various cups and mugs against the table tops. Robin struggled to meet the occupants' inquiring glances with an expression that communicated the proper degree of harmlessness without seeming too friendly, curious, or intrusive.

Robin crossed the floor to the bar at the opposite end of the room. A simple wooden plank atop a chest-height wall, it had long lost whatever luster it may have once had. Small wooden casks and jugs of different shapes and sizes were arrayed on its top. Shelves mounted on the wall behind the bar held more of the same.

Behind the bar stood a burly man in a colorful patterned blouse and leather jerkin. A matching kerchief held back white hair. Bushy white brows arched over bright eyes. Gold rings pierced his earlobes. On one of the rings perched a tiny gold parrot figurine.

"Good afternoon," Robin said to the barkeeper.

"Aye, Stranger." The barkeeper's reply sounded like a greeting.

"Yes," said Robin. "Stranger I am, new to this place. I have been on the road many days. From Allenton. Have you heard of it?"

"No, I hadn't but now I can say that I have."

"And what would be the name of this place?"

The barkeeper snorted. "Ah, you are indeed a stranger. Landlubber too, I reckon. That would explain the shoes," he said with a chuckle.

Robin looked down at his boots, then at the feet of the others in the room. Most wore turnout shoes and some others more curious footwear that appeared to be nothing more than a sole strapped to the foot with rope.

"This is Rocky Port," said the barkeeper. He held out his hand. "I am Lister."

"Pleased to meet you, Lister," said Robin. "I am Robin. Gabrielle said I could find food and drink here."

"Ah, our Gabrielle." Lister nodded. "Did you spend much time talking with her?"

"More like listening." Robin was unwilling to say more until he learned whether Gabrielle was mad, bewitched, or just strange.

"Gabrielle. A sad story. Her husband was a brave knight, you know. Liege to the lord of Lomroddoy Fortress." Lister tilted his head as if to indicate the fortress that loomed over the waterfront. "He returned victorious and unscathed from battle only to fall ill and he died. 'No rhyme or reason in that,' Gabrielle said then. She decided that if she could find the rhyme, she would find the reason. And so she . . ." Lister left the sentence unfinished but Robin understood.

"A sad tale." And one with which he could empathize, Robin thought. He knew from personal experience how misfortune could unhinge the mind.

"So, what would be your pleasure?" With a sweep of his hand, the barkeeper indicated the beverages arrayed on the bar. "Ale? Brandy? Rum? Madeira? Port? Sherry?"

"Ale will do fine," Robin said. "And to eat?"

"Sausage? Cheese? Bread? Whelk? Drum? Crawfish?"

"Bread and cheese and some sausage would do nicely," Robin said. He didn't know what the other items were and was not interested in embarking on any gustatory adventures. All he wanted to do was slake his thirst and fill his belly.

"Bets," his host called over the din. "Could you help our guest here?"

From a flight of stairs to Robin's left emerged a woman whose hair was as white as Lister's. Over her dress she wore an apron of the same brightly patterned cloth that made up Lister's blouse and kerchief. She had no earrings but instead wore many rings and strings of beads around her neck. "My wife, Bets," said Lister. "Bread, cheese, and a bit of that sausage if you will, dear."

With a small curtsy, Bets went back upstairs.

"Your cup, sir," Lister said and beckoned with his hand.

Behind Robin, the conversations and laugher had resumed. Bets returned carrying a trencher with a link of sausage, a roll, and a wedge of hard cheese.

Robin broke off the corner of the cheese and palmed it, then reached into his sack. He stowed away the cheese bit for Meeyoo and withdrew his cup, careful to present it with the crest facing away from Lister. The man filled it with ale and handed it back.

Robin tried to eat slowly and casually but he couldn't get the food and drink into himself fast enough.

"Looks like you needed that," said Lister. "More?"

Robin nodded. "I've been on the road a while." And spent a night in a dungeon where I was left to die of hunger and thirst, he thought but did not say.

"And where are you bound next?"

Excellent question, Robin thought. Would that he had an answer. Before he could frame one, Lister's attention was called to something happening at the front of the room. Following his glance, Robin looked over his shoulder to see a man enter and head to the bar.

The reedy young man settled on the stool next to Robin. His dark eyes were bright, his dark hair and beard closely trimmed. The particolored jerkin that he wore over his white blouse was like a quilt, composed of patches of material, all different patterns and textures. Entertainers at Robin's court had worn such clothing.

"Ale?" asked Lister.

"Of course," the man replied with a chuckle, and set his cup on the bar.

Lister said to Robin, "Glad Abner comes here quite often and always has the same drink. He's quite the storyteller. So good that sometimes we forget to charge him. He often serves at Lomroddoy and so brings us news of what transpires behind those fortress walls. Have you been to court lately, Glad Abner? What story have you for us today?" he asked.

"Ah, it is definitely worth a few drams," Glad Abner said, "Quite the uproar in the fortress. I wonder if I should even speak of it, for fear of bringing evil spirits to your door."

Lister shrugged. "I don't think that an evil spirit would stand much of a chance in this place. Some of these men need just the merest excuse to start brawling. What has got the fortress in a dither? Is it under attack?"

"Not from soldiers." Glad Abner leaned forward and spoke in a whisper. "A sorcerer."

Robin felt the hair at the back of his neck rise. He wished that he could lean in too as he wanted to hear what Glad Abner had to say but didn't want to appear overly interested.

"Yes," said Glad Abner, "a sorcerer. A sorcerer with a wicked familiar. The sorcerer tried all kinds of chicanery to get inside the gate. Who knows what malevolence he had in mind? The guards saw through his subterfuge and stopped him. Took his weapons and threw him in the dungeon and chained him to the wall."

Bets shrugged. "And so, danger was averted and all is well. Not much of a story, Glad Abner. I think you're going to have to buy your own drink this time."

"I'm not done," Glad Abner said, his voice getting louder as he warmed to the telling of his tale. "The sorcerer escaped his bonds. No one knows how. It had to be magic. He was alone in the cell. He had no weapons, no tools, no possessions at all save the shirt on his back. He freed himself from the chain and escaped the cell and is nowhere to be found."

"He had help. You said he had a familiar," Lister pointed out.

"He had the familiar with him when he was arrested. But the guards gave chase and threatened it with swords and lances and a great show of power. They frightened the familiar and it vanished," said Glad Abner.

Vanished, my ass, Robin thought. Meeyoo just ran and hid for a while.

"Maybe the sorcerer summoned the familiar to return and give him aid," Lister said.

"Maybe. Or maybe the sorcerer was powerful enough to free himself on his own. In any case, it was magic at work." Glad Abner folded his arms and smirked. "And now they are both at large, the sorcerer and his familiar. Now tell me that story isn't worth a drink."

"So far, I'm not impressed. No harm was done, was there? The sorcerer is gone, off to bedevil someone else. The fortress is safe once again. End of story."

Glad Abner held up an index finger. "Not quite. There's more. The guards were worried that from his cell, even chained, the sorcerer would inflict some curse, so they decided it was their duty to dispatch him. They created a deadly potion—"

Ah hah! Robin thought. So they had intended to poison me.

"—but when they went to administer it, the sorcerer overpowered them—"

Not quite, thought Robin. I overpowered only one guard.

"—and smote them all."

CHAPTER EIGHT

Now wait a minute! Robin wanted to cry. There was no smiting. I didn't smite even one guard, much less three. There was one guard and he was still breathing when I left him. Stunned, but breathing.

Had he died later, from injuries Robin inflicted? The thought made Robin feel unexpectedly queasy. Why, he wondered, should the death of a murderous enemy guard upset him? As King he and his knights had gone on offensives and there were deaths on both sides. Kings had to protect and preserve what they had as well as enlarge their kingdoms, often at the expense of others. Robin had never second-guessed the price paid for that.

Death had come at Robin's own hands and not just on the battlefield. As a dragon slayer, he had vanquished many a beast. Dragons were fierce and fearsome, the cause of much death and destruction. The people whose safety and peace of mind he had restored had been grateful. He had spared not a thought for the dragon. It had been a fair fight every time; Robin had simply been the better fighter.

Was there a message he had missed, a lesson here that he was meant to learn? Or was the bone-deep chill that he now felt simply the realization that he was now a marked man.

"And," Glad Abner said, "the sorcerer took the guise of one of the guards. He could be in the keep still or anywhere in the fortress, wreaking who knows what mayhem. It is feared that if the sorcerer and his familiar unite they will seek vengeance on the fortress."

I didn't take the guard's guise, I took just his jerkin and coif, Robin protested silently.

Bets took Glad Abner's cup, filled it, and passed it back.

Glad Abner took a healthy swallow. "Anyway, as I said, the fortress is in an uproar. They've got a massive manhunt, or should I say witch hunt, going. Door to door. They are determined to rout out this evil and powerful sorcerer."

"Well, not our problem is it?" said Lister. "I'm not sure the fortress's worries are any of mine."

"Unless," said Glad Abner, "the sorcerer escapes the fortifications. I hear tell that they are determined to find him, to avenge the death of the three guards."

Robin felt a little sick. Three guards dead? Massive manhunt? For him, when he was guilty of nothing, was in fact the injured party? They had denied him his rightful reward! Lomroddoy Fortress owed him the other half of the prize. Were the fortress's guards intent on his death to quash the complaint of a dragon slayer cheated out of his bounty?

From one of the tables a couple of men hollered for Glad Abner to join them. He picked up his cup. With a wink he said, "Let me see if I can parlay this story into some more ale," and went to join them.

Lister turned to Robin. "So, Robin, you were telling us where you are headed next," he said.

Robin took a swallow of ale to open a throat now pinched closed with fear. "I had thought to book passage on a ship," he croaked.

"Headed for where?"

Anywhere but here. "Anywhere?" Robin said wishing that didn't sound so feeble.

Lister laughed. "You're certain you're not a sailor?" He waved his arm to include the room. "If you're willing to work, you could probably get hired on just about any ship in port."

"I had thought to be a passenger," Robin replied. "Me and my horse."

"Ah, now that's a different matter. " Lister stroked his beardless chin. "What do you think, Bets?"

She pressed her lips together. "The Orion could handle that. Where's Captain Gregersen? I see some of his crew."

Lister squinted at the crowd. "And if he sees them here, he will be most vexed. Fortunately for them he is still aboard the ship."

"Speak of the Devil . . ." Bets said.

Coming through the door was a tall slender man with a tanned and weather-beaten face. A dark blue cap with a low flat crown and short bill topped his flaxen hair. A light blue vest was laced over his white blouse. Both the cap and vest were embroidered with a golden rope encircling an image. Wide blue-and-white-striped drawers flared to mid-calf and dark leggings covered his legs. Robin found the man's shoes almost as curious as Robin's boots. Ankle-high and shaped like typical turnout shoes, they were made not of fabric but of sturdy oiled leather. The lantern light glinted off a silver chain about his neck from which dangled a pendant: half a silver heart with a jagged edge. The newcomer's entrance was greeted with curious glances and the buzz of conversation grew louder.

Robin noticed two men slowly rising from their table. Behind the tall man's back, they sidled toward the door, one with his arm over the other's shoulder and leaning heavily, and with heads bowed, exited as the new arrival strode to the bar.

"Captain," said Lister with a big smile. The two men shook hands over the bar and the captain gave Bets a peck on the cheek.

"What can we get you, Captain?" Bets asked.

"I've had enough of cold dried meat and ship's biscuits for the last few days," he replied. "A hot juicy roast would be most pleasing."

"Coming right up," she replied. "Oh, but first, there is someone that you should meet. Or someone who should meet you, I should say. This is Robin. Robin, this is Captain Gregersen of the Orion."

What was the protocol, Robin wondered? Should he bow? Robin decided that a ship's captain deserved some sign of respect and so made a slight bow.

He got a close look at the embroidery on the captain's vest. Shaped much like a heraldic crest, the image encircled by the golden rope was of a boat with three white sails and a dark blue pennant at the top of the mast. The ship floated upon wavy bars of blue and white under a dark blue sky studded with white stars. The crown atop the crest was composed not of oak leaves or trefoils but of a ship's prow flanked by billowing sails.

Robin thought "Orion" to be rather an odd name for the ship. All the other vessels he ever heard of had intimidating names like "Avenger," "Defiance" or "Majestic."

The captain somewhat hesitantly extended a hand in greeting.

"Robin has been inquiring about booking passage," Lister said.

"Indeed?" said Captain Gregersen. "Why don't you join me, sir, and we can discuss it?"

Sir, Robin thought, feeling a flush of warmth. It had been a long time since someone had called him that.

Captain Gregersen chose a table. Several men came to exchange greetings.

Bets came to the table balancing a laden tray. She crowded several jugs of ale on the table top. "The gentlemen there wanted you to have the ale, sir," she told the captain.

"Your cup, sir," the captain said.

Robin placed his mug on the table and the Captain poured out ale.

"So tell me, Robin," said Captain Gregersen. "I take it you are new to Rocky Port."

"Yes," he said. "This is a part of the coast which I had not seen." Truth be told, other than Sea Gate he hadn't seen any part of the coast.

"It's fascinating, is it not? And you wish to see more of it?"

"I had thought to, yes," Robin replied.

Captain Gregersen took a swallow of ale. "What part?"

Robin could give the Captain only the same lame reply that he had given Lister. "Any part."

Captain Gregersen lifted his chin and laughed. "Passenger, eh? You're certain you're not a sailor?" he asked.

From Lister's and Captain Gregersen's comments Robin deduced that sailors didn't care what was the destination, it was the voyage that interested them. "Fairly certain," he replied. As Lister had accurately determined Robin was a landlubber. His first sight of the sea had unnerved him.

"We leave on the morrow. We have cargo to offload here and cargo bound for Hewnstone to load and off we go. Not much time to linger. Our services are in demand. Does that itinerary suit you?"

Hewnstone. Even far away in the Chalklands, Robin had heard of it. Once a quiet seaside hamlet owned by a fellow named Hugh, it had grown to a huge seaport city that became known for its granite and limestone architecture, its founder forgotten. Robin had never been to Hewnstone but King Bewilliam's steward had journeyed to Hewstone's markets for many of the goods needed and wanted by Bell Castle and its subjects.

Perhaps that was where Robin should head next. From what he knew of it, the place was populous. A man could get lost there and not be found by soldiers looking for a fugitive sorcerer. "It does indeed."

"And you will be prepared to depart tomorrow?"

Robin nodded. "And what would be the fare?"

"For you to Hewnstone—"

"Me and my horse."

"Horse?"

"And cat."

CHAPTER NINE

"The cat is no problem," said Captain Gregersen. "We usually have a ship's cat although we do not at present."

Robin smiled. No other cats aboard was a good thing. Meeyoo was coming of the age when she would be mating and having kittens, kittens he could not afford to be saddled with, nor would he have the heart to abandon much less—horrible thought!—drown.

"The horse, however . . ." The captain looked downward and his lips pressed together in a thin line. "Well, that is a different matter altogether. We can't take a horse."

"Is the Orion not a cargo vessel?"

"It is but this trip our cargo is dry goods and building supplies. We are carrying timber to the coastal settlements where there is little, and vegetable wool and lambs' wool to supply weavers. We're transporting furs and pelts, not livestock."

Robin recalled his sojourn at Sea Gate Fortress, where there was so little lumber that furnishings, furniture, even buildings were constructed of seashells.

"We'd need to carry food and water for the horse."

Robin thought of Thief with despair. The horse had been abandoned once already when Robin was arrested yet Thief had stayed close and found him again. Robin couldn't desert the animal but he couldn't stay here either. Rocky Port was a small enough place that the fortune teller Gerald knew everyone. The arrival of a newcomer wouldn't stay unnoticed for long.

If Robin left Thief behind, what would happen to him? Robin knew he would not return to Rocky Port. Perhaps he could get word to Gabrielle at the stables and bequeath Thief to her? Robin awaited Captain Gregersen's decision with held breath.

"I believe we will have room for a little extra cargo although that will incur an additional charge," Captain Gregersen said. "You have money, I trust, to cover not only your fare but this excess baggage?" The fare that Captain Gregersen named would take a sizeable portion of the advance Robin had negotiated for the dragon-slaying. He would have far less with which to ransom his kingdom but there was no help for it. The tale that Glad Abner had told of the hunt for the sorcerer had left Robin eager to get away—far, far away and quickly. Tomorrow might not be soon enough.

"You have a passenger," Robin said. "I am deeply appreciative of your hospitality," he said, "but if I may, I will excuse myself. I need to make arrangements for my lodging tonight." Robin reached for his purse to pay for his meal, but Captain Gregersen stopped his hand. "Nay, good fellow, supper was at my invitation. We will look for you and your horse on the wharf tomorrow at sunrise."

They shook hands. Robin collected his rucksack, excused himself, and found a stool at the bar where he arranged with Bets and Lister for a room.

"We would be happy to have you lodge with us," said Lister and Robin wondered if his association with the captain contributed to the man's enthusiasm. "Welcome. If you would set out your cup, I'll pour you a celebratory ale, on the house."

Robin accepted the drink but hardly tasted it, every muscle and nerve taut with anxiety. He had hardly arrived in Rocky Port and now he was impatient to be gone. He would not feel at ease until Rocky Port and the deadly fortress were well at his back. As the fortune teller's father, Gerald, had predicted, Fate had made a decision for him. Robin would not be going to the Chalklands, at least not yet. First he would visit Hewnstone. He would leave at first light.

*****

A sea-scented breeze wafting through the small window laved Robin's face. The well-worn linens were soft against his skin and Meeyoo a comfortable warm weight on his chest. He was a world away from the night of terror he spent in the fortress's dungeon. Robin felt that he could happily lie here forever but the darkness in the room was already thinning.

Would that he had time for a proper bath and a haircut but it was well past time to be on his way. Robin availed himself of wash water to bathe and shave and struggled into clothes still slightly damp from the rinse he had given them the night before. He packed up his gear and Meeyoo.

More of Gerald's words came back to him. This time Robin would prepare for the trip, would provision himself well with food, drink, tools.

The sun had barely ridden over the horizon yet people already streamed in and out of the shops, carpets and bolts of cloth on their shoulders and bundles under their arms. A clutch of customers crowded the food stall. Robin bought bread, dried fruit, cured meat, and a jug of ale for himself, carrots and sweet potato for Thief, and a wedge of cheese for Meeyoo. At a mercer he bought a scrap of bright yellow silk. It would make a nice hair ribbon for Gabrielle who richly deserved it for her kindness. He paid her for Thief's care and collected the horse, thinking that he would truly miss the woman's curious rhymes.

As Robin left the stables, the fluttering of red birds high on the bluff caught his eye. His breath stuck in his throat. The fluttering was not red birds, but pennants. Two riders stood at the top of the grade, their black and red livery a stark contrast with the blue sky above them. Red-and-black pennants streamed in the breeze from the tips of their lances. Soldiers from the fortress.

Robin hurried to the wharf where several ships had already entered the harbor. On the ships' decks, men hoisted crates and piled them onto smaller transport vessels. On the wharf, sailors

69

helped load merchandise into carts. Customers surrounded other sailors who sold baskets and strings of fish that glimmered in the sun like silver platters. In the distance, more ships awaited their turn to pass through the mouth of the harbor. Their sails gleamed bright white against a cloudless blue sky. The waterfront rang with the clang of metal against metal, the creaking of wood and leather, the flapping of fabric in the wind, the cries of birds, and the shouts of sailors hollering over the hubbub. The breeze made tiny waves in the harbor's water. A good day for sailing, Robin thought. Or was it? He had never been sailing. That was about to change.

He searched out Captain Gregersen's ship. Robin found the same blue and white crest he had seen on the Captain's clothes insignia emblazoned on the ship's single rectangular sail. The image implied that Captain Gregersen's Orion was a massive vessel with three sails. Instead, Robin found the Orion to be much less formidable a craft than he would have guessed, with one mast and the one sail. The vessel's sides were barely higher than the wharf to which it was anchored.

Robin tied Thief's reins to a piling at the foot of a wooden plank bridge between the wharf and the ship. Sailors hauling crates and tuns to the wharf passed others trudging across the plank with outbound cargo. Robin waylaid one of them. "Excuse me, where would I find Captain Gregersen this morning?"

"Amidships," the man replied without a glance behind him.

Robin didn't know where on the ship that was but apparently the captain was aboard somewhere. Robin crossed the plank dodging men with heavy pelts draped over their shoulders and bales of wool balanced on their heads. He immediately found the ship's subtle but constant rocking motion unsettling. Each step demanded that he make a conscious effort to stay on his feet. He spotted Captain Gregersen and picked his way across the deck, sidestepping coils of rope and grunting crewmen rolling barrels into position along the ship's side.

"Robin," said Captain Gregersen, pitching his voice above the noise. "On time, and I thank you. We must go with the tide. We need to get your horse aboard . . ." Gregersen turned his head to regard the lengths of wood, bundles of fur and textiles, and crates stacked on the deck. One of the crew members edged past. Captain Gregersen caught his sleeve. "What is taking so long, Hendriksen? We must set sail soon but half the cargo is still on board and we've hardly begun to take on the new load. As well, this gentleman will be our passenger and we need to load his horse. We're going to lose the tide."

"I'm sorry, sir," said the man Hendriksen. Unlike the other men who worked bare-chested and even barefooted, Hendriksen wore a tunic and long leather vest. "We're doing the best we can but we're shorthanded. Lute and Toby are absent without leave. No one knows where they are."

Robin pictured the two men he observed slinking away from Bet and Lister's establishment. "I believe that I saw two of your men last night at the alehouse. I'm fairly certain that they noticed you when you entered but they left."

"In the alehouse, you say?"

Robin nodded. "One appeared to be unwell."

"Drunk as loon no doubt." The captain looked as though he could spit. "Toby and Lute. They have tried my patience for the last time."

Robin could have sworn that he heard the captain growl.

"You don't suppose that you can get your horse aboard by yourself?"

Robin frowned. Captain Gregersen had demanded a pretty penny for Thief's cartage and now had the gall to put Robin to work? He was about to voice his objection when he saw that the fortress's soldiers had entered the waterfront street. "I am agreeable to that."

He started for the plank bridge when Captain Gregersen said, "Hold a minute." The captain scrutinized Robin from head to foot and his face took on a ruminative expression. "We find ourselves undermanned. Would you be willing to work on this voyage for your fare?"

If it would get them away from this port and out to sea before the soldiers found him . . . Robin had no idea what work on a ship entailed but how hard could it be? He doubted that it would be any more arduous than blacksmithing. That had been grueling but Robin had been desperate. Not having to pay for passage would leave money in his purse for the reestablishment of his kingdom. "Indeed, I would," he said.

"Excellent. Welcome aboard," Captain Gregersen said with a smile, and then the smile faded. "Hendriksen," he called.

The harried man hastened to his side. "Robin, this is Hendriksen. Hendriksen, this is Robin, the newest member of the crew. He will be replacing Lute and Toby."

Robin realized with some dismay that he had just agreed to replace not one but two able-bodied men who by all appearances had been at least fifteen years his junior. As he reconsidered the wisdom of the bargain that he had just struck he saw the fortress's soldiers in conversation with the grocer.

The captain departed and Hendriksen said, "Set down that pack of yours. You can stow your gear in the folk's cell."

Robin was certain that he looked as bewildered as he felt because Hendriksen said, "Fo'c'sle. I'm sorry," he sighed. "Forecastle?" He pointed to the front of the ship. "Forecastle." Hendriksen turned and pointed to the rear of the ship. "Aftcastle. Crew sleeps in the fo'c'sle. That is, when we sleep. Captain and passengers in the aftcastle."

The "castles" of which he spoke were small railed decks. Raised above the sides of the ship and reached by ladders they did indeed look a bit like crenelated parapets. The smaller castle fitted over the ship's V-shaped front while the aftcastle spanned the larger and more rectangular shape of the vessel's rear. Beneath them, dark cubbyholes were crammed with supplies. "You said passengers are accommodated in the aftcastle," Robin said.

"Aye, but you're crew now," said Hendriksen. "Leave that sword and that pack of yours in the fo'c'sle but make sure they're secure."

Robin patted his sword's hilt. "This is staying with me."

Hendriksen frowned. "I say it isn't. It's too long for shipboard duty. We prefer shorter weapons. They're more useful in close quarters. Yours will get in the way of your duties. Stow it. Tie down your gear well. Anything that's not lashed down is likely to go overboard. Then meet me amidships."

And just whom did this Hendriksen think he was ordering around? If only he knew. Stifling a protest, Robin ducked his head and stepped into the forecastle cubbyhole. Two rolled-up bolts of leather lay on the floor with four overstuffed sacks of rough fabric, their rope drawstrings looped through the ship's ribs. Robin shrugged off his rucksack and knotted the straps around the leg of a small bench. With reluctance, he threaded his weapon through the straps, securing it to the bench with leather laces.

He laid back the pack's flap. Meeyoo took a cautious peek at her surroundings. Her nose twitched and her ears laid back.

"This is home for the next few days, Meeyoo. Yes, I know, this is strange. But you'll be safe here. We both will," he said. Safer than they would on land. "You are welcome here and have the run of the ship. Just don't jump overboard."

Hendriksen had said that the crew slept here but Robin saw no beds, no pallets, no cupboards, just some of the cargo that had been loaded today and coils of rope.

He hurried to rejoin Hendriksen who assigned Robin the task of adding crates from a tall stack along one side of the ship to the pile already on the wharf. Robin had no idea what was in them but whatever it was, it was heavy. Nevertheless, as he crossed the plank he hoisted the crate to his shoulders, all the better to put something solid between his face and the searching eyes of the fortress soldiers who had worked their way further down the waterfront street.

Throughout an hour that seemed much longer than a mere sixty minutes, Robin hauled weighty loads to and from the ship, all the while trying to evade the soldiers' notice. His footing was unsteady on the slick deck that moved erratically under him. The other crew members shouted instructions to each other and Robin found it dizzying trying to sort out which order was meant for which man. Yet all seemed focused on getting the ship loaded and out to sea. Robin found the spirit of teamwork reminiscent of his battle training which emphasized the importance of every man working single-mindedly toward a shared goal.

Robin struggled under the weight of bale of wool when he saw something that nearly made him stumble. One of the soldiers eyed Thief. Robin wondered just how close a description had been issued of the sorcerer's equine familiar. The soldier seemed especially curious about the horse.

"Robin," called Captain Gregersen.

Robin nearly dropped his burden. "Yes."

"We are very nearly loaded. Let's get that horse aboard."

"Now?" The guard had dismounted and was making a circuit around Thief.

"Yes, now, unless you've changed your mind about taking him."

"Not at all." Robin slowly crossed the plank bridge. He was dismayed to see that the soldier was one of the guards who had first apprehended him. So much for him having killed three men, but Robin didn't suppose that this was the time or the place to plead his case. "Excuse me, sir," he said to the soldier, taking pains not to look the man in the eye. "I've been ordered to get this horse aboard."

The guard seemed to take little note of Robin and he was glad that he had shaved his beard.

"This horse is going aboard the—" the guard looked up at the ship. "The name of this ship, Seaman?"

"The Conqueror, sir."

"Indeed. And the captain's name?"

"Lawson," replied Robin.

The soldier nodded. "Tell Captain Lawson we wish to speak with him about an important matter. An escaped felon. The captain should be wary. This dangerous outlaw may try to sneak aboard the vessel. Send the captain down here so that we may inform him."

Robin untied Thief's reins from the bollard. "I will tell him forthwith," he said. "Sir," he hastened to add, and led the horse across the plank. Thief's steps were halting and when they reached the deck, the horse balked at walking on what proved to be a slick and unfamiliar surface. "Come along now, Thief," he said, and led the horse across the deck step by edgy step.

Hendriksen waved Robin over. "I saw the soldier talking to you. Problem?"

"Not at all," Robin replied. "He simply wished to remark on my adroitness with the horse."

"Adroit?" said Hendriksen.

"That I handle him well." Robin hoped that the Orion would put considerable distance between itself and the dock before the soldier realized that "Captain Lawson" would not be coming to speak with him.

"Indeed," said Hendriksen although he did not appear wholly convinced. "Well, come with me." Hendriksen strode across the deck to join three other men. "And by the way, when you speak to the captain, you are to address him as 'sir' as befits a commander."

And any minute, they'll all be expecting me to bow, too, Robin thought.

"This is Robin," Hendriksen said to the other sailors. "He's our latest crewman, replacing Lute and Toby. Well, then, let's get this horse in the hold. Then we'll raise the gangplank."

Whatever the gangplank was, Robin hoped that it wouldn't be too heavy. He had already lifted his own weight dozens of times this morning.

At Hendriksen's feet, a square cut in the deck opened to a dark space below. Robin peered into it and could barely make out the barrels and crates crammed into the ship's dark belly. Suspended above the opening, a leather sling hung by ropes attached to a beam that pointed skyward—a crane of sorts except Robin could see no treadwheel for raising and lowering the load. Hendriksen and other crewman hastened to draw the sling under Thief's middle and Robin realized the intent was to lower the horse into the space under the deck.

"He'll be housed there?" Robin asked in dismay. The cramped windowless space was worse than the fortress's dungeon.

"That's how it's done," replied Hendriksen. "Don't worry, he'll be fine. We do this all the time. Go, join those men at the capstan."

Hendriksen pointed to where three men stood alongside what appeared to be a large wooden spool with four long poles run through it. Each man stood at the end of the pole farthest from the spool. Robin deduced that this was the treadwheel after a fashion, laid sideways rather than vertically. It appeared to operate much like the wheel Robin had seen powering large grinding stones at a mill but this wheel was turned by sailors rather than horses. Robin took up position at the fourth pole. He no sooner found his place when one of the men shouted, "Alas, my love, I cannot stay." His cry had a cadence to it, like the beginning of a chant.

The other men yelled back, "Yo, heave ho!"

"I may be back another day," the first man sang out, and when the other men replied, "Yo, heave ho!" Robin realized it was a chant, with call and response.

"But I'm a sailor with debts to pay."

"Yo, heave ho!"

"So, my love, it's anchors aweigh!"

"Yo! Yo! Yo, heave ho!"

Robin marched forward in step with the other men, pushing the pole before him. The man's chanting set the rhythm making the task part Herculean undertaking, part dance. The men's combined effort caused the spool to rotate, which in turn took up the rope that operated the crane, lifting Thief over the hold's opening. Reversing their direction, they then lowered the horse into the space.

Hendriksen bolted a wooden cover over the opening. "There," he said, and with a wave of his arm indicated that Robin should join the men already standing alongside the plank bridge. "On my three, men," said Hendriksen. "One, two, three." Robin looked at the other sailors. They squatted, grabbed the plank with both hands, and lifted. Since "raising" seemed to be the order of the day, Robin did likewise. Together, the four men hoisted the plank, heaved, and pulled it fully aboard.

The Orion's crew took off in all directions. One raced to the side of the ship and reached across to the wharf. He loosened ropes from pilings, coiled them on the deck, then pushed against the dock. Hendriksen positioned himself at the rear of the ship while the captain stood at the front.

Robin tried to steal a look at the soldier on the wharf without catching the man's eye. He thought he saw the man waving and calling, but whatever he might have been saying was lost in the shouted commands from Captain Gregersen and replies from Hendriksen and the crew.

CHAPTER TEN

An oar was pressed into Robin's hand and he followed the lead of the other crew members, each of whom took a post at one side of the ship. To the tune of yet another chant they rowed in unison, guiding the boat across the harbor and out past the jetties. They had to dodge vessels both large and small, sailing ships like the Orion, and small rowed boats ferrying men and cargo between the dock and the larger ships, making their progress slow and painstaking.

Gulls and other sea birds fluttered and chattered overhead. As the ship plied the harbor water, Robin spotted the gray fin of some large fish. When its glossy curved back broke the surface, Robin recognized it for a dolphin which he had seen pictured in heraldic crests and works of art.

Out of the corner of his eye, Robin spotted Meeyoo winding her way around the barrels and coils of rope arrayed on the deck. Where the ship's side—gunwale, the crewman called it—dipped low to accommodate loading and unloading, she stretched her neck out to peer at the water. A moment later, she jumped back as if startled, then crept forward again. Wondering what had caught her attention, Robin stood in time to catch a glimpse of Meeyoo and a dolphin almost nose to nose before the big fish swam away. The animal hemstitched its way through the water alongside the Orion before submerging and disappearing from view. Robin found something delightful in the fish's leaps and plunges and hoped he'd see more dolphins on the journey.

Clear of the harbor, the crew stowed the oars and dispersed to their tasks on the deck. There was so much to learn about being aboard a ship, Robin found it a challenge simply to stay out of everyone's way much less be of real use. Like the servants of a castle, the vessel's crew members each had his responsibilities. Captain Gregersen had the command. He determined and set the course, assigned the various duties. Robin learned that Hendriksen would "take the helm," keeping the course and steering the boat by means of a tiller at the ship's rear. Three crewmen—Eli, Crank, and Cook—did whatever the captain or Hendriksen ordered when they weren't occupied with what Robin determined were routine chores: sanding and varnishing the woodwork, mending ropes, inspecting sails, and making any repairs. There seemed to be no end to the work, especially the Sisyphean task of polishing any metal parts. Rope rotted from the inside out and required constant care, as did anything metal. "Rust never rests," said Eli who was one of the two "ordinary" seamen, Crank being the other. As steward of the food supply and preparer of the meals, Cook was slightly less ordinary.

They all spoke a foreign language, of port and starboard, stem and stern, luff and clew, line and halyard. Simply trying to recall which was the left side of the ship and which the right gave Robin a headache.

"Here, look," Eli sighed, and pulled Robin to the right of the vessel. "Before ships got rudders, we used an oar to steer. Still do use it sometimes." He pointed to the long oar lying ready near an oar lock. "So, it's called a steerboard and this is the steerboard side."

"I thought you said 'starboard,'" Robin replied.

A forbearing smile creased Eli's round face and his hazel eyes were gentle. "Aye, steerboard, starboard, same thing. Now," he continued as he led Robin to the opposite side, "you don't want to damage your steerboard while docking so you always come into port on this side." He grinned. "Port side.

Robin nodded, massaging his aching temples. When his head stopped aching he would ask why the sail was called a sheet, and why the pole to which it was attached was called a yard, and why some of the ropes—no, lines! lines!—were called shrouds.

As bad as it was, his headache was less of a problem than his rubbery legs and queasy stomach which got worse the farther they got out to sea. At the mouth of the harbor where the waves were especially choppy Robin's stomach threatened to come up his throat. The urge to heave was almost uncontrollable.

"Seasick," muttered Crank. He had likely earned his name from the narrowed eyes and pinched mouth that gave him a permanently soured expression. "He looks green. Landlubber."

Cook threw an arm around Robin's shoulders. "Go lie down in the fo'c'sle. Close your eyes," he said in a lilting accent that sounded almost musical to Robin's ears. The man's dark skin came not from many days spent on the deck of ship but by virtue of his birth in a distant exotic land.

Robin staggered to the tiny shadowed space. He stretched out on the floor but couldn't get comfortable enough to rest much less quiet his stomach which seemed to twist this way and that in response to the rocking of the ship. The smells trapped in the close space—oil, pitch, wet wood, rusted metal—added to his distress. Meeyoo decided it must be time to retire and climbed as she was wont to do onto his chest. Robin shoved her off three times before she slunk under the bench and crouched there, glaring at him.

He drifted off and got a few moments respite only to be jolted awake by the ship's movement. He opened his eyes and saw that just outside the fo'c'sle Seaman Crank sat knitting. No, not knitting as he used no needles but instead his flying fingers tied many strands of rope into complicated knots. I must be truly ill, feverish, Robin thought. I'm having hallucinations. He rolled over on his side which only caused his stomach to roil. He turned onto his back and closed his eyes once more.

When next he opened them he saw Seaman Eli seated nearby on the floor, busy digging the point of a knife into a small white object.

"What are you doing?" Robin asked.

"Scrimshaw." Eli held up the object and Robin perceived the outline of an image carved into what looked like a bit of bone. "How are you feeling?"

"Like hell," Robin said. "I can't continue. We need to turn around and take me back to Rocky Port." He had come to believe that he would be better off wasting away in the fortress's dungeon.

Eli laughed. "I certainly wouldn't be the one to suggest that to the captain. I'm afraid you'll have to tough it out. Before long your mind will learn to rule over your body," said Eli.

"Maybe so but I think I've lost this round." Robin sprang up, raced to the side of the ship, and vomited into the sea until his stomach was empty and then he retched some more. He considered simply throwing himself overboard to end his misery.

"You might do better here out in the fresh air," said Eli. "Find a spot to sit amidships. Sit tall, keep your trunk balanced over your hips. Try to get along with the rhythm. Focus on the horizon. You'll soon get your sea legs."

If I don't die first, thought Robin. But he did as Eli suggested and found that it was a bit like learning to sit a horse. When he felt that he could stand without puking, Robin asked if he might have a minute to check on Thief. Eli unlatched the hold's hatch cover and Robin descended a ladder to the dark damp space crowded with cargo. The close and smelly quarters made him ready to retch all over again.

The horse seemed ill at ease, his eyes wide, nostrils flared.

"You're sure he's going to be alright here?" Robin said to Eli.

"You can come check on him when you're not working but be assured he'll be fine. We transport animals all the time," Eli replied. "Never lost a one and no one's ever complained that their cargo arrived in poor condition. Look here, the straps keep him in place. He'll get hay, water. He's got this mat to stand on, it's less slick than the wood so he won't slip."

Indeed, the floor beneath Thief's hooves had been laid with a sort of rug.

"What is that woven from?" Robin asked. "It looks like rope."

"It is rope. Hendriksen made it. We often have a need for something when we're far from land and we have to do what we can with what we have at hand."

Without much conviction, Robin comforted Thief telling him that he would be safe and that his needs were well met.

CHAPTER ELEVEN

Robin returned to the deck to find that the Orion had pulled some distance away from Rocky Port. As relieved as he was to have escaped the deadly fortress, the rapidly disappearing land made him uneasy. Before long they would be completely surrounded by water.

The Orion's crewmen seemed unconcerned but went about their work as though laboring and living atop a few planks of wood floating in the middle of the ocean was the most normal thing.

"From the way you've got your eyes glued to the harbor, I'm guessing you're still having second thoughts about coming aboard," said Eli.

"No, not at all," Robin said. "Well, maybe a little."

Eli chuckled. "This is your first time on a ship?"

"As a matter of fact . . ." Robin nodded.

Eli said, "You might surprise yourself and decide you like it. I've been sailing since I was a lad of ten. Oh, I kicked like a mule when I was first impressed into service. Started as a captain's servant. But by the end of the first voyage, I was certain that I did not want to go back to working in the mine." He clapped Robin on the shoulder. "You'll see. Now don't worry about that horse, he'll be fine."

"And my cat?" Robin asked.

Eli frowned. "You have a cat too?"

"Captain Gregersen said it wouldn't be a problem."

"And it won't. We usually have a cat or two aboard. They're good at keeping mice out of our food stores and keeping rats from chewing the lines. Had you in mind to put your cat to work?"

"By all means. Meeyoo's a good hunter," Robin said.

"Then let's see this cat," said Eli.

Robin led the man to the fo'c'sle where they found Meeyoo crouched in the deepest corner of the bow. "Meeyoo, it's OK, you can come out," Robin said in a soothing tone. "This is Eli." He put an arm across the man's shoulder, hoping that would give Meeyoo confidence.

Slowly she emerged from her hiding place and made a wide circuit around the Orion's crewman. Robin hoped that Eli wouldn't try to touch the cat which might startle her and earn the sailor retaliatory bites and scratches. At last Meeyoo sat on her haunches at Robin's ankle, her gaze fixed on Eli. Robin reached down and scratched her ears.

"Strong looking cat," Eli said. "I'll open the hatch to the hold. It would be good for her to find her way down there, keep the vermin down. Well, time for us to get to work. What was it that the captain assigned you to do?"

Work? Robin had done nothing but work since setting foot on the deck. There was more?

"Mend lines or sails?" Eli asked. "Patch the cladding? Swab the deck?"

It all sounded like heavy labor. The morning's efforts had already left Robin weary and his seasickness had drained him.

"Pump out the bilge?" asked Eli.

"Bilge?" Robin said, his ship-language learning headache threatening to return.

"The space under the floor of the hold, down below."

Robin had only just gotten his stomach to settle down and didn't at all fancy going below again. "I'm good at sharpening cutting edges."

"Are you now?" Eli said.

"Permit me." Robin withdrew his knife and held it out. "Do you need edges to be sharper than this?"

Eli had no sooner pressed his thumb to the blade's edge than a thin red line of blood sprouted on this skin. He pressed the fresh cut to his lips. "No, should I say not."

"I can get all your cutting tools that sharp."

"Well, that's a fine skill indeed. Find you a place to work and I'll round up whatever needs attention."

Robin fetched his whetstone and dragged a crate to a spot on deck where the sunlight was good. Eli returned with an assortment of knives, daggers, and shears, plus a sandglass and a brass bell.

"You can keep time," Eli said. "It's a job I was given to do on my first voyage. We take turns at a four-hour watch. Mark the time and sound a bell, one for each half-hour, until you've rung eight bells. That's how we'll know how much time is passing. At eight bells we start a new watch and change duties."

Robin nodded. He had heard the bell ringing but hadn't noticed that that it sounded on schedule. "When do you rest?"

Eli shrugged. "Sailors don't seem to need as much sleep as landlubbers, I guess. The work does keep us busy most of the time. Still, on some voyages even with all there is to do we have a bit of leisure." They spent it swapping tales from other journeys, he said, and when they got bored with listening to the same old tired story, they each had a little pastime. Eli said his was scrimshaw, his carving of pictures into bits of bone from large fish. Robin hadn't been hallucinating when he saw Crank knotting together bits of rope, something Eli called macramé. Even Hendriksen fashioned objects from rope, like the mat upon which Thief stood. "He said you'll be taking a watch, by the way. I'm guessing you've not done that before."

"Not on a ship," Robin replied, although he had stood watch many times at Bell Castle and on campaigns when someone had to be awake and alert at all times. "Who are we on guard against?" Robin had noted the masts of other ships plying the same waters as the Orion. Did Eli mean that other crews meant them harm, intending perhaps to take their cargo? The other ships seemed to keep their distance and even veered away rather than towards them.

"Not who," Eli replied. "What. Anything that could damage the ship. We don't often collide with another ship but it has been known to happen when another crew loses control. More likely we might run onto a sandbar or be struck by some flotsam. The sailor on watch keeps a sharp eye out, calls what he sees back to the helmsman."

And that, Robin realized, explained the nearly continuous shouting.

"'Cause you see," Eli continued, "from where the helmsman stands, the sail blocks his view. He can't see what's happening at the front of the ship. You've got to be his eyes." With that he took off to climb the ladder to the castle at the ship's bow.

Robin settled to his task as did the other crewmen. Crank and Cook attended to the deck, Cook pouring buckets of seawater on the wood while on his knees Crank rubbed its surface with a stone. Then in response to a shouted command that Robin didn't understand, Crank sprang up and climbed a rope net strung out from the mast like a huge spider web. Like some showman at a fair he clung to the yardarm, inched out on a rope strung below it and gathered in the voluminous sail.

Robin hadn't worked long before his rhythmic movements and single-minded focus lulled him into a detached state somewhat like a pleasant nap taken without sleeping. The smith who had instructed him in the art and science of blade-sharpening spoke of this detachment in almost worshipful tones and indeed Robin found it soothing. The vessel's constant motion, the clanging and shouting, the odors of pitch, wool, and lumber all faded from his awareness. Robin felt neither too hot nor too cold. The sun baked the top of his head but the sea breeze brought cooling relief.

He started out of the trance to find that the sand in the glass had sifted from the inverted top bottle through the narrow neck into the bottom bottle. He hastened to ring the bell, hoping that he hadn't let too much time pass. He smelled smoke and his stomach clenched with dread. On a vessel fire would be as deadly an enemy as storms, pirates, sandbars, and too much water in the wrong place. Robin scanned the ship behind him for the source. He spied smoke but before he could sound a warning, he saw Eli trotting toward him.

"Eli," Robin called. "I smell smoke! Fire—"

Eli nodded. "Not to worry. Cook is preparing supper. We don't always have a hot meal. But the weather's fair, the seas gentle, and we have fresh supplies. We will eat well this evening." Eli grinned and patted his stomach. He turned and pointed and Robin spotted Cook standing at a hearth of sorts. Coals glowed atop a bed of gravel in a rectangular iron brazier laid on top of the deck. Strong aromas wafted from the pot he tended. "Come and eat," Eli said.

Robin needed no further urging. His stomach was beyond empty.

The supper that Eli had so eagerly anticipated was a stew of mostly root vegetables and broth, with a few chunks of meat. Robin tasted sweet and salt, and then his mouth burned with some fiery seasoning. He guessed it was some unusual spice from Cook's exotic homeland. Robin had eaten only a spoonful when the strong flavors threatened to incite his stomach to revolt once again. Despite his gnawing hunger, he offered his portion to a grateful Eli. The speed with which the seaman gulped down the extra helping left Robin to wonder how such measly portions could sustain men who worked as hard as Orion's crew.

To drink, Cook gave him water. Robin realized that his face must have betrayed his surprise because Cook said, "You might have been expecting ale," he said. "No way to keep that fresh or make it on board. Later, when the water goes bad, we'll mix it with rum."

The crew made quick work of supper. Cook smothered the fire, packed away his cooking gear, and went to take the helm. Crank would stand watch.

Robin joined Eli at the bow. The veteran sailor described the many features of what seemed to Robin a featureless expanse of water.

Pointing to some floating lengths of wood, Eli said, "Jetsam. Sometimes in foul weather or shallow water, sailors have to lighten a ship to stay afloat," said Eli. "Times like those, the only remedy is to throw cargo overboard, like lumber they might be hauling. Jetsam. There be tales of latitudes where the winds die and ships become becalmed and livestock be cast into the sea rather than die of thirst or hunger when the food and water run out. Horse latitudes they're called because of that."

Robin didn't like the sound of that at all. Should the Orion find itself in such dire straits, there would be hell to pay before Robin would let Thief be put off the ship.

"Now should you see pieces with jagged edges, those are from a vessel that broke apart. Flotsam," Eli said.

Seaweed was vegetable matter that grew on the ocean floor but when detached rose to the surface to drift with the tide. "Seaweed's not usually a problem unless we run into a mess of it. Ships have been known to get snagged."

Robin thought of an ancient tale told him as a boy, that of a ship full of sailors that got so badly ensnared in the long hair of seductive sea nymphs that it could not move. The crew perished aboard a ship mired in place. A fanciful tale no doubt inspired by a tangle of seaweed.

"The clouds, the sky, the wind all tell us of good sailing or bad." Eli smiled. "Red sky at night, sailor's delight. Means we'll have smooth sailing the next day. But red sky at dawning, sailors take warning because a storm is brewing."

Robin rubbed his throbbing temples. However would he remember all this? He could hardly believe he was meant to take a watch and that Hendriksen intended him to be entrusted with the safety and welfare of the ship, its cargo, and crew. Robin reminded himself that not long ago he had led an entire kingdom. The lives of thousands had been his responsibility yet somehow being responsible for the compact Orion and its small crew felt more burdensome.

Eli said, "The waves hitting the ship now were formed by weather hours ago and miles away. They don't tell you much that you don't already know. But sometimes you see a wave shape that tells of good weather to come. We call them cats' paws because the little eddies look just like cats have walked on the water."

It was Robin's turn to smile. Meeyoo would like that.

Sea creatures plied these waters at depths far below the surface but now and then Robin spied not only the arching back of a dolphin but also the snaking shadow of an eel and the menacing fin of a dreaded shark.

A setting sun cast a warm glow on the deck's wood, glinted off the polished metal, and bled its color into the surrounding clouds, veiling the sky in red. Robin wondered if this was the "red sky" of which Eli had spoken, an assurance of a good sailing day tomorrow.

As abruptly as if someone had extinguished a candle, day turned into night. Lit only by the moon and stars, the Orion's deck was all dark shapes and darker shadows. Exhausted, Robin considered retiring to the fo'c'sle but the prospect of struggling to sleep in the dank and crowded space was repellent. Perhaps he could sleep out here on the deck. Robin spied a moving shadow—Meeyoo sniffing around amidships—and picked his way carefully across the deck to join her. Making a backrest of a coil of rope he sat and Meeyoo climbed into his lap. Robin sank lower against the coiled rope support, every bone and muscle aching. He wished that his body would stop berating him for taxing it so mightily such that he could get some badly needed rest. Would that the bells stop clanging, the crew stop yelling, the ship stop its constant pitching and rolling. How could he possibly sleep?

From where he sat, hungry, hurting, and weary, a future night spent in his restored castle tucked into his draped and cushioned bed, rested, fed, and garbed in soft linen seemed more like a fanciful dream than an attainable goal. While he did feel strangely safe on this fragile floating island, he also felt isolated and alone.

Robin stroked Meeyoo's back and whispered, "This will be a short journey. Eli said so. Then we will be in port. You and Thief and I will make our way to the Chalklands. We will find our deeds and titles, our servants. We'll enlist knights and bring the kingdom back to life. You'll like being a castle cat, Meeyoo."

She purred, whether in agreement or in appreciation of the petting Robin could not have said.

Above him, the sky with its myriad stars looked like a black woolen cloth riddled with hundreds of moth holes. Like anyone else he marked the passing of days and weeks by the phases of the moon, reckoned the seasons of the year by the appearance of certain constellations: the Big Bear, the Archer, the Twins. He had to chuckle. Orion had always been one of his childhood favorites; easy to spot with four bright stars at the Hunter's shoulders and knees, the slanted line of three stars that was his belt, and the cluster that was his sword.

Yes, tonight Orion could be seen clearly but Robin could see nothing of land. It might be near but in the dark it was out of sight.

He woke to a lightening sky and the chiming of eight bells. Silhouetted by the thin light of dawn, Captain Gregersen, Hendriksen, and Cook stood grouped around the brazier. Possibly there was breakfast. Robin hoped that his seasickness had abated enough to allow him to eat. He shooed Meeyoo from his lap and ratcheted his stiff body to a standing position, his muscles tight and throbbing, his head muzzy, and his mouth dry.

He stumbled to the brazier not knowing what to expect for a morning meal but after last night's meager supper he imagined that it would be substantial. Images of regal repasts danced before his eyes: generous portions of meat or fish, watered wine or ale, some white bread. Instead Robin found the brazier cold and Orion's morning offerings to be skimpier than last night's supper: a hard baked biscuit that had already gone stale and more tepid water that tasted of wood. He could imagine that after a few days of standing in the sun the drinking water would indeed be as palatable as the pond water he had drunk a couple of days ago.

"Robin," said Captain Gregersen, "I see you've acclimated to life aboard a ship."

If being cramped from sleeping on a hard deck, aching in every muscle and bone, and heaving up everything that had passed his lips meant Robin was acclimated he would have to agree.

"You will work today in the hold."

After making his initial acquaintance with the hold to check on Thief Robin had no interest in spending any substantial time there.

Cook said, "The Orion is a solid vessel but water that doesn't drain off the side seeps down into the bilge. And every ship leaks. It's vital to keep the hold dry by pumping out the bilge."

"I've been in the hold and I don't care to go there again. The odor made me quite ill," Robin said to the captain. "Sir."

Gregersen and the other sailors gaped and Robin realized that he had just objected to an order from the ship's commander. Had anyone dared to speak to Robin that way when he was king . . .

"It makes everyone ill but what would make us all far sicker would be to sink at sea," said Cook, his lilting voice softening the rebuke. "Let's hope that you do find it smelly down there. Stagnant water is a good sign. If it isn't, that means that fresh water is getting in and we've got a leak."

"He needs no explanation," the captain said, biting his words off like chunks of meat. "That wasn't a request, Seaman Robin, it was a command." Gregersen glared and thrust his head almost nose-to-nose with Robin. "May I remind you of your agreement to work this voyage? Do we find you not to be a man of your word?"

And so Robin found himself turning the latch, lifting off the hatch cover, and descending the ladder to the bowels of the ship. Although the open hatch let in some light it provided little ventilation.

For tools he had a bucket and a bilge pump, a wooden box with T-shaped handle, a wooden tube at the bottom, and a leather valve. Drawing on the handle operated the valve to suck water up through the tube, into the box, and out a spout into the bucket. Pulling up and pushing down the handle was like driving a bellows, reminding Robin of the long, hot, and hard days he had spent working in a foundry. Pumping out the bilge proved to be the more onerous of the two tasks. His eyes watered and he felt suffocated in the stuffy crammed space stinking of stagnant water, decomposing stores, and horse manure. Emptying the bucket necessitated climbing the rickety ladder with only one free hand in order to gain the deck and dump the bucket's contents overboard.

He could not remember a sound more welcomed than the eight bells ending the watch. His back and shoulders screaming and thighs trembling from exertion, he straggled up the ladder hoping he'd be assigned a different duty and indeed he was. He was sent back into the hold to check for leaks.

"You can hear a leak," Hendriksen said. He handed Robin a small earthenware pot. "You place the mouth of the pot over the wall and put your ear to the pot's bottom. If there is a leak, you'll hear a low rumbling. Just keep moving the pot around the walls until you're certain they're sound."

Robin sighed. At least this job wouldn't task his shoulders and legs.

It took the better part of the next watch to examine the entire hold.

"When Eli's watch ends, you'll take over," said Hendriksen. "Until then you can help Crank. He's mending rope."

Robin breathed a sigh of relief. At least he'd be on deck in the fresh air and bright light of a clear afternoon.

Mending rope called for an entire boatload of skills. Frayed edges had to be trimmed and kept from unraveling further using a knot that Crank called a whipping knot. Some damaged ropes could be repaired by splicing—partially untwisting the strands and then interweaving them. Though this resulted in a thickening of the line, Crank said that the splice made for a strong join. It sounded like a simple enough procedure until Crank told him there were eight different types of splices.

"Then there's lashing," Crank said, "where you wrap webbing or a piece of cloth around the two ends. And then there's knots.

Different knots for different reasons. Some we use to repair rope, other knots you need to know to tie things down."

Thus far Robin hadn't seen Crank's face wear any expression other than a wrinkled brow, narrowed eyes, and a turned-down mouth, but now he grinned and there was a sparkle in his eyes. "An overhand knot's the simplest. Even a landlubber like you knows how to tie that. Two overhand knots make a square knot. You can tie two ropes together with a square knot. But you got to make it correctly, right over left, then left over right. Otherwise you end up with a granny knot which is no good because it slips easily." Crank proceeded to demonstrate a figure-eight, bowline, clove hitch, and half hitch, his fingers flying so fast that Robin could barely make out how the knots came together. "But you got to remember, a knot can actually weaken the rope and if the rope is going to fail, it'll fail where the knot is. Splicing's better but sometimes all you can manage is a knot." He pointed to a pile of torn, frayed, and unraveling ropes. "See what you can do with those."

By the time the watch was over, Robin's head throbbed from the effort of trying to keep track of which was the standing end, which the running end, and which the working end. He had no doubt about the bitter end. Clearly that was where he had found himself. His fingers ached, the flesh rubbed raw by the ropes' coarse fibers.

Descending from the fo'c'sle Eli found his way across the deck. "You take over now."

Robin would have gulped had his throat not been so dry. "Now?" he asked, hoping his question hadn't voiced itself as a squeak.

"Unless you'd rather take the midnight watch," Eli replied.

Robin asked how he or anyone for that matter could keep an effective watch in the middle of a dark ocean.

"We get our fix from the position of the North Star. And the captain has a new invention called a compass. You might see him holding it. It's a small round box with a drawing of a star. The star's eight arms point to the different directions. A needle floats over the star and it always points north no matter which way the box is turned."

Sounded like magic to Robin.

"Don't worry," said Eli. "Captain Gregersen himself is taking the helm this watch."

Rather than finding this reassuring, Robin felt much as he had as a young prince knowing the man about to judge his swordsmanship would be his own father.

Eli clapped Robin on the back. "I'll stay with you until you've got your feet wet," he said, then chuckled at his own attempt at humor.

His belly rumbling, Robin dashed back to the fo'c'sle and raided his supplies for an apple before heading for the castle over the bow.

As he stood his watch, Robin hesitated even to blink for fear of missing some important information to call out to the captain. Trying to remember everything Eli had told him yesterday worsened his headache. When he wasn't scanning the water's surface for floating threats, Robin tried to peer beneath its silvered moving surface for hidden dangers. To his left —"Port!" Robin chided himself, "Port!"— land was just barely discernible as a thin dark line on the horizon. He couldn't at all make out the landmarks that Eli said they referred to in order to stay on course.

"We don't usually get too far from land," Eli said. "Many times we have several ports to call on. This trip we won't come into port till we make Hewnstone so we sail further out to sea. It's smoother sailing in deeper waters. Fewer chances of running aground and less traffic." Still, Robin hoped the captain wouldn't set a course that would put land completely out of sight. The thought of being surrounded only by water made Robin nervous.

At each bell, Robin cast his eyes skyward to study the clouds for any change that would foretell of bad weather to come. The fluffy white clouds that looked like cauliflower florets were reassuring indicators of continuing fair weather but Robin was on guard for any lifting or darkening that warned of a change for ill. He especially dreaded seeing the flat-on-top anvil shaped cloud that Eli said was a harbinger of rain, thunder, and lightning. Where in such weather did one take cover on the Orion?

And if the captain used the position of the sun to reckon their course, what did he do on cloudy days? Robin had asked.

The man gave him one of his patient smiles. "We use a bit of crystal. Even if the rays are too weak for us to see, they still shine through the crystal. The image it creates tells us where the sun is even if we can't see it."

More magic? Robin asked, but Eli had replied that it was simply a property of that particular type of crystal, a navigational tool passed down through several generations of seafaring Gregersens.

Robin scanned the water, called out that the waves were regular and gentle, the way ahead clear of debris with no other ships in view. He had to shout over the rattling, clanging, and swearing of a day's work going on behind him.

Were there shoals or rocky outcrops they were well hidden beneath waves. The possibility that he could miss a threat to Orion's safety made Robin anxious. He greeted each bell with mounting relief at the shortening of time for which he would be responsible.

He did enjoy one pleasant stretch when the sky was blue, the clouds white, the waves gentle, and the sails full, and he noticed that the tension that had knotted his shoulders for days, even weeks, eased as if carried off by the wind. Sailing under these conditions was not unlike a relaxing trail ride on a mild autumn day.

Eli left and Meeyoo joined Robin and sat for a while at his feet, squinting at the breeze blowing in her face and ruffling her fur until Robin's shouted status report startled her and she scampered away, off on another tour of the ship.

Crank came to relieve him. Robin could scarcely believe his ears when the man said, "You take the tiller for the next watch."

Robin's expression must have given away his surprise because Crank said, "We're in open water. It's not unusual for an ordinary seaman to take the helm. You shouldn't find the task more than you can manage and even if you do, there's no help for that. You'll just have to do your best. We're shorthanded and every man must take a turn at the helm. Just remember that to head toward starboard, point the tiller toward the port side. And the opposite is true of course; to steer toward port, drive the tiller starboard.

"Now, see that small pennant at the top of the mast? See how it's streaming out straight and centered between the two lines?"

Robin nodded.

"Say 'aye.' That means you heard and understood."

"Aye," Robin said. At least he hadn't been ordered to say "aye, Sir."

"All you have to do is steer the ship to keep that flag in that position. Hendriksen on watch will call out anything that you should know about and Captain Gregersen will tell you if there's to be a change in course. Got it?"

Robin mumbled "aye."

"You shouldn't run into any trouble. It'll be Hendriksen's job to see that you don't. But if the rudder becomes hard to manage, holler for help." With that he turned, headed for the fo'c'sle and a few hours' sleep.

Robin immediately found the ship's tiller hard to manage. It was like a live thing in his hand. The currents that he had observed at the water's surface clearly penetrated to its depths and he could feel them tugging at the rudder, conspiring to send the ship in a direction of their own choosing. It took all of Robin's strength to hold the tiller steady.

He riveted his gaze on the pennant streaming from the top of the mast. If it flagged or veered too far to one side or the other of the lines, he pushed at the tiller. It responded with reluctance, and resisted even more stubbornly when he had to direct it the other way to correct his initial error. After several wrong moves he felt as though steering in the opposite direction came more naturally, rather like directing a horse with a nudge of a knee. He found it helped not to think about it too much, the way he had learned to dance. As a young prince, his first few lessons had resulted in his treading on his master's feet. Then a maid who consented to be Robin's partner for extracurricular practice suggested that he relax, listen to the music, and move however felt right. Indeed he found that if he stopped planning his next step, his feet made the right decisions.

Robin took his cues from where on his face the sun burned the hottest and where the wind cooled it, how the water slapped the ship as the vessel plowed through it, as well as the shouted reports from the bow. Robin found it noisy, confusing, and draining, as if he were at a feast and trying to participate in several different conversations at once.

He became aware of the change in wind direction only when the first gust hit his other cheek and nearly knocked him off his feet, as if the ancient Greek god Aeolus had inhaled, turned his head, and exhaled mightily in the opposite direction. The rudder threatened to pull the tiller from Robin's hand. The blast pressed the pennant he had been watching flat against the lines.

Almost lost in the sudden wind was the captain's shouted command to gather in the sail. Robin saw Crank, who had probably just lain down and closed his eyes, race up the rigging and strain to get the huge cloth sheet under control. The frightening sound of fabric tearing rose over the clatter of metal and flapping of the frenzied sail. The ship rode a steep wind-whipped wave and then dropped with a jarring thump into a trough only to climb another.

"Drop the sea anchor!" the captain yelled and Robin watched as Eli threw a bucket overboard, playing out the rope to which it was attached.

Captain Gregersen appeared at Robin's side as he fought to move the tiller against an obstinate current. The captain called for aid. Cook and Eli joined them, tugged on ropes attached to the tiller, and helped to push and pull.

Robin gazed at the mast. Crank had wrapped the sail around it like bulky swaddling. Robin looked a question at Eli.

"We can't let out the sail, not in this wind," he said. "Now we go where the current takes us. The sea anchor will slow us some but . . ." He shrugged. "We may end up a little off course."

A little? Robin thought. He could no longer see the dark stripe that had been land. "The anchor doesn't hold us in position?"

"That would be a mooring anchor," said Eli, "but we would get rolled by the breaking waves. The sea anchor will help us to ride these rough waters, control our drift." His normally placid expression turned serious. "We're farther from shore than we would normally be for this route."

The captain shouted over the wind and slapping water. "Steady as she goes while I make the necessary corrections, get us back on course."

"Aye," Robin said, certain it wasn't going to be as easy as the captain made it sound. "Sir," he added.

Unsmiling, the captain nodded.

CHAPTER TWELVE

The wind continued to pound and Robin's face burned from the scouring. Even the clouds appeared to be blown across the sky with force, stretched thin and wispy.

Nearly as suddenly as it had begun, the windstorm subsided and Hendriksen came to relieve Robin at the helm. As he had been instructed, Robin reported the current rudder position and heading which Hendriksen dutifully echoed, adding "The captain said that you're to get supper, then help Crank with the sail."

Exhausted, Robin bit back a futile protest. "Aye," he muttered and headed for the brazier.

Cook had prepared a curious cold soupy stew from dried meats, biscuits, and fruits. Robin gobbled it down and followed Crank up the rigging. He felt the rope shudder under his feet and looked to his right to see Meeyoo climbing alongside him. "Meeyoo! Get down from here," he cried, and shooed her away. She turned and crept down the rope ladder with less alacrity than she had shown climbing up. Giving up on the lowest rungs, she simply jumped onto the deck.

Robin avoided looking down or even out at the endless expanse of water. Still he couldn't help but see the flotsam—or was it jetsam?—that now bounced on the waves. As he had been warned, anything that wasn't tied down had gotten tossed overboard. Was that Eli splashing around in the water, gathering up whatever he could reach? Cook stretched over the side and pulled salvaged cargo back into the boat.

As Robin drew near Crank, the sailor said, "We've got a bad tear. We'll have to fix it."

"Is there not a spare sail?"

"Aye, but it would be just as much trouble to hoist it as it would to mend this in place." He squinted at Robin. "You need a needle. And a palm."

What was the man talking about? Robin wondered. He had two palms. He held up one hand.

"No, no, that won't do. Get Eli's."

Robin had obviously looked as baffled as he felt because Crank said, "Go on, man. We've got to get this mended and unfurled. Time's a wastin'."

Wondering how he could take someone's palm without injuring the hand, Robin backed down the rigging and hastened to the side of the ship. "Give me your hand!" he called to Eli.

Wearing a puzzled expression Eli swam close and stuck his arm up. Robin grabbed his hand and yanked.

"What the—!"

"I'm sorry," Robin said. "I'm helping Crank mend a sail. He said to take your palm."

With a sigh, Eli hauled himself back aboard. "Follow me." His clothes dripping, he sloshed across the deck to the fo'c'sle where he grabbed one of the drawstring sacks. He rooted around and produced a wide leather strap something like a glove with no fingers. Attached to the leather was a bit of cork topped by a metal disk with several tiny pits. He passed Robin a heavy needle that was more triangular than round in shape and thick thread.

Robin returned to the mast and Crank showed him how to affix the strap such that the cork was positioned at the base of his thumb. "Sailor's palm," he said. "The cork helps to drive the needle through the fabric. The head of the needle fits into the pits and the cork takes the punishment instead of your hand," he said. "I'll start at the top of the tear, you start at the bottom, and we'll meet in the middle. Use tight, close stitches so that it won't tear again. I like to use triple-stitching. Not every sailor will go to the trouble but it does produce a stronger join."

Robin hadn't put very many stitches in the heavy fabric before he came to appreciate the difficulty of the task. It was like trying to sew tree bark while struggling to maintain his balance on his precarious rope perch with the wind making a sail of his tunic. He was grateful when Crank declared the mend completed and released him to return to the deck.

Captain Gregersen met him at the bottom, "Help Cook spread out the wet cargo so it can dry. Then go below and check for leaks," he said, "now that you know how." He handed Robin the earthenware pot, as well as several bits of frayed rope and a pot of pitch. "Repair any that you find."

Robin looked at the rope, then at the captain, and frowned.

"You can use the frayed ends as a brush to apply the pitch or, if you find a hole, plug it with a stub of rope and then seal that with pitch."

Robin had hoped to drag his beaten body back to the fo'c'sle and sleep until they reached Hewnstone. But he thought of poor Thief being tossed about in the dark close hold during the windstorm. If nothing else, while he was below he could check on the animal.

As he tested the hold's walls for weaknesses he had the strange sensation that he was being watched. Perhaps Gregersen hid in the shadows, evaluating Robin's performance. He whipped around several times but found nothing until finally the light filtering down from the hatch picked out a pair of eyes. He let out the breath he had held and went to stroke Meeyoo who had been observing him from a niche between the top of a cask and the ceiling.

Robin found both the ship and the horse none the worse despite the stress of the storm but the hours spent inspecting the hold gave him ample opportunity to stoke his anger over his treatment aboard the Orion. True, Captain Gregersen, I did agree to work, he said to himself. As a seaman, not as a slave! As Robin climbed the ladder to return to the deck, he framed his case for deserving at least a little rest. On his way to take the helm, Hendriksen waylaid him. Like a banking of the wind left the sail luffing fruitlessly, Hendriksen's words deflated Robin's ire.

"Best you get yourself a few hours rest," the helmsman said. "Eli has the watch next, then you."

By Robin's reckoning that gave him a watch that would start in the middle of the night and end shortly after dawn. With that to look forward to, he doubted he would get any sleep at all. He trudged back to the tiny dark space notched into the ship's bow. One of the bolts of leather had been unrolled and now lay stretched across the floor, stuffed like a sausage. Robin realized that one of the crew lay inside asleep, Cook or maybe Crank. The other bolt must be one of the other crewman's sleeping bag. Robin wished he had something like it. Instead he bunched his rucksack into some approximation of a pillow and tried to rest.

He didn't realize that he had drifted off to sleep until a bell woke him. He counted. Not quite time for a change of watch. He dozed off again until he felt a hand at his shoulder.

"The watch is over and yours has begun," said Crank, who had already left his sleeping bag, rolled it up, and stowed it away.

Robin rubbed his eyes but it did little to clear his vision. The overcast sky was as dark as a sea that was opaque as pitch. Only when a bit of moonlight broke through the clouds did the silver light reveal the rippling waves. Robin stood in the bow straining his eyes to see—anything. With reduced activity and little noise on deck, the sounds of the ship and the sea were more noticeable. Water crashing against the ship—or was it the ship crashing against the water?—struck many different notes.

Exhausted and still half asleep he found it difficult to keep a sharp eye out. He was almost grateful when the watch ended and he was sent aft to take the helm. Impossible to doze while wrestling with the tiller in an effort to stay on course. If he let his attention lapse for even a minute, a renegade rudder and tiller jerked him awake.

By the position of the sun Robin could tell that it was not quite noon yet he had already put in a good day's work. As he left the helm he wondered what insufferable chore the captain would assign him today. To Robin's surprise Captain Gregersen said, "If you'd like to get your horse up on deck, this would be a good time. The wind and seas are light."

Surely the other crewmen were as drained as he, yet they were willing to spend their precious energy on the behalf of Robin and his horse. Humbled by their generosity he joined them at the capstan to hoist Thief out into the open.

Thief could certainly use some exercise, which was the last thing that Robin wanted. For a second he toyed with the idea of riding the horse around on the Orion until the impracticality of the idea impressed itself on him. With a sigh, he took the rein and stood close to the animal as Thief took hesitant mincing steps on the slick wood.

They were on their third circuit and Thief's gait had become more confident when Robin felt a thump under his feet and the ship shivered. Odd, he thought. Had they hit something or had something hit them? Why hadn't Cook called out a warning from the bow?

The ship received another smack, stronger this time. Thief whinnied.

"I don't know what that was, Thief," Robin said. "I hope we haven't hit a rock or a sandbar." He called out to Crank. "What is going on?"

"I don't know. Mayhap we hit a shoal but I would be surprised. The Captain knows these waters. He wouldn't send us into shallows nor would Hendriksen steer us there. He's too good a helmsman."

When the third strike came it seemed less likely that they had hit something and more probable that something had hit them since the impact came from a different side of the vessel. Some large floating debris? By now Crank and Eli had drifted in from their duties and stood amidships, murmuring and speculating. Even Meeyoo had abandoned her haunts and wound herself around Robin's ankles. He scratched her ears to give her a reassurance he didn't quite feel.

"Big fish, I think," said Eli.

"Whale," said Crank.

Eli spat. "Don't be ridiculous. No whales in these parts."

"Shark, then," said Crank. "They can be massive and aggressive. Why, I remember once—"

"We have heard that one so many times, Crank," Eli said with a sigh. "If it's a shark, where's the fin?"

The men darted from port to starboard, fore and aft, and peered over the side of the ship. Robin had edged his way to the bulwark to get a better look when the mysterious aggressor rammed the ship again. The jostling made Robin uncertain of his footing and he didn't want to be close enough to the edge of the ship to risk falling into the sea. Floundering in water plied by a mammoth shark did not sound like a good idea. Just as he stepped back, another blow struck the vessel, throwing Robin off his feet. He landed with a thud on his rump.

From the deck he saw rising above the bulwark the tail of the Devil: thirty, maybe forty feet long and serpentine, red, with an arrowhead shaped tip.

CHAPTER THIRTEEN

The Orion was under attack by the Devil himself? Robin's heart beat so fast that he could feel it in his throat. Had he been asked a moment earlier if he believed in the Devil he might have answered "no" despite all the misfortunes that had befallen him. He would have said that those had been due to his own failings or had been the acts of men. To attribute them to the work of the Devil would have been to accept that they were beyond his ability to change.

Now confronted with irrefutable evidence Robin found himself more afraid than he had ever been before. What defense did he, did any of them, have against the Devil?

With a cry of horror the rest of the crew, equally terrified, backed away from the side of the vessel.

A second tail joined the first in waving many feet above the ship's bulwark. Two? Robin was astounded. Were there two Devils? He had thought that there was one and only one Satan.

Magic then. This was an apparition, a spell cast not just upon Robin but upon the entire crew. Robin couldn't have said which was more terrifying, Evil Incarnate or the dark arts.

The devil tails disappeared from view but something under the ship bumped the vessel.

"Captain," called Crank, "What is it? What should we do?"

"Shark," said Eli to Crank but his voice trembled. "Isn't that what you said?" He shook his head. "A shark, with two tails like that?"

Crank's face was pale. "We could chum the water. Bring him closer and gaff him."

"Are you mad? Bring him closer? How close do you want him? He could jump aboard the boat." He got up in Crank's face. "Are you volunteering to lean over the side with a twelve-foot pole and grab whatever that thing is? And if you catch him then what?"

"Gentlemen—" Captain Gregersen's voice died when the devils' tails reappeared and were joined by long red arms like snakes only longer, thicker, and more muscular than any serpent Robin had ever seen. Two of the snake-like arms hooked the edge of the Orion. The ship rocked, a wave of water swept in, and splashed across the deck, and drenching the crew.

Meeyoo howled and sprinted away for cover. Thief neighed in distress.

"I should get my horse below—"

"Not now!"

Robin glowered. "But—"

"Too late! Lash him down good. Now!" Gregersen yelled.

"Aye. Sir." Robin cast about for some stable structure. He grabbed some of the sea-soaked pelts that had been laid out to dry in the sun and draped them over Thief for cushioning. Then with heart pounding he secured the wild-eyed, whimpering, and stamping horse to the mast with lengths of rope.

The menacing devil tails and snake-like arms sank below the surface only to reappear a moment later, and now there were more than two. Robin could count the tips of eight serpentine arms. The arms stretched up and showed themselves to be tiled with hundreds of disks. The beast rose higher in the water revealing the arms to be attached not to some trunk but to a huge red bulb of a head studded with what looked to Robin's astonishment like two eyes big as cart wheels. A pungent odor that was part fish and part something else, something noxiously acidic, filled the air.

"It's a kraken," said Captain Gregersen, his face pale and eyes wide in amazement. "A giant kraken! I had heard of them but I did not believe they were real. I thought they were just a myth."

"What does it want with us?" asked Hendriksen.

As if in answer to his question the kraken's devil tails reached across the ship's bulwark. Crank jumped back just in time to avoid being touched by the tails' arrowhead tips, tips that looked strong enough to pierce flesh. Four tentacle-like arms crept over the edge of the ship. To Robin it appeared that the disks on the tentacles' underside had gripping power. Weighed down by the kraken's bulk the ship tipped dangerously close to the water. Cargo, ropes, tools, oars, and supplies skidded across the slippery deck and tumbled into the sea.

Dried meat spilled from a barrel and spread across the water's surface. The kraken reached out a tentacle and scooped up the morsels, pulling them to the crown of the bulbous head. The morsels disappeared somewhere in the center of the cluster of tentacles. Was that where the beast's mouth was? Robin shuddered at unbidden images of those gripping tentacles snatching up the crewmen and dropping them into that mysterious maw to encounter who knew what gruesome fate. Even if the creature was merely curious or clumsy, it could capsize the entire vessel but it was clearly more than simply curious. It was hungry and it liked meat.

"Can it be killed?" Robin called, scurrying along with the crew to secure whatever hadn't already spilled overboard.

"Of course it can be killed," said Captain Gregersen. "All living beings die."

Except those that have been bewitched, Robin thought, not quite convinced that the kraken wasn't the Devil or some other supernatural demon.

Captain Gergersen shouted, "All hands on deck! Crank, get the sail in. Hendriksen, pull up the rudder. Cook, Eli, get armaments."

Robin started for the fo'c'sle. "Seaman Robin, where are you going? I said every hand on deck."

"And you said to get armaments. I'm going to get mine." The captain nodded his assent.

As he dashed for the fo'c'sle, Robin saw a brown streak dart out and sprint toward the mast. Before he could stop her, Meeyoo had scrambled halfway up the rigging leading to the basket at the top of the mast, what the crewmen called the crow's nest. Many times in the past he had seen Meeyoo take refuge on a tree branch or other high perch. Indeed "in summa loco" was a good defensive position but he feared that the kraken's rocking of the ship would fling her off and into the sea. "Meeyoo, get down from there!" he cried and started after her.

"Robin, your weapon!" the captain called.

Growling with fear and frustration, Robin skidded to the bow and undid the laces securing his sword. He rushed past the mast where Crank frantically wrestled with the sail while Cook, Eli, and the captain arrayed themselves along the vessel and drew their swords. The inadequacy of the short blades became apparent immediately.

"Bows and arrows!" Gregersen commanded and the crew hastened to comply. At the captain's command, they let fly with arrows. Too weak to pierce the creature's thick hide they simply bounced off and fell useless into the water.

"Captain, sir, flaming arrows?" Eli said.

"Too dangerous to start a fire," the captain shouted back.

Once again, tentacles snaked toward the vessel and latched on as if to pull the ship under. Both hands on the hilt, Robin brought his sword down and sliced through the appendages. He would have expected a cry of pain, a roar of anger, but the kraken made a keening sound unlike any he had ever heard from an animal, even a dragon. Lengths of tentacle as long as Robin was tall dropped onto the deck and slid to the other side as the vessel righted itself. The kraken pulled away waving the severed limbs, wounded but by no means dead.

Had Robin been fighting a dragon, he would have known where to deliver the mortal blow but this was no dragon. Did the kraken have a heart that could be pierced and if so where on its barrel shaped body was it? Did it have a brain? Would an injury to its head disable it?

Perched on the rim of the crow's nest, Meeyoo crouched, her shoulders hunched, her hind quarters raised. Robin had seen her assume that posture many times as she prepared to launch herself at some prey. Oh, no, he thought, no, no NO! "Meeyoo, don't even . . ."

Horrified, Robin watched as Meeyoo catapulted herself towards the monster, legs spread and claws extended. She landed on its face, sank her teeth into its flesh, and dug her front claws into its eye.

The kraken thrashed about sending huge waves crashing into the ship and sweeping across the deck, knocking sailors off their feet. It waved its limbs trying to smack at a tiny assailant that it could not see and Robin feared that Meeyoo would be tossed far away and into the water but she dodged the frantic tentacles and hung on, scratching and biting at the kraken's eyes.

Though the crewmen's arrows had been too feeble to be effective, Robin thought he could do some damage with his sword, if he could get close enough.

Or get the sword close enough.

Seizing the longest line that he could find, he knotted one end around the sword's hilt and tied the other end to his belt. He wrapped the rope around his waist and jumped atop the aftcastle.

Holding his sword like a lance, he brought his arm back. If the kraken had a brain it might be in that bulbous head. Robin targeted carefully to as not to hit Meeyoo and hurled the sword toward the beast.

His aim was off. The blade struck the kraken but failed to pierce its skin. The sword bounced off and landed in the water.

Robin yanked on the line and reeled his sword back into the boat before the thrashing monster could snag it.

Again, Robin thought, and this time his aim would have to be true. He turned the hilt in his hand, feeling for just the right grip that would send the blade slicing like an arrow through air to pierce the kraken's thick hide.

Robin launched the sword a second time. It sunk itself between the kraken's eyes, prompting another unholy roar. Now more interested in extracting the offending weapon than the cat that clung to its head, the monster waved its tentacles toward its eyes while stretching a devil's tail out toward the Orion and Robin. Before the tail could reach him, Robin yanked on the line, extricated his sword, dragged it back aboard, and jumped out of the way, calling on years of youthful jousting practice dodging a quintain.

The kraken was no dragon but it appeared to Robin that the wound had weakened it. Its wild lurching became less forceful.

From his elevated vantage point Robin could see something of a ridge below the kraken's eyes. Could that be where the head and body were joined? Could that be the neck? Would there be a life's-blood vessel there where a sword could do some damage? He reached back and flung the sword once more, aiming for a spot between and slightly below the eyes. The blade hit home, sinking nearly to the hilt.

The kraken's thrashing turned to twitching until at last the creature became still. It began to sink and horrified, Robin envisioned Meeyoo sinking along with it. She clung to the kraken but her snarling had become whining.

"Someone, please, help Meeyoo!"

He didn't have to ask twice. A crew eager to rescue the cat who had helped save their lives scurried about the deck. "How about this?" each cried as he held up what he thought might aid her rescue and threw it into the water. But Meeyoo shied from jumping onto any of the planks or boxes and instead clung to the kraken which continued to sink lower into the water.

Robin jerked on the line attached to his sword but could not loosen it from where it had buried itself in the kraken's neck. Instead, to his dismay, he felt the line tugging on him and realized that if he couldn't dislodge the sword, he would be pulled off the ship and dragged down under the water by the sinking kraken. He untied the line from his belt but he refused to lose the sword, and he would not lose Meeyoo.

He spied the sea anchor and tossed it overboard, grabbed an empty sack, and threw himself into the water. Plunging straight down, salt, seaweed, and noxious kraken blood surged into his nose. Salt stung his eyes and burned in his wounds. He wished he had first taken off his leggings and boots. Sodden, they weighed him down but he thrashed his way to the surface. He wrapped an arm around the bucket and kicked himself closer to where the kraken's hulk floated like a partially submerged log. The tentacles hung flaccid.

"Come on, Meeyoo," he called. "Come with me. Jump onto me."

Meeyoo padded gingerly towards him but drew back when water splashed her paws. Crying, she pulled her legs close and clung to the last remaining dry spot on the top of the kraken's body.

Kicking his legs like a pair of shears, Robin drew so close to the kraken that he could feel its heat. The fishy smell nearly suffocated him. He turned his head, filled his lungs, held his breath, then lunged for his sword, pulling it free, and shoved it into his belt. The kraken moaned.

Wounded, not dead, Robin thought. He needed to get Meeyoo. He needed to get away!

Robin reached out for Meeyoo.

Water covered the cat's paws and she whimpered. Stretching his arm until he thought it would pull out of its socket, he reached out and got a handful of fur at the nape of Meeyoo's neck. He plucked her from the dying kraken and pulled her to his chest. She dug her claws into his skin and wriggled, trying to climb higher on him and get away from the water wetting her tail.

He thrust her into the sack. One arm around the cat, the other clinging to the bucket, Robin kicked as hard as he could, weighed down by the anchors that were his boots. He could already feel the suction of the sinking kraken pulling him down with it.

CHAPTER FOURTEEN

An even stronger force tugged Robin toward the ship. With swollen prickling eyes he saw the Captain leaning over the bulwark pulling the rope tied to the sea anchor. Hendriksen, Crank, and Eli grabbed the rope and helped to hoist Robin, Meeyoo, and the bucket aboard.

Robin laid the sack on the deck and Meeyoo wriggled out. Belly almost to the ground, she crab-walked across the wet deck littered with shattered crates, spilled and soggy cargo, and trailing rope until she reached the hatch. Finding it covered she let out a howl. Eli hastened to remove the hatch cover and she dove in to seek refuge below.

Robin collapsed on the deck and tried to catch his breath. The punctures and scrapes from Meeyoo's claws stung and throbbed and he wondered if the kraken blood was poisonous. Hendriksen helped him to a sitting position and pulled off the sodden boots. Crank brought a blanket, Cook a jug. Not water, not ale, but rum. It warmed Robin's blood and tempered the horrors of the battle and Meeyoo's brush with death.

On legs twanging like a lute string, Robin staggered over to Thief. "There, there, Thief," he said, struggling to keep his voice low and steady. "It's all right now. Everything's going to be all right." Stroking the horse's flank, Robin examined the horse. The horse was undamaged but he was traumatized, his mouth foamy, his eyes huge, and his nostrils flared. Robin patted the horse's nose and head and murmured to him until Thief stopped trembling. Then Robin draped an arm over the horse's neck and leaned into him, taking warmth from the horse's side, listening as the animal's beating heart slowed and its snuffling breath calmed. He could not have said who was comforting whom.

Behind him, Captain Gregersen called that they would celebrate their victory in good time but for now they had but a few precious moments to get seaworthy. He ordered that they return Thief to the hold, then repair damage and recover some of their supplies.

"Surely you jest," Robin said.

The captain glowered. "I find nothing humorous about wanting to make it to port, Seaman Robin," he said. "Now get busy!"

Eli tossed the sea anchor into the water to steady the ship. The crew made quick work of manning the capstan. Thief lowered below, Crank put one leg over the side, then the other, and slid overboard. He floundered around gathering up oars and pushed crates, tuns, trunks, and anything else that still floated close to the ship. With lines, nets, and buckets, Eli and Robin scooped as much of the spilled cargo as they could reach back into the ship. Now wet with sea water and stained with kraken blood, the wool and timber were heavy and reeking.

The deck too was slick with seawater and gore: more of the sea monster's sticky dark blood than the sailors' red. Captain Gregersen and Hendriksen set to work scrubbing it with brooms. As they worked their way around the vessel they picked up strewn bits of ship and sea monster. While Crank dried himself, Robin and Cook climbed the rigging and examined the mast and yardarm for damage.

From the deck Hendriksen cried, "Look at this!" He held up a piece of the beast's tentacle that Robin had sliced off with his sword. Hendriksen made to toss the piece overboard but Cook cried, "No! Wait!" He scrambled down the rigging, picked his way across the deck to Hendriksen's side, and examined the length of tentacle. "I have a use for this," he said.

Hendriksen gave him a skeptical look.

"Captain," called Cook. "Permission to be excused, sir, to give the kraken his just rewards."

Captain Gregersen looked just as puzzled as had Hendriksen but nodded his assent. Cook took the tentacle and headed for the hold.

Captain Gregersen stated that they needed to get the ship navigable quickly while it was still light, the wind was calm, and the tide had not turned. To settle jangled nerves and ease the burden, the captain distributed allotments of rum.

Robin climbed down from the rigging and hastened to get his share. Cook emerged from the hold headed across the deck with an armload of cooking supplies. Robin clambered down the ladder to the hold and found Meeyoo had burrowed into a bale of vegetable-lamb's wool. He stroked her head. "How can I thank you enough, Meeyoo? Again, you have saved me, saved the entire crew!"

"Me. You," she said with conviction, just as she had as a kitten. Robin's eyes stung once more, not with seawater but with salty tears.

He returned to the deck and was greeted by the smell of boiling oil. The crew had gathered at the brazier around Cook who manned the cook pot. Somehow he had gotten a fire going.

"We lost many supplies overboard but I had some charcoal, oil, and flour stored below," he said. One arm encircled a large bowl filled with flour-coated rings. In his other hand he held a long-handled pierced spoon. The pot gurgled.

The rest of the crew sipped from their cups. Hendriksen tapped Robin on the shoulder and handed him a jug. The sweet spicy scent of rum filled Robin's nose.

"Ready, men?" Cook asked and was answered with an affirmative murmur. Cook dumped the contents of his mixing bowl into the oil which bubbled, spurted, and popped. With the pierced spoon he stirred the pale-colored rings. An aroma evocative of fried fish filled the air. When the rings turned brown, Cook scooped them from the oil and returned them to the bowl. He picked out a ring. "Hot," he said, and blew on it before popping it into his mouth. "Hmm," he said as he chewed. "Not bad. I think you will find it edible. Sir?" He passed the bowl to Captain Gregersen who helped himself to a fried ring before handing the bowl to Hendriksen. The bowl circulated from man to man and each sampled the dish.

Robin found the morsel to be chewy with a fishy flavor that was very strong but not unpleasant.

"Calamari!" said Captain Gregersen, helping himself to another ring. "We had this at that southern port."

Cook nodded.

"How did you . . ." In mid-chew the captain said, "Oh, no. You didn't!"

"I did indeed, Sir," said Cook with a grin. "To me, that tentacle looked like squid. I thought that since the monster had sought to eat us it was only fitting that we eat him. Men, how do you like fried kraken?"

The crew was silent for a moment. Cook beamed and Robin hoped that the man's enthusiasm and pride of achievement would not be dampened by someone puking.

Captain Gregerson raised his cup. "To Cook!" he said. "To fried kraken!"

The other men joined in the toast. "To Cook!" More toasts ensued. "To Robin!" "To Meeyoo!" "To the kraken!" "To Captain Gregersen!" "To Hendriksen!" "To the Orion!" until the cups ran dry, the sky took on a rosy sunset hue, and Captain Gregersen declared it time that they head for Hewnstone. He would take the watch and Hendriksen the helm so the other men could get some desperately needed rest.

With Cook, Crank, and Eli, a drained Robin stretched out across the fo'c'sle floor. Before he could even say "goodnight" sleep overtook him.

*****

Robin found himself roused by the sound of eight bells. With the other men he emerged from under the fo'c'sle and under a starless night sky straggled to the helm for assignments.

"The good news is, we are not far from Hewnstone," said the Captain. "We ought to make it by afternoon tomorrow. The bad news is that we have got a leak but have no more pitch. Much went overboard in the fight and we have used what was left."

The men of Orion's crew fell silent. No one wanted to ask the obvious question which was would they sink before they made port. At last Crank said, "How bad is it?"

Captain Gregersen's expression was guarded. "It's at the waterline. It would be good if we could fix it. If it gets too bad, we can jettison some cargo."

Robin felt a chill at the back of his neck as he recalled what Eli had told him about "horse latitudes." The Captain wouldn't order Thief thrown overboard, would he? Robin would not allow that to happen.

His head ached much as it had his first day aboard when he was trying to learn the language of sailing. Like someone knocking on a door, an idea clamored for his attention. What was it trying to tell him?

"The lumber that we have on board," he said, "what wood is it? Is any of it pine?"

"No. We'll be picking up pine, bringing it back to Rocky Port. What we have is birch."

"Birch will work fine. Is it dry?"

Cook said. "There's some in the hold that's not too damp. Why?"

Robin grinned. "I can make you some pitch." He recalled his preparatory experiences at the forge's bloomery. Many men had spent long hot days driving bellows nursing the fires that turned wood into the charcoal needed to smelt metal. Pitch was a byproduct of the process. "I won't be able to make a lot, but I can make some. I'll need Cook's brazier and his charcoal. We'll have to start a fire. And I'll need a cup and a lidded pot that I can poke a tiny hole in."

While Crank and Eli took the watch and the helm, Robin and Cook worked through the night tending burning coals piled around a covered cook pot packed with birch bark chunks. The heat rendered sticky sap which dripped out of the hole in the cook pot's bottom and into the cup beneath it. By the time it was light enough to see, they had made enough pitch to patch the hole giving the Captain more confidence in the vessel's integrity.

"Well done," he said, and set a course for Hewnstone with no further talk of casting cargo into the sea.

Robin took the watch at the bow while Eli stayed at the helm, all the better to free up Cook and give him a chance to make breakfast. Much of the ship's food supply had been spilled overboard during the sea monster fight. Robin offered up the hardened stale bread, dried fruit, and meat that remained in his rucksack. Cook moistened it all with rum, combined it with the last of the ship's stores, and mashed it together. The salty sweet and barely-edible bun lay like a rock in Robin's belly and had him drawing up mental lists of the foods he would seek out the minute they made port.

When ahead of him he spied a darkening of the horizon that looked like land, his heart and his stomach leaped and he found himself salivating. Indeed, the thin dark line grew thicker and then took on contours. "Ho!" he cried out. "Land, I think. Land!"

The cry was passed from man to man along the ship. Soon after came the orders that hands would be needed at oars to guide the ship through Hewnstone's busy harbor. Hendriksen relieved Robin so he could help row. The Orion having lost an oar in the battle with the kraken, Robin improvised with a length of timber, his hands and shoulders screaming in protest.

When Hewnstone's harbor came into view, Robin could barely make out the port's features for the grateful tears that blurred his vision. He blotted his eyes with a shirt sleeve stiff with salt. Hewnstone's harbor appeared to rest at the foot of a long, pale gray bluff. As they drew closer Robin could see that the gray shape wasn't a bluff at all but the manmade structures of a huge seaport city. Hewnstone did not rest at the foot of a bluff nor did a fortress loom over it from atop a motte. Instead, buildings lined the shore as far to the right and left as Robin could see from his post at the bulwark. He longed to be in the crow's nest or even the fo'c'sle to get a better look.

Drawing even closer, Robin could see that while Rocky Port's harbor had been a rough basin encircled by jetties with docks along one side, Hewnstone's wharves lined either side of a long wide channel. Ships filled the spaces nearest the channel's mouth and the Orion's crew had to row a considerable ways into the channel to find a place to tie up. Once the ship was secured to the dock Robin joined the men to put the gangplank in place. Eli, Cook, and Crank scattered about the ship attending to tasks in what seemed to Robin to be the reverse of their departure from Rocky Port and Robin collected his belongings. He found Meeyoo in the hold, bundled her into the sack, and went in search of Hendriksen to inquire about offloading Thief.

"You are leaving us then," said Hendriksen.

"That was the agreement, that I, my horse, and cat would be transported to Hewnstone."

"Well then, since you're going ashore, might we impose on you to visit the ship's chandler and get them working on the supplies we'll need? Between loading, unloading, and getting the Orion shipshape we are pressed for time while in port."

"I don't see why I couldn't."

"That would help. Before you go, the captain would like a word."

Robin frowned. Exhausted, famished, he was in no mood to brook any delay. The captain had better not be planning to demand payment for the transportation, Robin grumbled and stomped across the deck with as much authority as his stiff, salt-encrusted and sun-dried boots would allow.

CHAPTER FIFTEEN

He found Captain Gregersen at the aftcastle. The man looked drained, thinner, even older than he had but a few days ago. "Ah, Robin. you are leaving us?"

"I have my things, my cat. All I need now is my horse. Sir."

"You're sure you won't stay?"

"Stay?" was Robin's dumbfounded reply.

"Might you not consider becoming a sailor? You, even your cat, have become part of the crew. The Orion and its crew are in your debt for your service. I believe I speak for all of us when I say it would be to our benefit if you would continue on with us."

"Aye," came a voice at his back.

Robin turned to see Eli, Cook, Crank, and Hendriksen grouped behind him. "Aye," they said in unison.

For a moment, Robin's throat was too choked with emotion to permit speech. He swallowed and said, "Men, I'm a landlubber. I . . . I have a mission to accomplish."

His lips pressed in a thin line, Captain Gregersen nodded. "Well, if you fail, or even if you succeed, know that you are always welcome here on the Orion."

"Hear! Hear!" cried the ship's crew.

Gregersen lifted the strap of a pouch over his head and handed the small bag to Robin. "Payment for your service above and beyond our agreement. And a token of my appreciation for saving my ship and crew." The bag was heavy in Robin's hand.

"And mine," said Eli. He handed Robin a small knife whose ivory handle was carved with the image of a sailboat.

"And mine," said Crank, presenting a pouch that was neither stitched nor woven but tied in elaborate tight macramé knots.

"And mine," said Cook, handing Robin a small drawstring pouch fragrant with some exotic spice from the man's personal store.

"And mine." Hendriksen's gift was a small jug of rum encased in a sheath of woven rope. "Now, men, let's get that horse on deck."

Hoping it would be the last time he would ever have to dance in that tortuous round, Robin helped to man the capstan. Once on deck, Thief lifted his head and snuffed the fresh air. To Robin the horse seemed perhaps a bit thinner than he had been when he first boarded and moved stiffly. Saddling and bridling the horse Robin said, "Looks like you and I could both use a good feed. Let's go ashore." He looped the straps of his sack over the pommel. His heart as heavy as the bag of coins that Captain Gregersen had given him, Robin led the horse across the gangplank. Keeping his head high, he fought the urge to look back and catch one last glimpse of the Orion and her crew.

Leading Thief, Robin stepped onto the dock and found his first steps to be strangely unsteady. The ground under his feet felt oddly firm and immobile and he realized that he had become accustomed to the ship's constant pitching and rolling, had learned to make continual small adjustments to balance his weight and keep himself centered and upright. Thief, too, needed a few moments to steady himself and get his bearings.

Clearly familiar with the needs of sailors making port, vendors of food and ale had set up stalls as close to the docks as they could get. With a bumbling gait, Robin approached the nearest one, bought a meat pie, and wolfed it down so fast he barely tasted it.

Wider than Rocky Port's waterfront street, Hewnstone's wharves were nonetheless crowded with sailors, cargo, donkeys, and carts. Grocers, butchers, linen-drapers, ship's stores, and other merchants lined the street but they were larger, more numerous, and varied. Not built of timber or wattle-and-daub the buildings were all constructed of large gray rectangular-shaped stone. Robin barely had room to mount Thief for the people who milled about. The Orion was certainly home to much that was malodorous, but at least the wind usually carried the smell away. On Hewnstone's dockside way the mingled odors of people, animals, and food hung like a miasma that was nearly suffocating.

Robin saw the flap over the top of the rucksack move. Meeyoo poked her head out, took one look at the unfamiliar surroundings, and burrowed back into the pack.

Astride the horse, having bested man and nature, Robin felt like a conquering hero. Caesar trotting down the streets of Rome on his war horse could not have sat any taller in the saddle.

Robin found the ship's chandler that Hendriksen had spoken of almost immediately. Robin dismounted Thief and tied the reins to a bollard. Several groups of sailors thronged outside and it seemed that every ship in the harbor had sent a crew to get supplies. Robin edged his way past to get inside.

The store appeared cavernous for the quantity of merchandise crammed into it. Goods were displayed on every surface: standing on the floor, arrayed on tables and in baskets, tacked to the walls, and hung from the ceiling. The place smelled strongly enough of old wood and old iron that the odors overpowered even those of Robin's own salty sweaty clothes and body. He threaded his way past barrels of oils, tar, and pitch, casks of glues, resins, and solvents, buckets of tallow and varnish. Ropes thick and thin of varying materials stood in coils on the floor next to rolls of paper. From the walls hung axes, hammers, and hooks. The store also sold items that could just as easily be found in any house. A boat being not only a vessel but a home, it had need for brooms, mops, pots, soaps, and mugs.

Displayed on a table was a curious assortment of jewelry. Gems set in rings, bracelets, brooches, and pendants glinted in the lantern light. A couple of necklaces appeared to have been made of pointed animal teeth strung on a cord and there were bracelets made of what looked like braided rope. Small bits of engraved bone looked like the scrimshaw craft that was Eli's pastime. There were model ships intricately carved from different woods and even one that resided inside a glass bottle. Though the model boat was tiny, the bottle's mouth was even smaller and Robin wondered how the boat had gotten into the bottle. Perhaps it was open at the bottom. Robin lifted it up to see but the bottle proved to be all of one piece.

In a corner sat a woman on a low bench. The simple blue bodice she wore was laced over a white muslin chemise and green skirt.

Long with a low back, the bench on which she sat stood on short pegged legs. Hanging from it like saddlebags were leather pouches filled with various implements. By the light of a lantern, the woman worked a length of sail with a needle. Her long blonde hair gleamed in the lantern light and around her neck glimmered a silver chain from which hung a tiny charm, half a heart with jagged edges where it had broken in the middle. Something about the charm seemed familiar.

Three men entered the shop. One of the men wore a long leather vest over a white blouse and wool pants while the other two wore simple tunics and leggings. Robin took the man in the vest to be an officer directing the other two as to which barrels and crates to haul to their ship.

The officer crossed to the seated woman who rose and handed him the sail she had been sewing.

"So soon?" asked the officer. "We gave you this just a few days ago."

"I confess that I put in some late hours to get it done, but I knew you were in a hurry for it and didn't want to hold you in port overly long." The woman stated her price and the officer held out a handful of coins. From her right hand she unwrapped a leather strap that looked similar to the sailor's palms Eli and Crank used and took the coins. "As always, I thank you, sir, for your continued patronage," she said, and returned to him one coin.

"You're most welcome. Don't know how you do it, Brandy, but you always seem to have what we need. Much to the chagrin of our seamen, our stay in port this time will be brief."

The woman Brandy and the officer shared a chuckle.

"And may I say that you are looking especially fine today," he said. "Is the Captain in port?"

"Thank you, sir," Brandy said with a slight curtsy. "Not yet, I'm afraid."

"Well, give him our regards when you see him next."

"I will."

The officer followed his men out the door and Brandy turned her attention to Robin.

"Wondering how the ship got in the bottle, are you?" she asked.

"I was indeed."

"Buy it, and I'll reveal its secret," she said. Piercing blue eyes in an intelligent face and a forthright manner tempered her flirtatious words.

Robin chuckled and set down the ship-in-a-bottle. "Much as I would like to know, I am not here to buy goods for myself, but for the ship from which I just disembarked. The Orion."

"The Orion is in port?" she asked, her face brightening.

"It is indeed and the crew sends greetings. They will be along later. They still have business aboard the ship. I am Robin."

The woman curtseyed. "Belle Randal is my name, but everyone calls me Brandy."

"We had a rough voyage from Rocky Port. They are still repairing the damage. The captain asked me to call ahead with the supplies they will need as the list is extensive."

"Damage, you said? You were caught in a storm? Is Captain Gregersen all right?"

Robin studied the woman's broken heart pendant which appeared to be the mate to the one worn by the captain. "Not a storm precisely. A collision. And while the boat sustained damage, the crew is uninjured." Robin knew the Orion's sailors would delight in telling the tale of the kraken attack. He would not steal their thunder.

Brandy clasped her hands and sighed with obvious relief. "But you made it into port. So, how might the Hewnstone's Ship's Chandler be of service?"

Robin recited the list of required equipment and services.

"It will take some time to gather all that. Will you wait or . . .?"

Robin shook his head. "The captain and crewmen will be along later. They are still assessing the damage and may have additional needs. I will be staying briefly in Hewnstone, then moving on."

"You're not a member of the crew?"

Robin shook his head. No, he thought. I am a king.

CHAPTER SIXTEEN

The shop's door opened to admit the newest customer.

"John!" cried Brandy.

Captain Gregersen strode across the room to join them. "Robin, thank you for attending to the ship's business," he said, but his gaze was focused on Brandy. He took both her hands in his and for a moment they stood in place staring at each other, not speaking. Were they husband and wife? Robin wondered. The broken heart charm they both wore suggested an imperfect love.

His attention still focused on Brandy, the captain asked Robin, "You're certain you won't continue on with us?"

"I am headed elsewhere." On the morrow, he would plan his journey to the Chalklands. For now he was grateful simply to be on dry land with Thief and Meeyoo safe, unhurt. Tonight he and his traveling companions deserved a good meal and a comfortable night's rest. "Where might I find a night's lodging for me and my horse?"

Brandy said, "There are several inns with stables a ways back from the wharf."

Robin thanked her for her advice and bid his leave. With eyes still only for each other, the captain and Brandy wished him farewell.

His purse bulging with the advance for his dragon slaying in Rocky Port and the gifts from Captain Gregersen, Robin and his companions could enjoy lavish accommodations. No more sleeping on hard wooden decks or in foul-smelling holds, no dining on hard biscuits and mildewed hay. Today was indeed the first of better days ahead. Robin splurged on an apple at a grocer's stall for Thief and cheese for Meeyoo, a chicken pie for himself. After days of dried meats and hardtack, sausage did not have its usual appeal. A jug of fresh ale proved a welcome respite from the stale water that they had drunk on board.

Next to the ship's chandler was a linen draper who sold not only cloth but a few items of ready-made clothing. Judging from the selection, Robin deduced that he wasn't the first sailor to make port in need of a fresh tunic and pair of leggings. He could certainly use new boots as well. When he got to the Chalklands, one of the first things he would do would be to visit a shoemaker.

Past the alehouse he came upon a shop with which he was unfamiliar. Like its neighbors it had a small arched door set into the street side stone façade. The open shutters presented a view of the goods arrayed inside on the windowsill: books. Books covered the table tops. The walls seemed to be built of books. Scrolls were stacked in heaps like small cords of firewood. Folios of pale parchment and vellum lying side by side made a light-colored quilt. Robin could see no merchandise other than books.

The sunlight streaming through the window showed an interior crowded with trestle tables. These too were piled with books. Toward the back of the shop, a man sat hunched over a worktable. He looked up, caught Robin's eye, and beckoned him in with a wave. Robin tied up Thief, shouldered his pack, and pushed open the door.

The man left his worktable, started toward the door and met Robin midway. A clean-shaven man of some forty-odd decades, the shop owner had the pale skin of one who spends much time indoors. His tonsured hair left the top of his head bald. Reading stones perched on the bridge of his nose.

"Greetings," he said. "I am Robert. How may I be of service?"

"Tell me about this place," Robin said with a sweep of his hand that included the long wooden trestle tables and benches, dark woolen rugs, and walls that were not made of books but might as well have been, lined as they were from floor to ceiling with shelves filled with tomes. Two worn wing-backed chairs flanked a small table that held a brass lantern, a pottery jug, and two pottery goblets. Atop Robert's worktable was a wooden easel against which was propped some written material. Sheets of vellum lay at the base of the easel. Cups filled with quills and thin narrow blades stood at the table's corner. "What is this shop?"

Robert's grin was both proud and smug. "It's a stationarius. Here I obtain exemplars, original masters of texts. I make copies which I then rent."

To whom? Robin wondered. Texts would be of use only to those few who could read. He looked about. Robert and the shop both appeared to be prosperous.

Robert answered the unasked question. "Hewnstone is a very big city with an impressive number of literate people. The lord and his court as well as masters and students at the university all have need of books. So do the clerics at the many chapels, a demand that exceeds the ability of the monks at the abbey to meet." He inclined his head. "That was where I learned my trade, you might say."

A defrocked monk? That would explain the tonsured hair. Robin wondered what had been Robert's transgression.

"I am kept quite busy making copies of Bibles, books of hours, liturgies, and calendars for the chapels alone. As well there are poets and storytellers who write tomes which I copy and rent for the entertainment of the nobles or anyone who can afford the price."

The door opened to admit a man, a nobleman by the looks of his clean white shirt, brocade vest, woolen breeches, and silver brooches on his shoes.

"Ah," said Robert, "if you don't mind? A customer with whom I have an appointment." Robert excused himself.

Robin nodded and took a seat on one of the chairs. He set his pack on the floor, turned back the flap, and gave Meeyoo's head a pat. "Soon, Meeyoo, we will be settled in an inn and have a nice long rest," he murmured. Meeyoo stepped out of the sack and climbed into Robin's lap. He stroked her head and back. She laid down making herself comfortable while keeping an eye on Robert.

Eavesdropping was not Robin's intent but it was a small shop and not difficult to overhear the conversation. From what Robin could discern, the nobleman was a poet. He had a number of poems of which he was quite proud. "I am certain many would find them entertaining and would want a copy such that they could read them over and over," he said.

The nobleman and Robert negotiated and finally fixed a price for Robert's services.

Robert escorted his customer to the door. He strode to the small table and filled the two goblets with liquid from the urn. He handed one to Robin. The fruity aroma suggested that it was wine. "A cat?" Robert said. "You have a cat?"

"I can put her outside with my horse." He moved to grab his pack.

"Oh, that's quite all right," Robert said. "My apologies for the interruption but the aspiring poet is a wealthy man. Unfortunately not as talented at writing poetry as he is at making money, in my opinion. I seriously doubt that I will get many interested in renting his book of verses. One look at the first poem or two . . ." Robert shrugged. "Were he anyone else I would not invest the time or labor, but what he is willing to pay will be sufficient compensation even if I never rent a single volume." He chuckled.

Robert's pale face took on a rosy glow and his eyes glittered with excitement. "Slow and painstaking work is copying, even slower the way I do it." He chuckled. "I keep getting distracted reading when I should be copying." Robert took a sip of wine. "I love reading. Too much, my superiors decided. They were right:

books are my vocation. When I left the abbey, I made myself available as a scribe for hire. I set up stalls at fairs copying documents, writing letters, whatever people needed that involved writing or books. After a while I had earned enough to open the shop."

He grinned and Robin couldn't help but smile too.

"I do have books of fine poetry that I am certain you would enjoy. Volumes of tales, some suspenseful, some humorous, some touching, some bawdy . . ." Robert winked.

Another customer entered the shop and Robert stood to usher him to the worktable. Startled, Meeyoo jumped off Robin's lap, scooted under the chair, and tucked herself up against Robin's ankles. As Robert conferred with his customer, Meeyoo crept out and took one cautious step at a time, sniffing and exploring the room. Robin wondered what she made of the scents of ink and parchment.

Having explored the perimeter of the room, Meeyoo jumped onto one of the tables and walked across rather than around the books arrayed there. "Meeyoo, get down from there," Robin hissed, loud enough for her to hear but no so loud as to draw the attention of Robert's customer. Robin hoped that Meeyoo had not soiled a book.

The cat leaped onto another table.

"Meeyoo!" Robin said between clenched teeth. With a glare, the cat hopped down to the floor.

Robert shook hands with his customer and escorted him to the door.

Meeyoo sprang onto Robert's worktable, padded onto the vellum laid out at the base of the easel, and stretched out across it.

"Meeyoo, no," Robin muttered and rose to pluck her from the table just as Robert bid his customer farewell and turned to rejoin Robin.

"What the—?" Robert cried.

Meeyoo stood and sprang from the table. Her hind legs sent leaves of parchment scattering and her shoulder jostled an ink bottle.

"No!" Robin and Robert cried in unison, diving toward the table. Landing on one foot, Robin caught the ink bottle and held it upright but not before some ink splashed on Meeyoo. She yelped.

Robert scrambled to retrieve the scattered pages.

Hunched close to the floor, Meeyoo scuttled across the room leaving inky paw prints on the wool rug, then launched herself out the window to the street.

"I'm so sorry!" Robin cried. Tossing a handful of coins onto the table he grabbed his sack and ran out after her.

Robin looked up and down the street. On Hewnstone's cobblestoned streets he thought he could make out the ink prints that Meeyoo had left in her wake. He set off in that direction and at last spotted her cowering in a refuse pile behind another shop.

"Oh, Meeyoo," Robin sighed and picked her up, not caring about the paw impressions she stamped on his tunic. He tucked her back into the sack and looped the straps over the pommel of Thief's saddle.

Eager as he was to journey to Mathus Abbey and search their archives that would wait until tomorrow. He needed rest, Thief needed rest, and they all needed food. He guided the horse's steps along Hewnstone's streets and stopped at each inn he found. True to the advice he had received from Brandy at the ship's chandler's, he did not have to travel far from the docks to find lodging for himself and his charges.

At a small home he was met by the owner's wife. Petite with blond hair, the woman's smile was friendly but the strain of working as hostess showed in her tired eyes. Her husband, a tall robust balding man, called to one of the young people busying themselves about the hall, a son by the looks of him, and directed the lad to see to Robin's horse.

His rucksack over his shoulder, Robin climbed the stairs to his allotted room. The tiny attic space was as low-ceilinged as the cubbyhole under the Orion's forecastle and there was barely room for him to turn around between the washbasin stand, the sleeping pallet, and a chair. He let Meeyoo out of the pack. After sniffing at every corner, she leaped upon the bed, and attended to grooming her fur. Robin attended to some grooming of his own. With soap, cloths, and fresh water from a bucket, he sponged away the salt crust that left his skin feeling tight and dry. He barely recognized as himself the image of the ragged man reflected in the polished brass mirror. On the morrow he would have a proper bath and a trim. A city as large as Hewnstone undoubtedly had a bathhouse.

From the bottom of his sack, he unpacked his other suit of clothing which had seen little wear: a pair of leggings; white bag-sleeved blouse, and a velvet-and-brocade jerkin with a bit of fine trim. The garments were wrinkled and musty. He shook them out and draped them over the chair to air out. Out of deference to the ecclesiastics of Mathus Abbey he would wear his best when he called upon the priory.

Robin peeled off his stiff stained tunic and leggings and slipped between the sheets. Though he had planned to take just a brief rest, he fell fast asleep almost as soon as he laid down.

He slept a dreamless sleep and awoke to Meeyoo's prodding and the thin light of an autumn morning through windows he had neglected to shutter. His body protested that a good night's rest had not at all made up for the recent days' exertions but his spirit was eager to journey to Mathus Abbey.

Hewnstone did indeed have a fine bathhouse. Fed, bathed, shorn, and shaved, Robin left not knowing if he felt like a new man or simply more like his old self. Either way, his spirits were lifted. He bought provisions for several days travel and headed north, away from the sea and inland toward the Chalklands.

The sky was just a little gray with a hint of winter to come. Were he sailing, Robin would have noted the fluffy white clouds with pleasure. Once he left the stone structures and fortifications of Hewstone the landscape softened. On either side of the track, stalks in harvested fields dried and browned in the autumn sun and leaves on the trees were as often yellow, orange, and red as they were green. The days were still warm enough but the nights would be cool, even colder as he got further north. Before too many days passed he would need a cloak. A cloak, embroidered with his crest and trimmed with the ermine pelts he had kept all this time. New boots, a younger horse . . . Robin chuckled. He could amuse himself all the way to Mathus Abbey by toting up the things he would need to transform Robin into King Bewilliam, the list was that long.

CHAPTER SEVENTEEN

Robin journeyed all day and spent the night in a small country church. He got little sleep. His restless mind leapfrogged from one possible outcome to another. He would find the records he sought at the abbey or he would not. He would be able to reassert his sovereignty or he would not.

Despite his weariness, at dawn Robin got up from his pallet. Perhaps instead of continuing north he should indeed return to Hewnstone. Would the Orion still be in port? Robin could accept Captain Gregersen's offer of a position on the ship. It had been hard work but one thing was for certain: it afforded him little time to ruminate about his lot in life. And sailing had provided moments of pleasure. He could learn the secrets of the captain's sun-finding crystal, how to make pouches and mats by knotting rope, how to carve pictures into sharks' teeth. He could learn the words to the sea shanties sung at the capstan and the oarlocks.

No, Robin decided. He wasn't at heart a sailor. He was a king. He would continue with his plan.

His heart beat with anticipation when the evergreen foliage, vivid autumn leaves, and rolling terrain told him he was in the Chalklands and it beat faster yet when the abbey came into sight. Its red brick and white stone walls crowned a hill bearded with trees and shrubs. Crenellated towers pointed toward Heaven. Though lacking the curtain walls of Lomroddoy fortress at Rocky Port or even of Bell Castle, the high straight unbroken walls enclosing the abbey's acres were sufficiently intimidating. Along with pilgrims, merchants, and others who had business with the abbey, Robin led Thief through the tall archway that was the only entrance. Spires, artful engraving, and embossing disguised the true purpose of the defensive tower shadowing the entry. Though dedicated to spiritual practice, the abbey had riches and treasures that others coveted and its friars were ready and able to spring to its defense.

Black-robed monks greeted visitors at the gate and Robin was directed to the stables. He left Thief and Meeyoo in charge of a young monk who looked barely older than a boy. In need of neither lodging nor alms, Robin explained that he needed to speak with someone about the abbey's archives.

"You'll want to talk to Brother Thaddeus," the young novice said. "I will find him for you. Perhaps you could wait in the refectory? Surely after your journey you are in need of refreshment." The novice escorted Robin across the abbey's grounds past small guesthouse cells for mendicants and grander ones for more distinguished visitors. Ahead, the abbey's wings surrounded a square cloister. Robin followed his young guide through an airy colonnade and into the refectory. "I will find Brother Thaddeus," the novice said, and departed.

Robin remembered the abbey's refectory to be much like Bell Castle's great hall, with benches pulled up to long trestle tables arranged in a rectangle and draped with white cloths, the abbot's seat at the head. Sunlight from the open windows glinted in brass and silver pitchers, illuminated the wall tapestries, and warmed the polished wood floor. Tall candelabras stood ready to light the room on overcast days and dark nights. The friar in charge offered him ale, a bowl of soup, and a portion of cold roast pig garnished with tart grapes and then left Robin to enjoy his meal alone. After the close quarters of the Orion it felt odd to have so much space and so much food to himself.

The soup smelled rich, the carrots and green beans were bright and crisp as if just picked, the pork moist, and the ale smelled almost fruity but Robin barely tasted the food, anxious as he was to meet Brother Thaddeus and have a final answer to his question. In the silence of the great hall Robin was certain the hammering of his heart would be audible to anyone who entered.

At a sound behind him he turned to see the door open. The sunlight framed a tall, slim man. The long black woolen robe and coif made him look like a pikestaff.

Robin felt his jaw drop. He stood but his knees were so weak and his lungs so empty of air he thought he might have to sit again. He could not breathe because his chest had turned to stone.

Because the monk was his son, Conrad. An older Conrad to be sure. Taller, a little broader across the shoulders and chest, with a longer face absent of the plumpness of youth but unmistakably Conrad. A fringe of hair the color of flame, pale skin that so easily reddened in the sun, the brown spots scattered across his cheeks and the bridge of his nose, the thin lips, and above all, the green eyes with unfathomable depths under pale auburn brows that always seemed drawn together in thought. All Conrad's.

Robin's heart which had come to a dead stop began once again, pounding extra fast as if to make up for lost beats. He felt lightheaded and forced his rock-hard chest to expand and draw a breath.

"Conrad?" he wanted to say but couldn't get his throat to work. He swallowed hard and squeezed out, "Conrad?"

"I am Brother Thaddeus," he replied, his frown deepening. He stopped and leaned forward. "Sir, forgive me my rudeness. You look something like—"

"Your father. Conrad, it is indeed I."

Conrad took two cautious steps forward. He peered at Robin. "How can this be? I would swear you are my father but he is dead. King Bewilliam is dead."

"No, Conrad, those were only rumors, false tales. I am not dead, but alive. And more truly alive now that I have found you, Sapling."

Conrad's mouth fell open again. "My father's pet name for me when I was a lad. How could you know?"

"I tell you, Conrad, it is I."

Conrad drew yet closer and squinted. With a gasp he said, "Your Majesty," and bowed.

It had been so long since anyone honored him that way Robin hardly knew how to respond. He wanted to wrap his arms around the boy, the man, or kiss him, or clasp his hands, but found himself rooted to the spot where he stood. "Your father, still and always."

And King? Yes, that too. A king with two princes, and Robin had found one of them. His heart swelled with joy. "I know you must have many questions, some of which I fear I cannot answer. You may have harsh words for me but before you speak, let me just say—" The words stung like shards of glass in his throat. "I wish I could turn back time. If I had known what was in store for us, I would have done whatever was necessary to keep that from happening. But I didn't know! It was never my intention to abandon you. You have been ever on my mind. Had I known where to look I would have found you sooner."

Conrad staggered to a bench, made as if to sit, and then observing courtly conventions, straightened.

Robin took a seat himself. He patted the bench beside him fearing that if Conrad didn't sit he might fall over. "Sit, please, Conrad."

Conrad lowered himself to the bench. "Your Majesty . . . Father, you look . . . different."

"I have been at sea," said Robin. He had been many other places all of which had taken a toll. "And I am older. You, Conrad, have grown so tall. You are . . . a man."

"Yes, I am older too. Please, tell me where have you been, Sire? What happened to my king, my father?"

"It's a long story," Robin said. He recounted what had transpired since they last saw each other. When he was done he asked, "Now how is it that you come to be here?"

"You mean an abbey of all places?" said Conrad. "Because we never were churchly people?"

Robin felt his face grow warm. He could not dispute that assertion. Of course Bell Castle had a chapel served by a member of this very order but Robin's attendance had been rare and his reverence, if it could even be called that, perfunctory. The preacher had on more than one occasion cautioned him against the sin of hubris.

Conrad said, "It's not what you think. Come, let's walk, if you're up to it."

"Do I look that badly?"

"Weary."

"Not that weary. Lead on."

He followed Conrad out of the hall and along the shady colonnades surrounding the cloister. "In the absence of King Bewilliam—"

Absence. The word stung.

"King Ulric, the Queen's new husband, sent me here."

Husband? "Ulric?"

"He claimed to be lord of a region far to the west called the Palisades." Conrad shrugged. "I really didn't know what was going on. I was but a lad, engrossed in my studies. The Queen did not make me her confidant and I was not privy to Her Majesty's personal matters. I remember first noticing foreign emissaries who called at Bell Castle. Then unfamiliar knights came, followed by an entire retinue and the man calling himself King Ulric. He was accommodated as a guest in the great hall. After some weeks, I learned there had been a marriage."

The Queen remarried? But that couldn't be, Robin thought. She already had husband—me!

Conrad's pinched expression alluded to the pain that accompanied this memory. "I heard there was a feast. Then this King Ulric took up residence in the keep."

In the keep? Robin thought, his ire rising. In the royal bedchamber? Slept in his bed? With the woman who had been his wife?

"You heard? You were not there?"

"I was sent here," Conrad said. "King Ulric had sons of his own, you see. I became the second son."

Robin bit his lower lip. A life dedicated to the Church was the usual fate for a son out of the line of inheritance.

Conrad said, "Your Majesty needn't feel badly about that. I didn't. The situation at Bell Castle was . . . distressing. I found peace here. Here I have time to myself. I have time to think."

That wasn't hard to believe. Even as a youngster Conrad could often be so lost in thought that he could appear to be by himself even in a roomful of people.

"I am encouraged to think."

Robin's face must have expressed his confusion because Conrad said, "Let me give an example. As a child I would look out a window at the sky and wonder why is the sky blue? Do you know, Sire?"

"Why the sky . . . it's because . . ." Robin paused. "God made it that way?"

Conrad gave him a patient smile. "Yes so I would be told but that didn't satisfy me. I would spend hours thinking about all possible reasons. I would make up answers. I really wanted to know. I asked everyone who would listen to me, all my masters, everyone who was older and wiser and should have an answer. But they didn't, not really. I even asked the abbot. 'God made it that way' may be perfectly true but that didn't answer 'why a sky? Why blue?'"

Robin found himself shaking his head. Why there was a sky and why it was blue wasn't anything he had ever questioned.

"I decided that I needed more people to ask. Somewhere there would be someone who could tell me why the sky is blue. Why water is wet. Why even if I climbed to the top of the castle, I couldn't touch the stars."

Robin tried not to chuckle but he could picture Conrad attempting that very thing, much to the consternation of his mother and his masters.

"I thought surely someone had answers to my questions. And I found them here."

"But this is a church. I would imagine that here more than anywhere else they would tell you 'because God made it that way' and that's all you need to know."

"That's partly true," said Conrad. "That is the answer that I get but here the brothers want to know more about God and His Kingdom so that we can better do our part to fit into His plan. And here there is one other resource. Here there are books."

"Books?"

Conrad's face took on a radiance that colored his otherwise pale complexion. "Books! The wisdom of the ages. Available to anyone who can read."

Robin felt a smile grow within himself. At least he had done something right, had given Conrad something he considered of value. He had made sure that Conrad learned to read.

"And here you also found God?" Robin asked.

Conrad looked puzzled. Then he nodded. "Oh, you mean the robe and the tonsure? I did become a preacher. I have duties here in this community, we all do. But because I am learned and literate, I received training as a scribe. So now I help make books. For the most part we make copies of the Bible and other religious texts which are then sold to other monasteries, to kings and lords for their libraries, to universities. But we also copy other books. It's very slow, time-consuming work, especially since I have a bad habit of reading what I'm copying."

Conrad's words echoed those of the stationarius in Hewnstone.

Conrad smiled the same sheepish smile he would give when caught skipping out on a fencing lesson to go stare at a painting in Bell Castle's great hall. "The abbot says not to worry as it is in this way that I am becoming intimately acquainted with the texts. It is akin to prayer, he says."

Mathus Abbey's abbot clearly had a different understanding of the value of reading than had the stationarius's superior, who had defrocked the poor man.

"So you joined an order for the opportunity to read books?" Robin asked, astounded.

They had reached the end of the colonnade. Opposite them in the cloister a stone fountain bubbled. Conrad bade Robin sit. "At first, that was my plan. It was pretty much the price I had to pay for access to the library. It didn't seem that high a price to pay.

"But the brothers are wise men. You would think that being secluded like this they would be sheltered, innocent, but you would be wrong. They are learned and astute and good judges of character. I did not fool them. They knew why I was here."

"However because they are kind and charitable they let you stay despite your ulterior motives."

Conrad said, "They are kind and generous but they are also sincere and committed to their faith. There is no room here for imposters."

Robin frowned. "So you . . . pay for your lodging? They put you up in exchange for your labors as a scribe?"

Conrad shook his head. "No, I am a true brother, a friar in good standing: Brother Thaddeus." A serene smile turned up his lips. "I see your look. You don't believe me. Because we had not much to do with faith at Bell Castle."

That was true enough. Robin had been King Bewilliam, responsible for running a kingdom. He strived to solve whatever problems presented themselves. Little could be left to Providence. The stakes were simply too high to wait for help to come from the heavens. What had been accomplished was the work of his hand; no need to thank any Supreme Being. Robin had raised his sons, princes, one of whom would one day be King, to be equally self-reliant.

As if reading his thoughts Conrad said, "You ruled as if you believed yourself to be the master of your own fate and raised us to believe that we were too. But I always knew there are more dimensions to Life. And now I know that I was right."

Robin could hear again Conrad's masters reporting on how poorly young Conrad was proceeding with his lessons. Though demonstrably intelligent in other regards, Conrad seemed to have little aptitude for the arts and sciences of being a ruler. Instruction in how to lead men, use weapons, discipline troops, plan a campaign, and negotiate pacts had to be repeated more times than should have been necessary for a boy of Conrad's acumen. Though successful at persuading the Queen to give him a day off from training Conrad was otherwise indifferent when it came to learning how to haggle. He would question why he should desire what another man had and would too often yield any advantage he had gained just to be done with the exercise, the masters would report.

Robin had chastised the masters for being incompetent and had dismissed several, had scolded Conrad for being lazy and lacking discipline. Many times he ordered the boy to attend court and observe how the business of the kingdom was conducted only to have Conrad plead illness. Too many times he would find the boy not resting in bed but sitting in the garden.

"And what of you, Sire?" Conrad asked. "Surely after what Your Majesty has been through you would agree that there are other forces at work."

Robin wasn't all that ready to agree but neither did he want to argue. "You might know something of this. The deeds and titles for Bell Castle and its holdings that have passed through the generations to me, to us . . . where would they be?"

"When I left, they were where they had always been. In the strong box with the royal treasury."

"Which I don't have. But monks would have made records of all those transactions?"

Conrad nodded. "We take our archival responsibilities very seriously."

It was as if the sun had risen in Robin's chest. He gripped Conrad's hands. "So all is not lost! Here? Would there be records here?"

Though he didn't seem to share Robin's exhilaration, Conrad nodded. "I would imagine so. We should visit the scriptorium."

Conrad stood and led Robin back through the colonnade and past the workshops that made the abbey a self-reliant community: mill, bake house, kitchen, buttery, and brew house. Tiny monks' cells hardly bigger than closets surrounded the cloister and above them were vestries, parlors, offices, and apparently the scriptorium.

Robin followed Conrad up a flight of stone steps. Conrad pushed open the door and crossed the room to light a lamp. To Robin the room looked much like the Hewnstone's stationarius's shop only three times as large. Bound books and scrolls filled cases that stretched from the floor toward the ceiling that were so tall ladders were propped against them to provide access to the highest shelves. As had the shop, this room held a bulky wooden desk with an easel and writing instruments while a trestle table was covered by a long unfurled scroll. Slightly stuffy, the room smelled of lantern oil, ink, and leather.

"This is the scriptorium?" Robin asked. "This is where you work?"

"No," Conrad said with chuckle. "I do my work in my cell as do the other copyists. This is the library. The scriptorium is our collection of manuscripts and books. It's here we will find Bell Castle's archives. I will see what I can find. Please, sit. Help yourself to some wine." He indicated an armchair with a cushioned seat. "Pick something to read." He grinned. "Read anything, anything at all."

Robin filled his cup from a pitcher on the table alongside the armchair and sat. "I'll leave you to your research, then," he said. As he sipped the wine he felt the tensions of many months of struggle and doubt slip away.

"Sire?"

Robin lifted his head and opened his eyes. "I'm sorry, did I fall asleep? Did I keep you waiting?"

"Not at all. I found the kingdom's records are in perfect order: marriages, births, acquisitions, pledges, contracts, bonds, debts incurred and discharged, all going back generations. Someone else claiming ownership to the kingdom of the

Chalklands would have a difficult case to make. Would have to take it by force."

Or chicanery. Robin closed his eyes and sighed. One battle had ended but another had begun. While he might have a fight on his hands, it was one in which he was eager to engage. "Conrad, come with me! We will go back to the Chalklands, reestablish the kingdom . . ." Robin stopped. Conrad's regretful smile deflated his elation like a knife piercing a bladder.

Conrad shook his head. "I will not go with you. This is my home, my life."

"Don't be ridiculous. You're not a monk, you're a prince, someday to be King." Perhaps sooner than later, Robin thought, if he continued to be imperiled by deceitful lords, hounded by vengeful fortress soldiers, and menaced by giant squids.

Conrad's face grew stormy, his eyebrows drew together. He opened his mouth to speak, then stopped. As if a cloud had passed before the sun and then moved on, his countenance softened. "I never was much good at being a prince. I would be even worse at being King. I am not fit—"

"No, no, it's not too late. You can still learn what you need to know." Never mind the court's masters and instructors. Robin would teach Conrad himself. They could ride together to the Chalklands and Robin would share with his son the lessons learned from a life on the throne.

"I am learning what I need to know here. It may not be what Your Majesty needs me to know, but . . ."

"I will buy you all the books you want," Robin said. "Hire the best masters. You could be the Bell Castle preacher."

Conrad dipped his head. "I took a vow. Your Majesty would not want me to prove myself to be a man who doesn't keep his word, would you?" He opened the library door. "The hour is getting late. I must be at prayer. Your Majesty is welcomed to join us, of course. Can even stay for supper, stay the night." Conrad started down the stairs and across the cloister to the church. "I'm sorry. I know you're disappointed."

Disappointed? Crushed was more accurate. Conrad could not have devastated Robin any more thoroughly had he ground him under his foot. Something like anger smoldered in his belly. "No, of course you would not break your vow," he said. "But couldn't you honor your vow by serving at Bell Castle? Speak to the abbot about it." If Conrad didn't, Robin would. "All this time you have said little of your brother. What do you know of him?"

"Ah, Zachary." Conrad nodded. "Just as I was no longer the first son, Zachary was no longer the second. It is expected that the landless and disinherited will seek adventures and explore new worlds. I believe that's what he's done. I don't know for certain. He was still at Bell Castle when I left for the abbey."

Robin followed Conrad into the church where Conrad joined the other gathering monks.

With its thick stone walls and stone-paved floor, the room was cool, would always be cool even on the hottest day. Robin wondered if that was deliberate, to create a chill in the visitor that might be taken for the fear of God or perhaps to keep worshippers from falling asleep during the less than mesmerizing sermons. Clerestory windows high on the walls kept the room from being completely dark but the light did not shine down on the benches, which were instead in shadow. Perhaps the intention was that the sole illumination should be the words of the preacher.

Robin had not spent much time here. The chapel at Bell Castle was served by visiting preachers who would attend to the spiritual needs of the kingdom's subjects. This rarely included Robin who hadn't had much more use for the pronouncements of the religious officials than he had for those of his seers. Had he been asked then he might have said that he didn't see much difference between the stories in the Bible and the fairy stories he had told to his sons when they were little boys.

Robin sat on the backless bench, struggling to sit straight although his lower back hurt from the lack of support.

With its incense, bells, and chanting, the service had enough to hold his attention but Robin found his mind wandering. Speak to the abbot, he had said to Conrad. Indeed, at the conclusion of the service, Robin would do that very thing.

CHAPTER EIGHTEEN

Robin stole a look at Conrad riding astride Thief. Conrad's expression was sullen unless he caught Robin looking at him, at which point he would flash a forced smile.

Robin knew Conrad wasn't pleased with the turn of events but didn't care. He had confidence in the agreement that he had made with the abbot. In time Conrad would see that it was right, would come to appreciate the arrangement, and see that it met his own goals as well as Robin's.

Robin understood that Conrad had made an oath and didn't want to break it but as the firstborn son of King Bewilliam Conrad had already had a duty. That preceded and precluded any pledge that would prohibit him from fulfilling his destiny. To Robin's way of thinking, the abbey was wrong to have accepted Conrad's vow in the first place.

The abbot of Mathus Abbey been far more agreeable to Robin's proposal than had Conrad. Upon learning that one of his friars' father, a king, was on the abbey grounds the abbot invited Robin to sup with him at his table while Conrad—Brother Thaddeus—ate with his brothers. It gave Robin ample opportunity to test his idea without objections.

A mission of the brothers was indeed teaching said the abbot who agreed that it was the friars' charge to bring instruction to the people rather than wait for people to come to the abbey. It would not be a renunciation of Conrad's vows to serve at Bell Castle, rather it would be a fulfillment of them. Robin's pledge of financial support for the chapel proved to be persuasive.

Now Robin and Conrad made their way to the castle. Despite Conrad's simmering bad temper Robin's heart was light, buoyed by the sight of familiar plants, animals, and terrain.

Burdened by Robin's weight and pulling a heavily-laden cart, the quarter horse that Robin had bought from the abbey set a pace that didn't present much of a challenge for Thief to match, especially considering all the rest the horse got with Conrad's frequent stops for prayer. Not a warhorse by any means, the abbey's mount that Robin had decided to name Hope would be good for riding and work. Battle stallions would come later. Robin had thought to leave Thief with the monks who out of charity would have cared for him as he lived out his days. However, as Robin and Conrad drew away from the abbey's stables, Thief's mournful expression had tugged at Robin's heart.

The abbey was able to supply Robin with much of what he knew they would need upon their immediate arrival at the wreckage of Bell Castle. That Robin had sufficient means to pay for it all hadn't stopped him from dickering and striking a bargain.

When Conrad could be budged from his sulk he was willing to speak of his life at the abbey but declined to talk about what had happened at Bell Castle after Robin left. "I have nothing good to say and my negativity would serve no one," he explained. "It won't change what happened." He gave Robin a sober look. "Understanding and accepting that I can't change the past enabled me to embrace the future."

True enough, Robin thought, finding that even after all this time he still seethed at the thought of the deception and betrayal that had stolen his life. That smoldering fire did not need to be fanned into flame. His energies were doubtless better spent building a future than reliving a hurtful past. Much as he craved the details he preferred not to aggravate Conrad's already sour disposition with bitter recollections.

Meeyoo proved to be a help in lightening Conrad's mood. At first Conrad had found Robin's choice of traveling companion strange and Meeyoo had been equally leery about Conrad. But after several stops for rest, refreshment, and prayer, Meeyoo's purring and prodding for pets finally won Conrad over and earned her a perch on his saddle as they rode. Now and then Robin would look over and see Conrad observe how Meeyoo busily surveyed the passing landscape. She would glance up at Conrad as if seeking commentary about their surroundings which brought an amused smile to the young man's face.

Bell Castle's keep materialized on the distant horizon. Bell Castle had never been a bustling city like Hewnstone or a forbidding fortress like Lomroddoy. It didn't control an important travel route or harbor. Bell Castle was still the biggest structure in the area, impressive perhaps because of its rural setting.

Robin warned Conrad of what they were likely to find when they arrived at the castle, or more to the point, what they wouldn't find: stores, furnishings, food. All had been removed, leaving just the shell of a castle.

Conrad shrugged. "I took a vow of poverty, Your Majesty. I don't need much."

As true as that might be, Robin couldn't help but imagine that Conrad would be shocked at the sorry condition of what had been his home.

What Robin noticed first as they drew near was the quiet. No one else plied the road—what was left of the road. Overgrown with grass and weeds it was barely distinguishable from the surrounding meadow. Rotted and desiccated fruit hung from the highest branches of trees in need of pruning.

The drawbridge over the dry ditch between them and the gatehouse was nowhere in sight.

"I think it's a sign from God that we should turn back," said Conrad.

"Nonsense," said Robin, who had scaled more than his fair share of dry ditches lately. They and the horses could manage it. The only problem was the cart which filled wouldn't make it up the escarpment. That had been built steep not so much to keep out foot soldiers but to obstruct machines of war. "We'll have to unload it and carry everything across."

Conrad greeted the news with a frown then composed his face. Item by item they unloaded the cart and piled everything on the opposite side. The two horses leaped down one slope and clambered up the other. Robin tied the cart to Hope and pushing and pulling, he and Conrad helped the horse to get the empty cart through the ditch leaving them both sweating despite the coolness of the autumn day. Conrad brushed at the now dingy hem of his white habit.

The first portcullis gate stood in a raised position. Robin wondered if the metal parts might be rusted and seized in place. Rust, he remembered Eli telling him, never rests. Leaves and dirt filled the gateway corridor and clung to spider webs in the corners.

To Robin's surprise the second portcullis gate was closed. He remembered it as being open.

"Ah, a second sign. Now surely we will be turning back," Conrad said.

Now it was Robin's turn to scowl. "Maybe this is a challenge from God," he said, "to test the strength of our commitment."

Conrad opened his mouth, closed it, then opened it again. "How do you propose to raise the gate?"

"What would you suggest?" Robin asked, curious to see if Conrad had retained anything from his princely lessons.

Conrad folded his arms. "I could pray."

"You do that," Robin said and turned to study the gate. Through the wooden slats Robin could see that one of the two ropes leading from the top of the gate to the winch in the gatehouse had snapped and lay on the ground. He scaled the latticed grid as if it were a ship's ladder. At the top he could see that the gate's rope still ran through the pulley with a ragged stub hanging loose. The second rope was still intact, the counterweight attached. He hoped that it would be enough.

"Hand me up the longest rope we've got," he called to Conrad. He would join the fresh rope to the end of the frayed one. The mend would have to be small and neat to pass over the pulley. He made a mental inventory of all the knots that Crank had demonstrated aboard the Orion. This join would require a splice, Robin decided. Strand by strand he wove the two rope ends together.

He climbed down the grid putting one hand through the grid and then the next to keep the mended rope from drifting out of reach. At the bottom he pulled the rope through the space between two of the spikes arrayed along the lowest rung.

He and Conrad tugged on the rope, pulling it down toward them and raising the gate by fractions. Robin tied the end to Hope's saddle and leading the horse back down the gateway path got the gate raised enough to allow Conrad to pass through. "Lock down that windlass," Robin said, thinking at the first opportunity he should change out the ropes for chains. He hastened to thread the mended rope back through and attach it to the second windlass to secure the portcullis gate in the raised position.

As he and Conrad piled their belongings back into the cart for transport inside the curtain wall, Robin noticed the boy regarding him with a strange expression.

"What?" he finally asked.

"I just . . . I wouldn't have thought it possible, to open the gate from the outside. If it's that easily breached, what good is it for defense?"

Robin tried not to grin, although Conrad's words were as balm for every strained muscle. Despite his protestations, apparently Conrad did have some interest in the workings of a castle.

"Normally, defenses would include men stationed in the gatehouse. If invaders made it this far, past the drawbridge and first portcullis gate, our men would be positioned above and would throw rocks and boiling water on the invaders. They'd be very vulnerable in the gateway passage and would likely retreat. They'd be too busy trying to save themselves to mount the kind of offensive that we just did."

"The way you figured out how to raise the gate. How did you know how to do that?"

It was good for a king to know the mechanics of a castle's defenses, but he wouldn't tell Conrad that. The young man was already resentful of the responsibilities that would come to rest on his shoulders one day. "Maybe God put the notion in my head," Robin said.

Conrad nodded but Robin was fairly certain Conrad had been willing to give his earthly father some credit.

"We should start a fire and draw some water before it gets dark. Get the stables cleared out and get the animals fed and watered."

"There's something that I need to do first," said Conrad.

Robin imagined that he wanted to visit what had been his room. Instead, Conrad turned toward the chapel.

With a sigh, Robin led the horses to the stables. The tack, tools, and equipment had long since been carried off, as well as had any food but the stalls needed to be cleared of the rodents that had built nests in the corners. It was a task to which Meeyoo eagerly applied herself. Robin and Conrad had brought all the feed that they could carry from the abbey but Robin could see that they would need more, as soon as tomorrow depending on the condition of the pasture. He cleared the scum from the surface of the well and drew water with which to fill the trough.

He drifted across the bailey. It surprised Robin that despite the lack of furnishings no one had made use of the abandoned buildings which while empty still stood and could at least provide shelter. Perhaps rumors had spread that the castle was cursed or haunted. It would appear to be if not for the golden light of a fall afternoon. He regarded the inner bailey, the empty structures, and untended farmland, and tried not to think of the work that lay ahead.

A light glowed faintly behind the chinks in the chapel's clapboards. Robin entered the small building to discover that Conrad had found candles and lit one. Some of the floorboards were loose but the benches still stood in place. Perhaps the thieves, for that's how Robin thought of them, had feared reprisals from God.

"I thought we'd build a fire in the great hall," Robin said. "Have supper there, the first of many to come. Or if you'd rather, we can spend the night in the keep. You could reclaim your old room."

"This will be my room, Your Majesty," Conrad said. "I'll spend the night here. The first of many to come."

"As you wish." The chapel was not meant as a habitation. There was nowhere to build a fire. As winter approached, Conrad would likely find the nights chilly and change his mind about where he would sleep.

Robin had to admit that he was reluctant to spend the night in the vacant keep. There was something forbiddingly lonely about the tall cylindrical building perched on its own motte in a corner. Memories of warm fellowship, food, and merriment made the great hall more attractive. Recalling the condition in which he had found it when last he saw it Robin made his way there with some trepidation. Time and inattention had not been kind and Robin was shocked to see how quickly even the sturdiest structures could decay if left unattended. Peeled plaster gave the walls a piebald appearance. Paint had faded, wood rotted, metal rusted, and fabric disintegrated. After another week of neglect seemingly the entire castle would be just a pile of rubbish.

He collected fuel for a fire, food, ale, and scooped up Meeyoo. He remembered how alone he had felt the last time he had been in the great hall and how much he missed the cat's companionship. "I told you that you would like being a castle cat," he said, releasing her to inspect the surroundings. "I know it doesn't look like much now but in time . . ." He took a seat on the dais that had supported his throne, ate his supper, and drank his ale. Tomorrow would be time enough to begin the reconstruction of Bell Castle. Tonight he was just glad to be home.

From the bottom of his sack he unearthed the ermine pelts, all that remained of his royal cloak. They were crushed and matted and some of Meeyoo's fur clung to them. Robin sat and stroked them. He would get a new robe, have it trimmed with the pelts, have it embroidered with the domain's heraldic crest. Get a suit of armor made complete with an ornamented helmet, a crown so there would be no mistaking his sovereignty . . .

He woke to Meeyoo's prodding to find himself sprawled across the dais, stiff and sore from the previous day's exertions and a night sleeping on the floor in a cold room. The bright light of a new day streamed through the window only to be lost in the dust dulling the marble floor. Over a mug of ale Robin considered what should be his first move. He and Conrad needed somewhere other than the floor to sleep and not only a place to eat but food. The stores were barren.

A wild fall crop had grown scraggly and stunted, overshadowed by weeds. The closed portcullis gate had kept gleaners at bay and some fruits and vegetables remained to be picked, but most were overripe, rotten, or had gone to seed. The plots needed clearing and winter crops started. There was no time to waste; it was almost too late. They needed flour, ale, and wool, clothing and blankets, furniture, and tools.

The castle grounds had been abandoned but the Kingdom of the Chalklands claimed fertile lands for many miles around. Surely serfs still made a living from land that Robin owned and for which they owed him rent, taxes, or tribute. What had happened to the kingdom's servants? It was doubtful that this King Ulric of the Palisades had made off with them for the servants were bound to the land. Nor had he bought their service from Robin. He had found no evidence of that in the records at Mathus Abbey. Instead the archives accurately noted bonds still in force.

Robin needed his masons, carpenters, blacksmiths, weavers, tailors, painters, not to mention farmers, millers, butchers, bakers, and brewers. They would have to be reminded of their obligations, a job for a corps of knights. Robin pressed his lips together and shook his head. Rallying Bell Castle's servants presented a daunting enough challenge. Confronting his errant knights was another matter. Robin might need that armor and helmet sooner than later.

He needed help which by rights should come from his sons. Conrad wasn't proving to be any kind of a secondary. Robin wished Zachary were with them. Zachary hadn't been any more dedicated to his princely studies than his older brother. However now that Zachary would someday take the throne he might see the value of his lessons.

Robin sighed. Conrad had no better notion than Robin of what fate had befallen the younger son.

Robin stood. In the coming days he would find those servants and knights as he would find Zachary but some needs had to be addressed today. To meet them he would strike agreements with freemen, merchants, craftsmen, and free tenants. He'd have to draw up contracts . . . He grinned. Sounded like a job for Conrad.

Robin started across the bailey to find Conrad emerging from the chapel, book in hand.

"Today we are setting out to find those who owe us service," Robin said. "Recruit additional help if we need it. We'll take both horses, look for a blacksmith. Thief is overdue —"

"I am staying here, Your Majesty," Conrad replied.

CHAPTER NINETEEN

Conrad quickly tempered his challenging expression.

Robin felt his anger spark. At first he had found himself amused by Conrad's obvious struggle to master his emotions. The young man met every assignment with a petulant scowl. Then as if aware that such was not becoming of a man of the cloth, Conrad would visibly soften his countenance and put on a benign expression.

However Robin had become impatient with Conrad's resistance. Conrad and Mathus Abbey's abbot had both maintained that Conrad's vocation was genuine but Robin had his doubts. Conrad was a prince, not a priest, with responsibilities. "It wasn't an invitation, Conrad."

"You are commanding me to accompany you, Sire?"

Coming from anyone else, the words would have been confrontational, but Conrad's tone and mien were even. I am your father, Robin thought. I am your king. He considered ordering Conrad to come along but instead asked, "Are you not concerned about being here alone?"

"Not at all. I am prepared to defend myself as I was at the abbey. As for defending the property . . ." Conrad shrugged, "there's not much here to defend."

"What will you do here all by yourself?" Robin asked, tamping down his annoyance.

Conrad held up his book, a Bible. "Read."

"Fine," Robin said with a grin. "After you draw up these contracts."

Robin traveled to the lands that he owned around Bell Castle, presenting himself as Sir Robin, a knight of King Bewilliam's. He would pull from his pack a scroll, one that Conrad had found in Mathus Abbey's scriptorium, and unfurl it. The document said nothing about a Bell Castle knight named Robin but that mattered not since most people could not read. The embossing and wax seal was impressive enough.

The subterfuge granted him a more favorable reception than would have riding up in modest attire on a swaybacked horse and claiming to be their king. He was not surprised that his servants didn't recognize him as Their Majesty even though in pledging their fealty his subjects had put their head in his very hands. Their king was a much changed man: older, wizened, yet also leaner.

He discovered that servants still lived on his land. Some still paid taxes and tribute, only not to King Bewilliam, not to Bell Castle. They had been told that King Bewilliam was dead, that the land now belonged to King Ulric.

Not so, "Sir Robin" told them. "You shall resume working for, paying taxes to, and remitting your tribute to Bell Castle."

Some expressed concern about reprisals that King Ulric or his knights might visit on them for nonpayment. Robin assured them that they would be protected. For the most part, however, Bell Castle's servants seemed relieved to learn that the king was not dead and that he had resumed rule. A few even pledged to report to Bell Castle on the morrow to work or to deliver food or supplies, which warmed Robin's heart. He had always thought of himself as a just and amenable lord. Apparently that opinion was shared by many who considered King Bewilliam's governance fair compensation for their labor.

He also came to agreements with unlanded folk who were more than willing to entertain his proposal, especially as the proposal included an offer of property. He found a number of bordars, half-villeins, and serfs who had a semblance of a roof over their head and not much else.

Land Robin had aplenty, it was people he needed.

By day's end he had arranged for a couple to serve in the kitchen, the husband as baker and the wife as cook and brewer of ale. Their son would work in the stables and the daughter the scullery. Another family with three children and one on the way agreed to tend the fields in exchange for more land and a larger home to support their growing numbers. Robin found a young carpenter with more skill than equipment who was eager to advance his trade if Bell Castle's king would provide the tools. Few of which Robin had. They would have to be purchased or made, lengthening the list of items he needed from a blacksmith.

The smoke he spied billowing from a forge aroused both nostalgia and aversion. The clanging of a sledgehammer against an anvil flooded him with memories of the grueling months he spent laboring in an ironworks.

The tiny forge was little more than a small shed at the back of a smaller half-timbered house. Having spotted the smoke, Robin expected to see a furnace and indeed there was one backed up to the rear of the house. The shared warmth would be welcome in the cold months but Robin thought the heat from the smith's furnace would render the inside of the home sweltering in the summer. Smoke plumed from the chimney that poked through a small pitched roof sheltering the workspace in the ell between the house and the furnace wall. Tongs, mallets, and hammers hung on the house's rear wall while a work table stood at the center of the covered space as did as an anvil, a water bucket for tempering the metal, and several stumps that served as work surfaces. At one side of the table, the mouth of a bellows pointed to the base of the furnace, the handle for driving the bellows within easy reach of anyone working at the table.

This smithy looked just slightly less harsh than the one in which Robin had labored. Open on two sides, the work area would be less dusty and smoky.

A tall, white-haired man plucked metal scraps from the ground and placed them in a bucket. Nothing was wasted; metal scraps would be melted down to make new stock and bits of wood would kindle the next day's fires. It was a lesson Robin had paid something of a price to learn.

While not a young man the smith seemed aged even beyond his years. The work did that to a man, Robin knew. Blacksmithing meant long days driving a bellows, swinging a heavy sledgehammer, all in the blistering heat of a furnace. He had been jubilant to finally be relieved of that duty only to discover that there was even more punishing work, that of the ordinary seaman.

The man spied Robin and straightened. "Good morning," he said. "I am Gregory. What can I make for you? A hinge for your door, a shoe for your horse, hooks, nails? Spikes of all sizes."

"I do need nails and hammers as well as my horse reshod. But I also need something else. I need an entire blacksmith shop."

The blacksmith Gregory stepped back with a wary look, eyes agog.

"I am Sir Robin, a knight of Bell Castle as this document attests." Once again, he exhibited the impressive document.

The blacksmith's bow was nevertheless tentative. "How may I serve you, sir?"

"We are in need of a blacksmith and would like you and your wife—"

"Passed away, some years ago, I'm afraid," Gregory said.

"That is hard. My condolences." All the better, Robin thought. Gregory had no encumbrances that might make it difficult for him to relocate.

Gregory still looked skeptical. ""I have heard of Bell Castle. There is no one there. Some say it's bewitched."

"I can assure you that it is not. I just came from there. Do I look bewitched?"

Gregory shook his head but his brow was still furrowed.

"Yes, there was a . . . difference of opinion about possession, but King Bewilliam proved victorious and wishes to restore the fiefdom. As you can imagine there is much that needs to be rebuilt."

"Indeed," said Gregory. "My apologies. Please, sir, take a seat. And then please give me leave to sit. I have been on my feet all day and one is plagued with gout."

The "disease of kings" it was called but Robin knew men and women who were afflicted with the condition and they were not royalty. Some wanted to attribute the ailment to the consumption of alcohol, but that couldn't be the cause either. Everyone drank ale every day and not everyone got gout.

"By all means," said Robin.

"Thank you, sir." Gregory limped over to a bench, sat, leaned against the wall behind him, and propped one foot on a small stool.

"That must make it difficult to do your work. I was about to suggest that you could use a hand but it appears that what you need is a foot."

Gregory chuckled.

"A stand-in, so to speak," said Robin.

Gregory's chuckle became laughter. "All right, sir, you have my attention. But I'm confused. A castle should already have a smithy."

"And indeed it does, but it is empty. No tongs, no anvils, no hammers. No smiths." Robin looked about at the tiny shop and the even tinier house hoping that Gregory could be persuaded to abandon it in favor of working at Bell Castle.

From a wooden door leading into the house stepped a young man carrying two mugs. His short dark hair stuck out from his head in spikes and his chin was stubbly. A heavy leather apron covered his front from chest to knees. He handed one of the mugs to his Gregory.

"Greetings," said the young man to Robin.

"My son, Maxwell," said Gregory. "This is Sir Robin, a knight of Bell Castle. He needs his horse reshod."

Maxwell gave Robin the same skeptical frown that Gregory had but like his father, bowed. As he straightened he scrutinized Robin, his gaze lingering on Robin's sword. He then regarded

Thief and then looked at Robin with raised eyebrows that clearly said "not much of a horse for a knight."

In response to the unspoken criticism Robin said, "Not my usual mount. This is an old favorite of the king's. It actually did save his life once and he is sentimental about it."

"King Bewilliam has reassumed power," Gregory told his son. "He is rebuilding and has need of our services. Wants us to set up shop at the castle."

"Move? Live there too?" Maxwell's expression did not convey enthusiasm.

"There is much to be done at Bell Castle. Horses to be shod of course, as well as all manner of ironworking," Robin said. "Nails, locks, chains, lanterns, door handles, sconces, shovels and farm implements, hammers, cook pots and kettles . . ."

Maxwell's guarded expression did not change.

"Knives, daggers, and swords, of course." Robin thought he detected a glint in Maxwell's eyes, a quickening of interest. "For the soldiers and knights."

"Swords, you say?"

"For the knights." What young man wasn't fascinated by swords and didn't dream of the one that he would someday wear at his side? "Such as this." Robin withdrew his sword and laid it across his knees.

Gregory and Maxwell stretched their necks and peered at the weapon.

"A handsome blade. Quench-hardened?"

"Work-hardened," Robin replied.

Gregory nodded. "Produces more strength. As do the fullers." He fingered the groove that created a channel down the length of the blade, then tested the edge. He pressed his lips together. "This is indeed a fine instrument."

Maxwell looked it over, then gave a smile that could almost be called wistful. "Finely made indeed but I'm afraid we don't do much with blades."

"Yet you do seem to know your metalworking. And everyone has a need for a sharp edge be it a sword, a knife, or simply shears."

Maxwell had drawn closer. "Well, that's true. We could do more sharpening, I suppose. We just . . . don't."

Robin suspected it was because they weren't very good at it. He had discovered it was a time-consuming craft requiring much learning and practice. "It is a useful skill. I could teach you to do it efficiently and well."

"You, sir? You're a blacksmith? I thought you were a knight," said Gregory.

"I've done some metal working in the past. I made the sword."

"Yourself?" Now Maxwell's eyes were bright and his face wore a hint of a smile.

"From scratch," said Robin. "I smelted the alloy for the blank. I put the edge on it."

"Why?"

"Maxwell!" Gregory said with a frown. "Such impertinence. Yours is not to pester a knight with silly questions."

"Not at all," Robin said. "It's a good question. I was curious, Maxwell."

"Curious?" Maxwell seemed unfamiliar with the word.

"I wanted to know more about the sword than just how to wield it. Such as why some were more effective than others. It couldn't all be about the swordsman." Robin said to Gregory. "Sharpening is work you can do seated. Let me show you."

Gregory got settled at a worktable and Robin demonstrated basic techniques on one blade of a pair of shears. "Now you try it," he said.

"Maxwell, see to the man's horse," Gregory said and then tackled the other blade.

When he and Maxwell had completed their tasks he said, "Sir Robin, blade sharpening is not easy work. My back aches, my eyes feel like they've been tugged out of their sockets, and my hands are cramped."

It wasn't easy work Robin knew, and it didn't get easier. He waited wordlessly for Gregory's next pronouncement.

"But you were right. My foot pains me less. I think I would indeed find bench work more manageable."

Robin breathed a sigh of relief. Work for Gregory now held the prospect of being much less arduous than driving a bellows or a sledgehammer.

Maxwell chewed on his lower lip. "You say the king would like us to set up shop at the castle." Maxwell frowned and looked at his father. "We have barely enough time as it is to make what we need to keep a roof over our heads."

"It is the king's land that you're on," Robin said. Should it come to that, he could command their services but he would prefer to have their willing cooperation. "I will propose to the king that for the labor you would provide the kingdom, you would live on Bell Castle's grounds and have no rent," Robin said.

"Maxwell, go get some ale for the good knight," said Gregory.

Maxwell started for the house. He turned and asked, "And we would make swords? For the knights?"

"Indeed," Robin replied.

Gregory said. "I think we can come to an agreement."

CHAPTER TWENTY

Weary from a long day of arm-twisting and fast talking, Robin turned Hope towards home. Home. Robin allowed himself a small smile even though Bell Castle still looked nothing like the home he remembered. So much needed to be done and it seemed that it all needed to be done at once. Which should he have made first, a bed in which to sleep or a table at which to eat or a throne from which to rule? Until he furnished the great hall with tables and chairs, Robin found himself taking his supper from a tray while seated on the ornate upholstered seat he had placed on the dais to serve as a throne.

In the weeks that followed he fanned out in ever-widening circles, reclaiming servants, renewing compacts, and drafting new agreements. It was an undertaking befitting a knight, but Robin had none. He still smarted from his betrayal at the hands of those who had pledged allegiance to him. They would have to be found and punished. As for recruiting new ones, Robin discovered that while his need for support was unquestioned he had little enthusiasm for the task.

When he did not travel Robin put in long hours managing Bell Castle's servants. While their commitment to the castle's rebirth was gratifying, the work of setting priorities, acquiring and apportioning raw materials, and approving finished products never ended. Would that Robin could charge his princes with the responsibility but Conrad continued to maintain his devotion to his vocation, and Zachary . . . Robin tried not think about Zachary.

Few were kept busier than the blacksmiths Gregory and Maxwell. It seemed that everyone who worked at Bell Castle from the baker to the carpenter to the farmer needed something made in the smithy. The carpenter needed a hammer, the farmer a shovel, the cook a pot, the painter a scaffold, the stable boy shoes for the horses, and on and on.

Looming in the back of Robin's mind was the castle's lack of weapons. That there had been no incursions didn't keep Robin from worrying about defense. As word of Bell Castle's burgeoning prosperity spread the likelihood that someone would think it a worthy target grew greater every day.

Out of necessity Robin found himself lending a hand in the forge. At first the smiths found it uncomfortable to labor alongside not the man they had thought to be "Sir Robin" but their very king. Gregory was the first to abide a little awkwardness. Grateful to relieve the pressure on his swollen foot he quickly became at ease with sitting in the king's presence even if the seat was in front of a grindstone.

Maxwell on the other hand drove the bellows and wielded the sledgehammer with a sulky intensity that hinted at an unvoiced anger or resentment that Robin found baffling. Could it be the long hours at arduous labor? It was true that Robin tasked the smiths hard but he took pains to make sure they were well compensated, with comfortable lodgings, generous food, and title to their own land. Perhaps Maxwell faulted his father for his disability which laid the heaviest burdens on the boy's shoulders. Robin shrugged, applied himself to blade-making and showing Gregory the finer techniques of edge-sharpening, and left the sullen boy to his labors. Now and then Robin would look up to find the young man regarding him intently from across the room, whereupon Maxwell would quickly look away.

As the sun set on one long but productive day that had Gregory standing on his gouty foot for far too long, the man begged leave to retire. Robin was prepared to call it a good day's labor as well. He wiped his sweaty brow with a rag and took off the leather apron that kept his tunic from being singed. No crown or royal cloak needed here in the smithy. He had left them behind in the great hall where they were unlikely to be damaged or get in the way.

Maxwell stepped away from his anvil but only to light a lamp.

"You're going to put in some more time?" Robin asked.

"I should finish this, Sire," he said without looking up.

"Your dedication is admirable. Your productivity will stand you in good stead when you take over for Gregory." Which, given the man's health might be sooner than later.

Maxwell simply shrugged. The prospect of stepping into his father's shoes did not seem to generate enthusiasm. Were all sons like this, Robin wondered, disdainful of the legacy their father had strived an entire lifetime to bequeath them?

"You think perhaps that should be now?" Robin asked. "That given his gout, you should be in charge?"

Maxwell looked genuinely shocked. "No, Sire. My father is a hard worker, despite his pain. If you are finding fault with his—"

"Not in any way. You have accomplished much, you and your father. He has taken to sharpening quickly."

Maxwell nodded and turned his attention to his work, his lips pinched.

Perhaps Maxwell resented his father getting a chance to learn a new craft? Robin recalled their first meeting and the youth's interest in swords. Maybe Maxwell had expected that he too would get to work with weapons. "When you are done, there's something you can help with."

"Certainly, Your Majesty," Maxwell said with a bow and setting down his mallet, started across the room.

"When you're done," Robin said.

"As you wish, Sire."

Robin laid his file on the workbench. "What are you making?"

"A cook pot for Susan. She says she has outgrown the first one that I made."

Robin had to smile. "Indeed, there are more people to cook for at Bell Castle than even just a few weeks ago. But if you finish it tomorrow that will be soon enough. Come over here."

Maxwell bowed and joined Robin at the bench where he had been putting the finishing touches on a sword. "Your father is getting quite good at this but you should learn as well. Just as we need more and bigger pots for our cooks, we need weapons for our knights."

"Knights?"

"Yes," Robin said, smothering the nagging voice that questioned why he didn't as yet have any knights.

Robin had not found the art and science of making metal sharp easy to master at first nor had Gregory and he wondered if Maxwell understood any of the instructions at all since the lad watched but made no comments.

Finally, the young man said, "Sire, a question if I may?"

"Ask away," Robin replied, relieved to learn that Maxwell hadn't been standing at his shoulder wool-gathering.

"Why put all this work into making the edge sharp? Doesn't a knight simply . . .?" Maxwell made a stabbing gesture.

Robin tried not to chuckle. "Stab is only one of many offensive moves. Knights also use a sword to slice, cut, and chop, all of which call for a sharp edge. Slice—that will cut the skin. The enemy will bleed. If the slice and the bleeding are severe enough, that may be sufficient to win the contest. Cut— that will separate sinew or muscle from bone. Again, disabling the adversary. Chop—with full force, a strong knight can sever a limb. You can imagine that will slow the opponent."

Maxwell's eyes were wide.

"By way of demonstration . . ." Robin stood and held the sword over a sack of sawdust and by turns, sliced, cut, and chopped it to shreds.

"How does the knight know which to do?" Maxwell asked.

"It takes years of training and practice," Robin replied. And padding. Lots of padding.

Excitement briefly lit Maxwell's face before it settled into a crestfallen expression. His shoulders drooped. With a sigh and a bow he turned toward the anvil.

All these questions about knights and swordsmanship . . . Robin realized it wasn't swords or sharpening that had captured Maxwell's interest, it was knighthood. "You'd like to be one, wouldn't you? A knight?"

Maxwell's head whipped around. "A knight? Sire!" Again eager eyes and a face lit with enthusiasm darkened quickly. "That could never be. I come from a humble background."

"That matters not. Knights are made, not born. They earn their title through service to their lord, through bravery in battle."

"I could be brave, I know I could. I would fight to the death for Bell Castle!"

Robin tried not to chuckle. How eager the boy was to give away a life he had not yet lived.

"But my job is here. Bell Castle needs smiths."

"Indeed it does, but it needs knights, too. I could train you." Even as he said it, Robin realized it was really Conrad that he wanted to train, or Zachary. But that was not to be.

"You, Sire? Me?"

The thought of sharing what he knew, passing on skills learned through near-lethal experience, quickened Robin's pulse. Robin regarded the youth with a sternness he did not feel. "You would not start as a knight. A knight in training is a squire."

"Squire Maxwell," the lad murmured, and licked his lips.

"You think you have been working hard here in the smithy. Being a squire is even more demanding. You would serve a knight. Carry his armor, shield and sword, all very heavy."

Maxwell hefted the sledgehammer. "I am strong!"

Indeed, the lad was reedy and not overly tall but years of lifting heavy loads had built up his shoulders and arms. "Make sure that armor and those weapons are always in good order, ready for battle. His horse, too. Help the knight outfit himself for combat. Rush to his aid on the battlefield without hesitation, to replace his sword if he drops it or it breaks, to replace his horse if it's wounded or killed. All at the risk of your own death."

Maxwell nodded vigorously.

"Hold any prisoners the knight takes and if by some chance the knight is taken prisoner, you must rescue him."

"I would stay by his side, close as a shadow," Maxwell said.

Robin frowned. "You would still have to meet your obligations here." His words echoed a bargain that he himself had been offered, and accepted, not long ago. "Your father—"

"Would be so proud! Oh, yes, he has always expected that I would follow in his footsteps. But to be a knight—sorry, Sire, a squire of Bell Castle . . . I vow I would not shirk my responsibilities."

"Your father would not have to take on your obligations here?"

"No. I promise."

"You will be held to your vow. Should there be any complaints about your performance in the shop—"

"There will be none," said Maxwell. "I will make you both proud, Your Majesty."

"Well, then . . . normally you would be knighted on the battlefield or if not then we would wait until a feast or festival to award you an accolade." The ceremony was also more typically performed to dub a man into knighthood. "But there is no time like the present. Maxwell, please kneel before us," Robin said, letting the majestic plural lend weight to his words.

The young man hastened to comply. Robin tapped the flat of his blade to Maxwell's right shoulder, then lifted it over his head and tapped the left. "You are to be known henceforth as Squire Maxwell."

Maxwell looked up and beamed, then rose and with a bow, returned to the anvil and smacked the pot-in-progress with vigor.

Robin left the smithy to get a very late supper. Then more than ready to retire, he started across the bailey toward the keep. A movement in the darkness caught his eye. In the moonlight, a strange figure with a spiky head hummed and performed a jerky dance, looking for all the world like a woodland sprite. For a moment Robin was taken aback. How had such a creature gotten past the castle walls? Robin stopped and peered into the darkness and caught the words to the sprite's curious song: "Slice! Cut! Chop!" It was Maxwell with a broom handle practicing his swordsmanship against an imaginary foe.

Robin shook his head and thought, I'm going to need another smith.

CHAPTER TWENTY-ONE

The autumn air was invigoratingly brisk as Robin strode toward the gatehouse and he was grateful for the warmth of his cloak.

Admit it, Robin, he chided himself. You're not just warm, you're proud and indeed he found himself standing tall, his shoulders squared, the better to display the royal crest embroidered in the center of the garment. Kept his chin up and his head high, too, adorned as it was with a bejeweled gilt band tied around his brow. Barely a coronet much less a crown—that was still being made—the diadem nevertheless adequately identified him as person of royal authority.

Today he was bound for the Marlborough Fair. In the past few days, several of his servants had requested permission to attend it.

Trade fairs were nothing new to Robin. In years past they had had market days at Bell Castle when merchants from all points of the domain would bring their wares. As well, he had sojourned at a settlement that had held many market days.

His interest in this one stemmed not from idle curiosity or a simple desire for diversion. He had authorized no free fairs nor had he granted anyone a franchise. An abbey might be sponsoring this fair but if this was being held on his property, he was due a fee for the license. A knight or a prince could easily have executed the investigation but Conrad could not be persuaded to go.

Robin found his son as usual in the chapel. What had once been a somber windowless room with a few plain benches and a simple altar now seemed larger and brighter, inviting. The whitewashed walls shined with the sunlight streaming in from a newly-created window. Robin wasn't aware that any servants had been pulled away from their tasks and could only assume that Conrad had done the work himself, quite well from what Robin could see. Set atop the altar, a simple ceramic pot filled with sprigs of dill, rosemary and thyme lent the room a pleasant herbal aroma. At the back of the altar stood a plain wooden table and chair. The table held a writing easel, a cup filled with pens, books and papers, looking much like the work area of the stationer in Hewnstone.

Robin explained his errand. "You should come along. Think of all the people who will be there to whom you can preach."

"Indeed, but I have other plans today," was Conrad's reply. "I am working on a concordance."

Robin figured he must look puzzled. In response to his unasked question, Conrad said, "It's a listing of every word in the Bible, in alphabetical order, with definitions and commentaries about why those words are important or how they are used."

Robin decided he must still seem baffled because Conrad said, "A brother might want to present a lesson or give a sermon about oh, let's say patience. With a concordance he can easily find every mention of patience and the context in which the word appears. He can compare the different ways in which the word is used, see how often it's used. A concordance is a very useful tool but demands much time and diligence to compile. To provide worthwhile commentaries requires a thorough understanding of the Good Book."

The mere idea of assembling such a document made Robin's head ache. He could hardly imagine that Conrad wouldn't much prefer going to a fair, but he bit back a retort or a command. He had another idea.

Leaving Conrad to his work, Robin approached the smithy to find it radiating warmth and ringing with the sound of metal on metal. Gregory and Maxwell already had a fire going in the furnace and were hard at work. His fists wrapped around the handle of a hammer, Gregory paused in mid-swing and Maxwell set down his tongs. Gregory bowed to greet his king and Maxwell nearly went down on one knee.

"Greetings," Robin said. "We have a special task for Maxwell, if he can be spared. How fare you, Gregory?"

Gregory balanced on one foot and wiggled the other. "Very well, thank you, Sire. I think today I might even be spared the usual pain."

Robin noticed that the man did not stand on the affected foot which looked as swollen as usual but Gregory's smile was brave and his eyes pleaded almost as much as his son's.

"If you need my son's services, Sire, by all means. I can manage most capably."

"Then Maxwell, go get our horse and a mount for yourself. We will journey a few hours distance."

The track was busy with wayfarers bound for Bell Castle and also away from it. The further Robin and his squire got from the castle, the more congested became the road. Travelers on foot and on horseback jostled for space. Donkeys pulled carts carrying entire families. The fairgoers entertained themselves and each other, playing instruments, singing songs, telling tales. Along the way, vendors hawked sweet treats, beverages, and savory pies. The road was no less dusty than any other but many had apparently been willing to risk a little dirt in the name of sartorial splendor and were dressed in fine clothes.

Riding alongside Robin, Maxwell's head swiveled as he scanned the road, the other travelers, and the woods, his expression alternating between watchful and enthralled.

Robin had heard that Marlborough Fair was too big to be contained within any castle's walls and as he drew near he could see that was so. The Fair spread for hundreds of yards in all directions. Ahead of him rows and aisles of carts and stalls fanned out to the right and left making a sea of color, their canopies undulating like brightly-patterned waves in the breeze. The smoke of many fires streamed upwards and he smelled the mingled scents of sweet and savory cooking, the tang of ale, and the fruity aroma of wine as well as pungent herbs, flowery perfumes, musky incense, and the odors of the throngs of people and animals. Maxwell's jaw dropped and his eyes were agog at the scene before him.

Tradesmen and craftsmen on the outskirts of the fair undertook to meet the immediate needs of arriving travelers. Ale was for sale to fill jugs that had been drunk dry. If the road had taken a toll on a horse's feet, a blacksmith could repair shoes. A carpenter could fix damaged carts and wheels, a tailor could sew torn canopies. Indeed there were many here whose talents could serve Bell Castle. Robin hoped that somewhere he would find a responsible party or someone in charge who could answer his question about how the fair came to be. A gathering this large could not be impromptu.

A young man rushed to Robin's side.

"Your Majesty," he said with a bow. "If you would care to leave your mounts with me, I will watch them most vigilantly and see that they are watered and fed."

The fee seemed well worth the value as the aisles were so packed with people there was no room for horses.

They had no sooner started down one aisle than Robin was tempted to buy them an ale and a baked bun filled with chicken and cheese. To their right was a potter, to the left a basket weaver. Next they came upon a leatherworker, followed by a tailor. A woodcarver offered small trinket boxes crafted from exotic woods. Jewelers had gems and silver and gold finery. There were sellers of fruit, soap, eggs, clothing, spices, perfumes, flowers, oil, pies, poultry, wine, and wood. If it could be sold apparently it was for sale at Marlborough Fair.

In the small plazas between the rows and columns of stalls fairgoers could sit for a moment, eat their food, and enjoy entertainment. Each plaza offered a different amusement. In one, a stilt walker performed a dance upon legs that made him twice as tall as normal. In another, a mummer acted out a little play without saying a word. Musicians played lutes, harps, pipes, drums, and fiddles, or sang. Tumblers leaped and sprang. Jesters juggled and told jokes. Puppeteers held children enthralled while a performing bear and a talking parrot delighted the adults.

The very center of the fair held the largest plaza of all. In the middle stood a stage with painted sets and drapes behind which actors could hide until it was their turn to appear. The play in progress was apparently a comedy judging from the audience's laughter.

Robin couldn't remember the last time he had a hearty laugh. He found a tree stump on which to sit for a moment. He said to Maxwell, "We will linger here for a moment. You may continue to explore the fair if you wish."

"I would stay by Your Majesty's side as befits a squire," the lad replied.

Robin chuckled. "That's quite all right. We give you leave to wander. Come fetch us should you learn who has put on this fair."

Maxwell bowed and backed down an aisle, away but not quite out of sight.

Robin smiled and turned his attention to the stage which held two actors, a comely woman and a young nobleman. The woman apparently was smitten with the man who was clearly indifferent to her. She proposed all sorts of enticements to earn his favor, each one more generous than the next, much to the amusement of the audience. When none of those worked her invitations became earthier, escalating from romantic to risqué to raunchy, her actions matching her words as she sidled up close to him. Every thrust of hip or bump of breast drew hoots and whistles from the men in the audience, titters and disapproving clucks from the women.

The male actor remained steadfast in his refusal which Robin found hard to believe. Had an attractive woman such as was portrayed on the stage thrown herself at him, he would have mounted no protest. Women were not permitted to be actors and the female temptress was played by a man which was about the only thing that kept Robin from being truly titillated. He had to admit, the actor had done an outstanding job of transforming himself into a female. His long lithe body was swathed in soft fabrics, gathered and cinched to create curves where they were expected. Long dark red hair under a hennin with a diaphanous veil framed a fair complexion. The actor's husky voice was pitched to be tantalizingly throaty and it was only the actor's Adam's apple that gave away his true gender.

The play ended with the female humiliated, all of her attempts at seduction completely rebuffed. The actors drew to the side and the narrator took center stage to deliver the moral of the story, something about the valor of a virtuous woman, and to announce that another play would commence any minute. "Meanwhile, we ask your support of our theatrical endeavors. It's true that we live for your applause but we have to eat, too."

The two actors from the play that had just ended leaped down from the stage and circulated among the audience, mugging, holding out baskets, and collecting negotiable tokens of appreciation.

Robin thought the chuckles had been worth a coin. He stood and beckoned to the veiled actor who had so convincingly portrayed a woman. The actor caught Robin's eye, jogged over to him, and bowed. "Your Majesty," he said then stopped, mouth agape, his shocked expression genuine. The hand holding the basket fell to his side, spilling the coins at his feet.

CHAPTER TWENTY-TWO

"Father?" said the actor, the voice no longer seductive.

"Z—Zachary?" Robin dropped to his seat, the breath knocked out of him as if he had been punched in the chest.

He stared at the actor. A man who had not left boyhood far behind, he had Zachary's gray-green eyes and mahogany-colored hair but this could not be. Zachary, here, at a trade fair? An actor? His son, the prince, an actor? Robin couldn't have said which was more shocking: finding Zachary, finding him at a fair, or finding him an actor dressed as a woman. It was outrageous. Had Zachary fallen under an enchantment?

The young man stared back, his jaw hanging open.

Zachary's fellow actor hurried over. "Dale? Something wrong?"

Zachary shook his head and Robin did as well, trying to joggle his swimming thoughts into order. Dale? Had that been the name of the female character that Zachary had just portrayed? There was something familiar about the name. Robin thought it might have been the name that the child Zachary had chosen for his make-believe sister.

Zachary's fellow actor retrieved the coins that Zachary had spilled and tugged on his sleeve. "Come along, Dale. We have another play to perform."

"Ask Marion to stand in for me, please," Zachary replied in a strangled voice.

The actor shrugged and scurried back to the stage.

Zachary said, "How can this be? We thought you dead, Your Majesty. We were told the king was dead. How come you to be here?"

For a moment Robin was at a loss for an appropriate response. He felt lightheaded and couldn't decide which he felt more strongly: relief to see his youngest son alive and healthy or dismay at seeing him here, like this. "No, I am not dead although . . . You have many questions, and I will answer them, but tell me, what are you doing here, dressed like that? Please, put on your clothes and let's return to Bell Castle. As we ride I will tell you all that has transpired." His heart resumed beating with a vengeance, his breath came quickly. His eyes stung with tears of joy. He had found Conrad, and now Zachary.

"These are my clothes," said Zachary.

Robin was confused. Did Zachary mean that he had not yet stepped out of the skin of the character Dale? Perhaps he had no other clothes save this costume.

"And I don't wish to go back to Bell Castle. There is nothing for me there."

"When I laid eyes on the devastation, I had thought the same," said Robin, "but there is hope. I have started to rebuild it. I need your help. Come with me, we will make it as it was before. Oh, Zachary!" Robin moved to embrace his son but Zachary took a step backwards.

"If it was as it was before, I don't want to be there." Zachary tipped his chin up.

Robin could hardly believe his ears. First Conrad, and now Zachary had refused him. He had not gone through what he had, gotten this far only to be rebuffed. "I'm not inviting you to join me for an ale," he said. "I'm your father. I'm your king."

Zachary replied, "I will not go with you, but I think you must come with me. Perhaps I can make you understand although I doubt it."

Zachary turned on his heel and weaved his way through the crowd, the veil flowing from his hennin like a pennant, his skirts raising dust. There was nothing for it but to follow him. Robin trailed after him with a feeling of dread.

Zachary led them through the fair, out toward the road, and then into the woods. They had not walked far before they came to an encampment. Small donkey carts painted in bright colors and covered with fringed and beribboned canopies encircled a campfire. A few people milled about. Robin found it difficult to distinguish the men from the women as all wore colorful headscarves and jangling gold hoop earrings. Their billowy and flowing clothing was all wide skirts and floppy breeches topped by long tunics cinched with fringed scarves and woven belts. The encampment smelled of smoke and a pungent perfume.

Were they gypsies? Robin had heard tales of the strange dark-skinned folk who had originated in a faraway country and traveled in close-knit groups throughout the land. They kept mainly to themselves which was a good thing because they were rumored to be swindlers and scoundrels at best, witches and wizards at worst. How had Zachary come to be with them?

Conrad had said that disinherited sons set out to seek adventures and make their own fortune and that was often the case. But this?

Perhaps the gypsies had kidnapped Zachary and held him for ransom. They would have sent a ransom demand to the court and with King Bewilliam gone, gotten no response. Zachary was fortunate that they hadn't simply killed him. Perhaps they had pressed him into serving as a performer to ransom his own life. But why hadn't Zachary tried to escape?

With mounting terror, Robin wondered if Zachary was a changeling. Had the gypsies stolen him from Bell Castle and replaced him with one of their own? To what end? Had they thought thereby to gain the kingdom's riches? Had they been successful? Was this after all the answer to all Robin's questions about what had happened to his domain?

Robin shook his head. It was hard to imagine a raid by these eccentric people being victorious against Bell Castle's considerable defenses. How had they bested Bell Castle's soldiers and knights? It had to be magic. The gypsies had placed everyone under a spell. How else could they have vanquished Bell Castle's army and taken Zachary? Horror wrapped around Robin with a grip stronger than even a kraken's tentacles.

Poor Zachary, left defenseless without his father to protect him and now pressed into service, forced to masquerade as a woman, humiliating himself in public for a few coins. Guilt stabbed at Robin like a thousand knives and he felt dizzy as though from loss of blood.

One of the gypsies spotted them and approached. Robin slowed his steps. He should grab his son, pull him back to the road, to the fair. They could escape.

"Zachary," he said to his son's back. "Let's leave this place, go back to the fair. I have a horse. These people have only donkeys. We can make much better speed, gallop away, and put miles between us and these people. Perhaps once we get you away from their influence we can find a way to break the spell."

Zachary turned and gave Robin a puzzled look. "What are you talking about? I'm not under a spell. I have no need to escape. These people are my friends."

Robin gripped Zachary's arm. "You only think that they are your friends. They have bewitched you. I know something of enchantments. You can be under a spell and not know it. You think everything is the way it should be."

Zachary shook off Robin's hand and sighed. "I suspected that this would be difficult. I doubt that I'll be able to make you understand but I feel that I should try." He opened his arms and greeted the approaching gypsy with an embrace.

Robin shuddered. He had heard that changeling children could forget their true lives and spend the rest of their lives with the monsters who had stolen them.

"Who have you brought, Dale?" asked the gypsy man. "A king, by the looks of him." The gypsy bowed. "Your Majesty, welcome."

"This is my father, ruler of the Chalklands, the King of Bell Castle," Zachary replied. "We met at the fair."

The gypsy man took a step back. "How can this be, Dale? I thought you said that King Bewilliam was dead."

"Such had I been told. Clearly he is not."

The gypsy frowned. "Take care, Dale. The lawlessness and bedlam of the fair attracts all types. Not just those who do not wish us well but also those who practice the dark arts: witches, and wizards. Perhaps he is not your father, but a shape shifter."

Robin bristled. Was the gypsy wizard calling him a sorcerer? His head swam as he considered the possibility that he was under a spell. Perhaps Marlborough Fair was an enchanted realm and once he had stepped inside its borders, he had become bewitched.

"I appreciate your concern but I think I would know my own father, Quinn," Zachary said with a gentle smile. "I have yet to hear the tale of what transpired but I can assure you, this is King Bewilliam."

"In that case . . ." The gypsy man bowed. "On behalf of the Traveling Thespians, I bid you welcome, Sire. Please, may I offer you hospitality?" With a sweep of his hand, he invited Robin to take a seat by the fire. Zachary lifted the flap of a tent seemingly made of many overlapping rugs and scarves and returned with two bronze goblets and a wine bottle. He lifted the bottle. "Country fruit wine. One of our troupe members makes it herself while we travel between performances." He poured a cup and held it out to Robin.

With a trembling hand, he took the goblet but he did not drink. "Zachary," Robin pleaded. "Enough of this play-acting. We left the stage far behind at the fair. Can you not now come with me? Put on your real clothes? It is too strange to see you dressed this way. And why are these people calling you Dale?"

Zachary sighed and bowed his head. "Because that is my name. That has always been my name. I have always known it and tried to show it but no one would listen. Quinn, Marion, the others in this troupe, they listened.

"You were dead . . . well, gone. Conrad had been sent away. The Traveling Thespians came to entertain us at Bell Castle and I felt that they were kindred souls. I talked to them and they listened. They heard." Zachary put his arm around the gypsy Quinn's waist and Quinn returned the gesture. "When they left, I left with them. I am happy with them."

"Happy? How can you possibly be happy? You are a prince. You were born to rule, not to prance around in a dress acting the fool. You are needed at Bell Castle, more than ever."

Zachary frowned. "I was not born to rule. I was the second son. Conrad was born to rule." Zachary's frown deepened.

Conrad did not want the crown but now was not the time to discuss it. "That's not why I want you with me. You're my son."

"Would you still want me as your son if this is my life?" He waved his arm to embrace the gypsy camp and then swept it down his dress.

Robin's throat squeezed closed and his mouth went dry. He raised the goblet to his lips and then stopped. Part of him cautioned that the wine was a magic potion and that to drink of it would mean his doom.

But he had nothing to live for so why not drink it? The things that Robin thought were matters of fact—his lineage, his kingdom, his very name—had proved to be no stronger than the leaves of parchment on which they were documented. When he believed those to be gone, he had clung to the one thing he thought no one could take away: his fatherhood. Now that too threatened to be a title empty of meaning and substance.

He could not convince Zachary to leave, not with pleas or money. That left one last maneuver. "As your king, I command you to come with me."

Zachary folded his arms across his chest. "You are not my king. The Queen rules by the side of another."

Whether that union was legitimate was a matter for debate, but not here and not now. Robin seized Zachary's arm. "You will come with me!"

"No!" Zachary wriggled, trying to escape Robin's grasp.

"What seems to be the problem here, Dale?" The gypsy Quinn appeared at Zachary's side, his hand propped at his waist, near if not quite on the hilt of a dagger. Others from the encampment crowded around him wearing scowls and brandishing various blades.

Robin no sooner heard a rustling behind him than he felt his sword being pulled from its scabbard. He spun around to face the smirking gypsy who had so adroitly disarmed him.

You've lost your edge, King Bewilliam, he berated himself, in more ways than one.

"We welcomed you as a guest," Quinn said, "but you are no longer welcome. If you take your hands off Dale and leave now, you will not be harmed."

Weapons drawn, the gypsies inched closer.

Outnumbered, but not defenseless, Robin thought. He still had his knife and his wits. Slipping his hand under his cloak to grasp the knife's hilt, he slid his eyes to the right and left, searching for a bush or tree to guard his back.

A dark shape sprang from the shadows at the outskirts of the campfire. As quickly as the gypsy had disarmed Robin, Maxwell snatched the sword from the gypsy. "You're damn right he won't be harmed!" he cried. He handed Robin his weapon and stood at his side, his own dagger drawn. "Your Majesty, I am ready and at your command."

Robin regarded the clouded and glowering faces of the gypsies. His son's was pale and anxious, filled with distress and despair.

"We will withdraw," Robin said to Maxwell. "This is a fight for another day." And another time, another place, one without an audience.

The gypsy circle parted. Robin turned his back on the encampment and set off striding down the road back toward the fair, Maxwell at his heels.

"This was my fault. I should never have left my king's side, Sire," said Maxwell.

"Not at all," Robin replied. "We gave you leave to do so." He looked aslant at the lad. "How did you know where to find us?"

"I was at a stall and saw Your Majesty following the tall woman. I didn't want to interfere but a knight is supposed to keep his king in sight. I meant to withdraw once I was assured that your safety was not in question."

"Thank you, Maxwell." Robin felt as though he owed the lad an explanation but he understood nothing of what he had seen in the gypsy camp. Not gypsies, Zachary had insisted but what else could Robin make of a troupe of men who dressed and behaved so outlandishly? How much had Maxwell heard?

"I assure you, Sire, it was not my intent to eavesdrop or spy. I kept my distance. I simply wanted—"

"You acquitted yourself admirably," Robin said with an inward sigh of relief. Perhaps no explanation was required.

They retrieved their mounts and left the fair. Travelers continued to flock towards it even as the day's light faded. Headed back to Bell Castle against a tide of people, conveyances, and beasts of burden, they rode in silence, Robin with head hanging and gaze turned inward. He thought of the times he denied himself, even risked his life in the name of a kingdom that his sons would one day rule. Some would call those sacrifices but they never seemed that way to Robin. Fathers did everything in their power to make a good life for their children, to ensure that their lives would be easier and richer, even at the parent's own expense and peril. He thought of the blacksmith Gregory. He even now no doubt suffered a foot that throbbed with pain after a day's labor he had taken on so that Maxwell could accompany Robin. Neither Conrad nor Zachary wanted what Robin could give them, what he had worked his entire life to nurture and grow. He saw his dream of restoring his kingdom with his two sons by his side slipping away from him like a ship sailing away from land. His kingdom would die with him.

CHAPTER TWENTY-THREE

"**Your** majesty wished Dale to accompany us," Maxwell said.

"We do," Robin replied.

"We can get more men, go back. Just say the word, Sire."

"We'll be doing just that." Robin had been inventorying the able-bodied men at Bell Castle who could be called up at a moment's notice.

"Minge, in the stables, Sire," Maxwell said, echoing Robin's thoughts. "And Reggie, the farmer. The baker. My father, of course. We have armaments, Your Majesty. My father and I have been working on them."

It wasn't a strong force but it might be sufficient to extricate Zachary from a band of gypsies. Robin quickened their pace. They arrived at Bell Castle's gate and Maxwell slid from his horse. "I'll see to fresh mounts, Sire," he said. "I'll round up the men."

Men, Robin thought. Half the force was practically still boys. Robin dismounted. "We'll meet you back here."

Robin pointed his leaden feet to the chapel where a candle glowed in the window. Despite the chill of the evening, the door stood ajar.

Conrad sat on one of the benches, a cloth of some kind across his knees. He worked it with a needle and bright blue thread, his long fingers flashing white in the candle glow. At Robin's entrance he set the work aside, stood, and bowed. "Your Majesty."

"Your door was open," Robin said.

"I don't want anyone to hesitate to enter because of a closed door," Conrad replied. "I want everyone to know that they can come in, any time."

Robin didn't miss the unspoken invitation directed to him. "Aren't you cold?"

Conrad shrugged. "I stay busy and give it no attention. My comfort really is of little importance."

Easily enough said when you never spent weeks sleeping out in the open or on the deck of a wind-tossed ship. "What have you there?" Robin pointed to the cloth a section of which was clamped in a small square wooden frame.

"I'm embroidering a cushion cover for the back of one of the benches." He held up the cloth which pictured a cross ornamented with flourishes and swirls in blue, silver, and gold threads.

"We have servants who can do that," Robin said. Do it quite well, too. He had been pleased with application of the royal crest to his cloak.

"I know. Manual labor is honest work and I am honored to be able to do it."

Spoken like a man who hadn't spent his days sweeping in a barbershop or a steamy summer working in a forge just to have something to eat.

"Besides, it's a devotional exercise."

Robin sighed. "Please, be seated."

Conrad remained standing, his expression forbearing, his hands clasped over his belly.

Fine, Robin thought. He'd be sitting soon enough. "I found your brother."

Conrad's jaw dropped. His already pale face blanched and he sank onto the bench. Robin sat beside him.

"Where? How? Is he—"

"Alive and well. Yes. Alive, anyway. I found him at the fair."
You should have come with me, Robin thought. You may never
see your brother again.

Robin described the surprise and shock of the meeting but
not the skirmish or his embarrassing retreat. "You knew nothing
of this troupe of actors?"

Conrad shook his head. "I had already been sent away and
Zachary was still at Bell Castle. When I next heard of my family
it was to learn that they had left the Chalklands for the Palisades.
I assumed Zachary had gone with the Queen." Conrad frowned.
"You say he is bewitched? You think it's magic?"

Robin felt a chill that had nothing to do with the draftiness of
the chapel. "I can think of no other reason for his behavior."

Conrad pressed his fingers to his lips and thought for a
moment. "We discussed the dark arts at the abbey."

"It's the work of the Devil, right?" Most people attributed
otherwise inexplicable misfortunes to the acts of Satan. To
believe in the Devil would be to believe in some master
manipulator who could curse even the hardest working most
virtuous man leaving him powerless to steer his own course,
something Robin was unwilling to accept.

Conrad shook his head. "I don't believe in the Devil. Not the
way that you do, Sire."

You couldn't possibly know what my beliefs are, Robin
thought, but now was not the time for a spiritual debate. Still,
Conrad's admission surprised him. "You don't?"

"Satan is not some immortal imp, some cruel and petty
schemer who throws obstacles in our path for his own
amusement. We cause our own misery when we lose sight of our
duty to God and to each other."

Robin's head throbbed. Even if that were true and he wasn't
quite ready to agree that it was, he didn't see how it could help
Zachary.

"Would you take me to him?" Conrad asked. "I can try to get
him to see where he has gone astray, that God has a plan for
him."

Robin didn't know about God's intentions but he certainly had plans for Zachary and they had nothing to do with traveling about with a band of gypsies. "Zachary's captors have already demonstrated a capacity for violence. This is likely to require a show of strength. We will be met at the gatehouse by additional forces."

Conrad's raised eyebrow seemed to say "We have forces?" and Robin was grateful his son hadn't voiced it.

At the gatehouse, Robin found Maxwell and his hastily-mustered comrades already mounted and ready. Once they had ridden outside the range of the sconces lighting Bell Castle's gates, the night was dark but both horses and riders quickly adjusted to the low light. Using his memory of the trail he had taken to the Marlborough Fair, Robin took the lead. They galloped along at a pace that did not lend itself to conversation for which Robin was thankful. For the most part he was too preoccupied with watching the trail and plotting what they would do upon reaching their destination.

Despite the late hour, as they neared the fair they found the trail still busy with fairgoers. Wavering candle and lantern light gave the fairgrounds a surreal look. The music and merriment rang out just as boisterously as earlier in the day while the aromas of food and perfume seemed even stronger in the crisp night air. The aisles were slightly less packed than they had been during the day. Fairgoers looked up with annoyance as Robin and his men pushed through but bowed and made way when they recognized a king and clergyman among the riders.

They pressed their way toward the exit and into the penumbra beyond the light of the fair. Robin scanned the trail right and left seeking out the glow of the gypsy campfire but the further they rode from the fairgrounds, the darker became the woods.

Robin slowed his horse and finally brought it to a halt. "Gone," he said. "I think they're gone. We should have found them by now."

Conrad regarded him with an even gaze and made no comment.

"There were here, I tell you."

"Yes, Sire."

"You don't believe me."

Conrad frowned. "I—"

"Why would I make up a story like that?" Robin asked.

"I never said you did."

Tired, angry, frustrated, and fearful for Zachary, Robin turned his horse and headed back to the fair. At the central plaza, the stage on which he had first seen his younger son stood empty. Robin dismounted and approached a nearby stall.

The merchant bowed. "Your Majesty. How may we serve you on this most pleasant of nights?"

"The actors who performed here earlier today, what do you know of them? Will there be another play later? Have they left the fair?"

"I know not, Your Majesty. I guess I have just been too busy to notice. Come to think of it, I haven't seen any of them since midday, since . . ." he tapped his chin, "since they performed 'The Woman of Virtue.'" The merchant chuckled. "That was some play."

Robin turned and glared at Conrad. If his son had doubted Robin's story, at least here was some corroboration.

"It would be strange indeed for them to leave before the fair is over. Perhaps they are performing somewhere else on the grounds." The merchant tipped his head to one side. "Then again, actors are an impetuous and unpredictable lot. Perhaps they have already made their nut and moved on to the next fair or wherever performers go."

Robin thanked the man. Every muscle tense with anxiety he said to Conrad, "We will scour this fair for them."

Robin ordered his men down one aisle and up another, asking fairgoers and merchants for news of the theater troupe. As the night wore on the crowds thinned and the going was easier. Nevertheless it took hours to cover the entire fair. Some of the merchants recalled serving the actors food or drink. A few fairgoers well remembered seeing a performance and some even recalled enjoying the same play that Robin had. Robin winced when one man remarked on the beauty of the female character. No one, however, would swear that they had seen the actors after that.

With Conrad, Maxwell, and the other men plodding behind him, Robin arrived back at the fair's entrance defeated, despairing, and exhausted. He had lost Zachary again.

CHAPTER TWENTY-FOUR

Robin would die before he admitted it to anyone else, could barely admit it to himself, but truth be told, there was something he had been avoiding it. He could put it off no longer.

The rebuilding of Bell Castle and the reestablishment of his kingdom had called for labor, skill, and ingenuity and for that he had legions of servants and tradesmen. They were willing enough to stop serving King Ulric but their fears of reprisal were well founded. It wouldn't be long before King Ulric's knights would come around to collect taxes and tributes. They would be unlikely to take "no" for a response. Even more provocative would be the explanation that the servants were making payments to King Bewilliam, believed by all to be dead. The servants would need to be protected. When word got back to King Ulric that King Bewilliam had returned, the usurper would likely mount an offense against Bell Castle. The preservation of all Robin had accomplished thus far, the furtherance of his kingdom's restoration, would require muscle and for that he needed his knights.

His hasty preparation for the futile raid on the gypsies at Marlborough Fair had proved that.

Like his servants, Robin's knights had years ago pledged him fealty and in return had received grants of land. Also like his servants, his knights were still bound, needed to be reminded of their obligation, and pressed into service. Would he find that they shifted their allegiance and now served King Ulric?

Even if they hadn't they were guilty of dereliction of duty, a felony punishable by death. Knights were to cleave to their lord's side. How came it to be then that King Bewilliam had wandered for months lost, alone, defenseless, and beleaguered? Why had not a single knight come to the aid of his king?

Culpable of the most egregious offense were the four knights who had abandoned him and left him in peril at Grimstaff Castle. Were it not for the bitter hurt Robin felt whenever he thought of it, his ire would have been enough to carry him to the furthest reaches of the earth to take revenge against them.

The errant knights had put their honor, title, lands, and even lives in jeopardy. Calling them to account and pay for their crime would be no minor confrontation. Robin was unlikely to survive it without adequate support. His ragtag army of serfs would need to be headed by more than one competent leader. Conrad had exemplary training but had never been tested in battle. It was high time that he was.

And while Robin was thinking of Conrad, there was another matter of vital concern to them both.

With dread, Robin headed for the chapel.

It took him a moment to recognize his son among the crew of carpenters framing an addition. Conrad wore not his usual costume of white habit and black robe but instead was garbed in leggings and a simple tunic. Only his tonsured hair distinguished him from the other workers.

Robin stood at the base of the ladder and called "Conrad" to which he got no response. Stifling a grumble, he said, "Brother Thaddeus."

Conrad turned, smiled, and descended the ladder. "Your Majesty," he said and bowed.

"You are expanding the chapel," Robin said, phrasing the observation as a challenge.

"We need more room," Conrad replied. "Bell Castle has grown and more people want to come to learn, to worship. My scribal undertakings have expanded in scope. I need more room for writing and copying and to store research materials." Tipping up his chin he regarded the work in progress. "I daresay the chapel is becoming a church."

His face was placid but the set of his shoulders and squaring of his chest divulged his pride.

Robin was about to ask who had authorized the expenditure of labor and material when he realized that he had pledged to the Mathus Abbey's abbot to do that very thing.

As if in answer to Robin's unvoiced objection Conrad said, "The carpenters have already met their obligations. They are contributing their labor above and beyond their week work, as a gift to God. The materials, too, were gifts."

There was nothing smug about his expression or his tone which for some reason only infuriated Robin further.

"They're doing a wonderful job, don't you agree, Sire?" Conrad asked.

"It will be a credit to Bell Castle," Robin replied. "Our craftsmen are very talented."

"For God, they give their best efforts."

But not for their king? Robin felt his blood getting hotter by the minute.

"Was there something you needed, Your Majesty?" Conrad asked.

"Your sword arm. We are going on a campaign to seek out and punish the knights who neglected their duties and thereby betrayed the kingdom. You said you were prepared to defend Bell Castle."

"Indeed I am." His mien grew serious. "That is not just dereliction of duty, Sire, it's a moral offense, a sin against God. They pledged their loyalty in His name. The Church should issue a summons. They should do penance."

"Penance? I want their heads," said Robin, surprising himself with his anger.

Conrad nodded. "And Your Majesty would be within his rights to take them. But if I may be permitted, I have a suggestion."

In the end, Robin acquiesced to Conrad's proposal if only for the lack of trained commanders to lead raw recruits against seasoned warriors. Conrad would draw up a writ and a summons ordering the truant knights to appear at court where they would account for crimes both civil and spiritual. Robin would dispatch servants throughout the kingdom to deliver the demand.

Over the course of the days following the issuance of the summons the clanging of the gates being raised to grant entrance to the knights echoed throughout the inner ward. The barracks bustled with activity as they were pressed into service after having stood so long vacant. As befitted their rank, the knights no doubt expected more luxurious accommodations on the upper floors of the great hall but Robin wanted there to be no mistake: they were not guests. They should consider themselves lucky, he thought. He had been tempted to house them in the dungeon.

On the day of the audience, Robin sat on his throne and perused the great hall with satisfaction. It did not look the same as it had before. Instead, it was more majestic, more imposing. Knowing that the hall would have to speak for the renewed power and majesty of the kingdom he had taken great pains to furnish it with laboriously-carved seats of dark gleaming wood upholstered with lustrous silk cushions brocaded with gold and silver thread. Massive candelabra stood on long polished tables supported by trestles burly as Atlas's arms. Suspended from rods mounted on the wall, hangings told the story of the kingdom's history, assets, and bounty in weavings and needlework. The large room smelled of fresh varnish and new wool.

Behind his throne sat a small item of furniture few were likely to notice: the bottom quarter of a barrel with a cushion pressed into the base. When Robin held court, Meeyoo liked to watch the proceedings from the "throne" the carpenter and seamstress had made for her. Had anyone spotted the oddity they had the presence of mind not to remark on it.

At the appointed hour, a servant pressed into service as an officer of arms paraded the knights single-file into the hall. Robin observed their reactions as they took in the grandeur of the refurbished room. As hard as they tried to face forward, their eyes darted left and right.

One by one they approached the throne and bowed. Robin evaluated the expression of each man as he raised his head. Unblinking, Robin met each pair of eyes. They conveyed astonishment, embarrassment, and fear. He took their measure from the condition of their uniforms. Some wore polished helmets and spotless coats lined with iron plates while others had unsuccessfully tried to hide rusting chain mail under faded tabards. Some had kept their battle-fit physique while others had grown thicker in the waist.

Conspicuous by their absence were the worst of the traitors, Sirs Louis, Henry, Simon, and Walter.

The final man performed his obeisance and took his place in a formation facing the dais. Robin's tall seat atop the riser allowed him to look down while his audience had to look up. He sat and regarded the knights without speaking. He allowed the silence to build until the shrugging of shoulders and cranking of necks disclosed that the men had succumbed to their private anxieties. Then he stood.

"We are not dead," he said, "no thanks to you."

Robin saw many pairs of eyes darting about. The assembled knights could only be wondering what had happened to the four who had accompanied Robin on the campaign to slay a dragon at Grimstaff Castle's King Reynold's behest. Robin would let them fear that the four had already been punished and that they were next.

"But we are here. Alone, we eluded King Reynold's murderous intent. Alone, we escaped Grimstaff Castle. Alone, we fought to return to the kingdom of the Chalklands and Bell Castle where we rightly belong to shoulder once again our responsibilities to those who depend on us. We should not have been alone.

"It's true enough that you were not chosen to journey to Grimstaff Castle. Those who were are not here today. They will answer for their failure. But you failed, too. You failed to come to our aid." He stepped to the edge of the dais. "You pledged your lives, your very souls, to the service of this kingdom. You sacrificed them both when you defaulted on your vow. The kingdom of the Chalklands has survived, is thriving, and aided by the loyal—by the loyal!—will continue to flourish. They will prosper along with it. Traitors will be punished."

In the silence that greeted his words, Robin could almost hear pulses pounding. He could smell the tang of their tension.

And then a knight cleared his throat. "Permission to speak freely, Your Majesty?"

"Sir Albert, you may."

The man stepped forward and bowed. The son of a barrel-maker, Sir Albert was a valiant and bold fighter with the scars to show for usually being the first to charge into the fray. One particularly brash move had him on the battlefield before he even had a chance to put on his helmet. He had lost part of an earlobe to the well-placed slash of an enemy's sword.

Again taking the lead Sir Albert said, "Believe what you will but we did not desert you. Sir Henry returned from the mission and reported that it had been a rout."

Sir Henry had returned? Why then had the knight not answered the summons to appear today? Robin wondered.

"Sir Henry spoke of the treacherous and antagonistic behavior of King Reynold's knights. They resented Your Majesty's interloping, the implication that they were not up to the task. Sir Henry said that you had been victorious but then suddenly, unaccountably, you went missing. He told us that he and Sir Louis, Sir Simon, and Sir Walter searched for you but you were nowhere to be found. They came to fear for their own lives and fled King Reynold's domain."

Behind him, the other knights confirmed the account with nods and murmurs.

"Of course we were not content to let the matter lie, not with Your Majesty's welfare in doubt and so many questions unanswered. We left our homes and families and journeyed long and far, asking for news of Your Majesty, of Sirs Louis, Walter, and Simon."

The nods became more vigorous, the murmurs louder.

"We learned nothing of Your Majesty or of the three missing knights. We suspected they had been murdered by King Reynold's traitorous knights but there was no way to prove it. We thought to challenge King Reynold but without our Leader to command or guide us . . ." He spread out his hands in a gesture of helplessness. "Had Your Majesty ordered it, we would have made war on King Reynold but in the absence of any real information about what had transpired . . ."

In low voices, the other knights said, "Aye" and "True" and "What could we do?"

Sir Albert said, "We fanned out and combed the country searching for our King, sadly to no avail. We couldn't find a soul who had seen anyone meeting Your Majesty's description."

Robin could find that easy to believe. His mind gone, for many months he didn't even recognize himself.

"We thought perhaps Your Majesty had gone into hiding somewhere, the better to evade King Reynold who clearly meant for harm to come to Your Highness. Until we knew more, we thought it best not to try to expose Your Majesty's sanctuary. We returned to our homes waiting for news. Then even the Queen gave up hope for the King's return. A new king assumed rule but we did not swear allegiance to him. We swore allegiance to you, Your Highness. Had he commanded us to fight in his name, we would have refused. We even considered launching a resistance but in the end, decided lay low and bide our time in hopes of Your Majesty's return. I know it makes us all sound like cowards but we knew not what to do. We've never had our King simply vanish."

Sir Albert went to his knees. "Sire, we men are all unworthy of calling ourselves Your Majesty's knights. We neglected our most important responsibility. We beg your forgiveness and mercy and plead to be given another chance to prove our loyalty."

One by one, the other knights knelt as well.

Robin tried to imagine what it had been like for the knights of Bell Castle, fed only rumors and hearsay. In his absence, had his knights not been trustworthy, any one of them could have seized control of the kingdom. They had not. Upon his arrival Robin had found his kingdom waiting as if with baited breath for his return.

"We have decided to give you a second chance. You may keep your land but for dereliction of duty, for one year in addition to your military obligations you will perform week work. As a sign of your commitment, you will renew your pledge of fealty—"

"In the name of God," came a voice from the rear of the hall.

CHAPTER TWENTY-FIVE

Robin looked over the heads of the kneeling knights to see Conrad not so much stride as glide across the room. In his simple white habit and black robe he carried himself with a bearing just as noble as any knight in armor or king cloaked in velvet and ermine.

The knights half turned. "Brother . . .?" one said.

"Prince Conrad?" said Sir Albert.

"Brother Thaddeus," Conrad replied inclining his head like a benediction. He came to stand beside Robin and bowed, then turned toward the knights whose faces displayed varying degrees of confusion. "Yes, in the name of God. You swore a most holy oath of loyalty to your King long ago and then left your King to flounder. You broke your promise not just to your earthly king but your King in Heaven, a crime of immorality for which the Church metes out severe punishment. Think carefully before you make another vow and imperil your soul as well as your integrity."

The knights' heads swiveled as they looked one to the other and for a moment no man spoke.

Then Sir Albert turned to Robin and bowed his head. "In the name of God and everything I hold dear, I pledge my fealty to you, Your Majesty, King Bewilliam. Should I fail, take my head.

Stick it on a pike as a warning to all who disrespect their title and their king. Bury my body in an unmarked grave."

The silence that followed his pronouncement was so profound, Robin could hear the wind whistling outside the hall. Open-mouthed, the other knights stood and stared.

Sir Alan broke rank and knelt before Robin alongside Sir Albert. One by one, Sirs Michael, Kenneth, Ellery, and Howell followed suit. Under Robin's steady sword and Conrad's equally steady gaze they swore a solemn oath to God and King, then stood and came to attention.

Robin stepped off the dais to face them eye to eye. "Your pledge gratifies and emboldens us. We have accomplished much to restore Bell Castle and the kingdom of the Chalklands but our work has barely begun. You will be critical to our future success.

"As we said at the outset, we are not dead although for a time we may as well have been. Your faith that all is now as it should be is all that you need. You need no further explanation." He smiled. "But, we wish to satisfy your curiosity, put your mind at ease, and answer your lingering questions." With that Robin gave his knights an abbreviated account of what had transpired at Grimstaff Castle and its dire consequences. He felt vindicated as their expressions shifted from astonishment to dismay to anger.

"Sire, if I may?" said Sir Albert, his face stormy.

"Sir Albert?" Robin frowned.

"What of Sirs Henry, Louis, Walter, and Simon?"

The other knights set to murmuring again.

"We failed you, Sire, but they betrayed you."

The murmuring became grumbling. "For all we know they colluded with King Reynold and his perfidious knights. Should they not be punished?"

The knights sent up a chorus of maledictions.

"Punished they shall be if they are proven guilty of betrayal. We will seek them out and get to the truth of the matter. If they are found to be blameworthy we will visit on them the most severe of reprisals. You men will go and find them. Bring them to court to answer for their behavior, to be judged and sentenced. The property of those who are disgraced and proven to be traitors will be divided among those who demonstrate their loyalty beyond a doubt."

With cheers and roars, the knights drew their swords, thrust them into the air, and brought the tips together in a steeple. Then with a bow they broke formation and headed for the door.

"Sir Albert," Robin called.

The knight turned and bowed. "Yes, Your Majesty."

"Those were brave words you spoke and a grave vow you took."

"Yes, Sire, but I meant what I said. I was honored when you first made me a knight. I have tried to give good service but even I would admit my performance has been lackluster. When Your Majesty vanished it was easy simply to go on, to disregard the matter of Your Majesty's welfare, to not ask questions of myself or of anyone else. I silenced my fears and my responsibility to my king and gave all my attention to looking after my land and my family. I was wrong." He dipped his head and looked at the ground for a moment, then lifted his chin. "But when I came through the gate, as I crossed the bailey and saw all that had been achieved, when I stepped into this room and witnessed the transformation . . .When I looked up and saw you, my King, brought back from the dead, fit and hale, I felt that I too should aspire to greatness.

"So, yes, Sire, I made a bold vow. But I promise to make Your Majesty and myself proud. I will renew my efforts to find Sir Walter."

The two had served together on several campaigns. If anyone knew Sir Walter's whereabouts it was likely Sir Albert.

The knights filed out and Conrad started for the door.

"Brother Thaddeus," Robin said, "a moment, please."

"Yes, Your Majesty."

Robin looked about for any unwitting eavesdroppers, his heart heavy, but he and Conrad were alone. "It's about your . . . it's about Queen Daya."

Conrad's normally placid face turned stormy. "The adulteress."

Robin lowered himself onto a chair. "She may not have known that we were still alive."

"Even if she didn't it's still adultery. There is no doubt. There were witnesses."

"There were?"

"Zachary."

"He actually witnessed—"

Conrad's cheeks reddened. "Well, not the actual traitorous act I presume but there was a marriage or so I learned from one of the brothers at the abbey. There was a wedding feast. King Ulric did move into the keep, the royal bedchamber. There is no question. Or to be precise there are now, lots of questions. Matters of sovereignty, ownership, inheritance."

"I thought you didn't care about that."

"For myself, no. As for Zachary—" Conrad sighed and shook his head. "I couldn't speak for his concerns. It doesn't matter. Our personal ambitions are not important."

They're not? Robin wanted to retort. Your personal ambitions and those of your brother have put the kingdom of the Chalklands' future in jeopardy.

But Conrad was saying, "Charges must be filed and punishment exacted. It is a sin for which she and Ulric must answer. For the salvation of her soul, we should send out a summons and get to the truth."

A trial. Robin would need an advocate for what promised to be a long, bitter, and contentious proceeding with the most dire consequences for kingdoms, lives, and souls. Robin's agent would have to be a skilled reader and writer, learned in matters of church and civil law, experienced in the conduct of judgments. Conrad was literate, could handle a pen, and to Robin's knowledge had done little in the past few years but read the Bible and commentaries about its application.

"True, but I cannot," Conrad said. "Except for minor cases, clerics are not permitted to serve as advocates."

This was no minor case. Robin wracked his brain for an individual with all the necessary training and talents. "Ah, we believe we know of someone with outstanding credentials. Years of training and experience. He would have our complete confidence."

"Excellent." Conrad nodded. "Shall I prepare a letter?"

Robin clucked his tongue. "Except we don't know where he is or how to contact him."

"An experienced advocate yet . . ." Conrad frowned. "How does Your Majesty know of this advocate?"

"We met . . . in a public house."

Conrad rolled his eyes. "Yet Your Majesty has confidence—"

"We do." Robin related his meeting with Terrowin, the itinerant lawyer whom he had met at Sweet Water, and described the young man's curriculum vitae.

"Did he mention what university he attended?"

"He did."

"We will send the letter there. They should be able to contact him and tell him that we have need of his services."

Weeks passed without word from either Terrowin or his university. Robin despaired of locating the young advocate especially as he could think of no one else with such impressive credentials or drive and cringed at even the most polite inquiry about the progress of action against Queen Daya.

When the chamberlain presented a missive sent from the university, Robin grabbed it from his hand and in breaking the seal nearly tore the vellum. Terrowin had been contacted, the message read, and told that his services were needed at Bell Castle but days passed without any further communication.

Nor did any word come from Sirs Albert, Kenneth, Alan, or Howell. Robin tried to keep his gnawing worries at bay by focusing on the kingdom's affairs and Squire Maxwell's training. The young man had stayed true to his word not to let his preparation interfere with his duties. On many an evening Robin would cross the bailey to see the smith aglow with light and smoke billowing from the chimney, gray against a darker night sky, and hear the clanging of ironworking.

This night Robin found that Maxwell had banked the forge's fire for the day, swept, and put away tools. Seated at a grindstone, he sprang to his feet and bowed. "Your Majesty. I am done with my work. I was sharpening my sharpening skills," his cheeks flushed with embarrassment over the pun, "but I am ready for, well, whatever you need me to be ready for."

In spite of himself, Robin smiled. "If you're up to it we can begin your studies of siege warfare."

"I am indeed, Sire,' Maxwell said.

The lad probably would be less enthusiastic if he knew that the study of siege warfare was more about the design and construction of castles as defensive structures than it was about fighting and weapons. Robin was pleased to see the young man apply himself to the academic aspects of his training with the same zeal as he did the physical ones.

One afternoon when Robin and Maxwell were practicing jousting the officer of arms announced the arrival of Sir Howell. Robin told Maxwell to quicken his reaction time by practicing with the quintain and hastened to the gatehouse to meet Sir Howell.

"I found Sir Louis," the knight announced.

Sir Howell's flat tone did not bode well. "Let's repair to the hall," Robin said and ordered that refreshments be brought to him and the knight.

"I did my best to be methodical about the search for Sir Louis," Sir Howell said.

Yes, that would be Sir Howell's approach. Sir Howell's strength lay not in a robust physique but in his intellect. A brilliant strategist, Sir Howell was almost better in the war room than he was on the battlefield. Never completely comfortable seated on a horse, he owed much of what horsemanship he did possess to his wife who was herself quite the equestrian. Dismounted, he was light and agile on his feet. Always on the lanky side, he looked particularly tall and thin today, his cheeks somewhat sunken, his eyes set more deeply than usual and shadowed.

"I took what I knew of the man, the campaign to Grimstaff Castle, and the territory into account to decide where to look. Nevertheless I found him quite by accident. My men and I had been searching for days with no success. We were exhausted, hungry. We decided to bivouac in a glade, refresh ourselves, review our strategy. We had used most of our provisions and had little left but what we would need to return to our domain. Certain we were not on anyone's private property, we decided to see what sort of game we could hunt. Before long we heard a rustling and spied a boar rooting in the undergrowth."

Sir Howell looked at his feet and sighed. He raised his head. "The boar had already found Sir Louis and hadn't left us much."

Eaten by a wild pig, Robin thought. A fitting end for a traitor.

Sir Howell continued. "We found it impossible to determine with any certainty what had caused Sir Louis's death. We saw no signs of a battle near the area. Our guess is that he was on the run and was taken by the elements, a large animal, or some other misfortune. We gave a proper burial to what we could find of him, there in the wood. There being nothing more that we could do, we returned home to refresh ourselves and restock our provisions for the journey here to report.

"We did find his tabard, his armor, and a standard. Should Your Majesty think it appropriate we could have a memorial service."

Sir Howell's words were generous but the unsmiling mouth that formed them said that Sir Louis's traitorous actions had alienated him from the brotherhood of knights and left him undeserving of any but the most perfunctory rites.

Like Squire Maxwell, Sir Louis had been a young and ambitious man of whom Robin had high expectations. Robin hoped that Squire Maxwell's career would not come to such an inglorious end.

Sir Louis had not been married but his parents would mourn his death. Their loss would be even harder to bear because their son had died in a state of dishonor and sin.

"We will take that under consideration. Meanwhile I will direct Prince Con— Brother Thaddeus to transfer the deeds and titles to Sir Louis's lands to you. Well done, Sir Howell."

Several weeks each of which felt far longer than seven days passed before Robin heard from Terrowin himself. The young advocate wrote, quite eloquently, Robin thought, that he had already accepted a commission from a nobleman who wished to wed his son to a neighboring lord's daughter. It was a thorny matter involving complex exchanges of property and cash and, Robin assumed, stubborn and haughty men each determined to have his own way. Terrowin had been hired to attend the negotiations and record the agreements should there be any question later about what had been said.

Robin snickered. It used to be that a man's word was his bond. Apparently in these all-too-modern times one needed a record of what that word had been.

"I am sure Your Majesty can appreciate that I have committed my full attention to the matter at hand," Terrowin wrote, "and would not expect me to short-change my current employer any more than Your Majesty would wish anything less than my complete devotion to his case. I recognize the urgency and importance of Your Majesty's exigency and will call at my first opportunity."

Gone also it seemed were the days when a King's request was filled without hesitation or delay.

As the days passed, Robin found it increasingly difficult to concentrate. Being unable to take even the first action against Daya and Ulric was like having an itch in the middle of his back that only someone else could scratch. Many times he was tempted simply to mount an offense against the adulterers only to be stopped short by the realization that most of his knights were still scattered about the land.

The news that Sir Alan had returned was music to Robin's ears. Even more encouraging was that he had Sir Henry with him.

Sir Alan strode into the great hall and bowed. Sir Alan stood tall at attention with hands behind his back, his head high and his chin up. His forthright gaze and unsmiling countenance made Sir Alan appear to be a man to be reckoned with even under the most benign of circumstances. In the past he had proved himself to be a fearless and competent fighter but he had another talent that proved useful especially during long campaigns and fierce combats. His expert drumming kept soldiers' feet moving on marches and blood boiling on the battlefield.

On his knees at Robin's feet, Sir Henry cut a less imposing figure. He looked up, an aggrieved expression in his watery blue eyes. "Sire," he said, "I am troubled at having caused Your Majesty and my fellow knights a single moment of doubt. This is a terrible misunderstanding."

"We are listening," said Robin.

"King Reynold's knights regarded the appearance of the Bell Castle knights as interference. Worse, an insult. They were angry with their king. They thought he had called on us to shame his knights, to prove them unworthy so that he could take their title and land from them."

King Reynold had said nothing of the sort to Robin but that didn't mean it wasn't so. Robin's focus was doing the job he was hired to do, receiving payment to augment his ailing treasury, and returning to his kingdom. Another ruler's internecine issues hadn't been his concern.

"For King Reynold's knights, it was vital that they appear to be the champions of the dragon slaying. They offered us bribes to step aside, to falter. To flee, even. I took the bribe." Sir Henry looked down. "Yes, I did." He raised his head and said, "We all did but we never intended to follow through with it. We would never abandon our king. But in taking the bribes we thought to placate the other knights. Otherwise, we feared, they might bring harm to us, disable our company leaving you with only King Reynold's miscreants to watch your back."

"It was King Reynold's knights who had fled the dragon slaying," Robin said.

"Indeed," replied Sir Henry with a vigorous nod. "That made it even worse. They could not allow King Reynold to learn of their cowardice to which we had been witnesses. We returned to Grimstaff Castle and we should have been celebrated as victors but we were doomed men. King Reynold's knights said that we would never make it to the celebratory banquet, never tell our tale. They said that if we valued our lives we should flee the castle, leave the kingdom.

"The minute King Reynold's men retired to their quarters, we Bell Castle knights met in secret to decide what to do. How best could we protect our king, preserve Bell Castle's honor, and save our lives? It was never our intent to abandon our king but . . ."

Sir Henry looked down and wrung his hands.

"Go on."

Sir Henry pressed his lips together. "Your Majesty, I don't want to defame a fellow knight. Could Your Highness not ask the other knights for an accounting? Sir Louis—"

"Is dead," said Robin.

"Dead, Sire?" Sir Alan said, his voice strained.

"Sir Howell and his men found his body. Apparently he never made it far from King Reynold's domain," said Robin.

Sir Alan looked a question and Robin dismissed it with a wave of his hand. "It was not an honorable death." Sir Alan blanched.

"Sir Simon?" asked Sir Henry.

"Has yet to be found. Nor has Sir Walter returned from that mission."

Sir Henry licked his lips. "So much tragedy. But you, Your Highness, you returned. You have retaken the throne, brought Bell Castle back to life. Our hopes and prayers for you have been answered a thousandfold."

"No thanks to the knights who were supposed to stay by my side."

"I can explain that, Sire," said Sir Henry.

"Please do, then."

"It was Sir Walter, Sire. He said that we should flee, put some distance between us and Grimstaff Castle, then regroup. Use the bribe that Sir Reynold's knights had given us to procure more weapons, then return to the castle to defend our honor and expose King Reynold's knights for the cowards they were."

"Leaving your king behind," said Sir Alan.

Sir Henry turned his head toward the other knight, then toward Robin. "We searched for Your Majesty but Your Highness was nowhere to be found."

Ironic, thought Robin. While he sought his knights they were looking for him. Not finding them Robin had done some fleeing of his own.

"I always intended to join the other men and return to Grimstaff Castle but when I reported to where Sir Walter had told us to assemble, no one was there. I waited and waited. I found lodgings nearby where I hid, telling no one that I was a knight of the Chalklands. I returned every day to the secret meeting place but no one ever came. I prayed that Sir Walter and the other men had reunited with Your Majesty and that you all had made it home safely. I returned to the Chalklands, told the other men what I knew. Then I went back to my lands, er, your lands, Sire, to await further developments."

Sir Alan's brow was still furrowed and his mouth turned down.

"And when you received the summons to report to the muster?" Robin asked.

Sir Henry dipped his head. "I was ashamed, Your Majesty. I had failed as a knight of Bell Castle. I couldn't believe that Your Highness meant to include me."

"You were afraid that you would have to answer for your crime," said Sir Alan, his tone almost a growl.

Sir Henry nodded. "I suppose I could be called a deserter although I didn't. Quite the opposite. I stayed faithful to the charge that Sir Walter had given me. I stayed near Grimstaff, waiting. Reported every day to the meeting place. Tried asking for news of my king and my fellow knights without betraying my position.

"If that is a crime then answer for it I must. But I beg Your Highness for mercy. If I could be granted a second chance, I can prove Your Highness's trust is well-placed in me."

Second chance? Sir Henry would be considered fortunate to have his life spared. "We think a stay in the dungeon will give you ample opportunity to consider from whom you take your orders," Robin said. "Sir Alan, you have succeeded in your mission. Sir Henry's holdings will be transferred to you."

Sir Henry looked at Sir Alan with dismay.

"We will continue to investigate this matter. Sir Henry, should you be proven blameless, you may indeed be given that second chance." Robin directed Sir Alan to escort the knight to the prison. Robin needed to buy himself some time. Sir Louis was dead and could not corroborate Sir Henry's story but Sir Walter and Sir Simon were yet to be found.

CHAPTER TWENTY-SIX

When the gatekeeper passed word that a man calling himself Terrowin the Advocate had arrived by invitation, Robin could barely remain in his seat. "Grant him admittance," he said, "and bring him here."

The young man who entered the great hall seemed just as weary albeit a little less travel-worn than the one Robin had met months ago in Eian's public house. If Terrowin's fine clothes were any indication, the past few months had been good to him. His cloak even bore a coat of arms, a silver shield with three black martins. The symbolism of the birds spoke of a son who owned no lands and was forced to obtain his possessions by the sword. The landlessness was consistent with what Terrowin had told Robin of the sacrifices the man's humble parents had made for his education. As for the swordsmanship Robin would hazard the guess that the sharpest object the advocate wielded was his pen.

Terrowin strode to the base of the dais and bowed. "King Bewilliam." He straightened and his expression shifted from politely expectant to puzzled. "Sire, I don't recall ever being at Bell Castle or even the Chalklands and we have not met, yet Your Majesty appears familiar to me."

Robin lifted off his crown and mussed up his hair. "Picture us with a beard, in a plain tunic."

Terrowin's brows drew together in a frown, then rose and his jaw dropped. "Robin? From Sweet Water? You . . . Your Highness asked me about copies and archives. I didn't know—"

"That Robin was a king?" Robin replaced his crown and smiled. "The information you gave us served us well. Now we again have need for your knowledge and skill. Please, be seated."

"Thank you, Your Majesty."

Robin sent for refreshments to be brought for the newly arrived traveler.

"Would Your Majesty like to tell me something of the legal matter for which you need my assistance?" asked Terrowin.

Robin held up his hand and didn't speak until the servant had delivered food and drink and departed. "We have your assurance that everything we say will be held in confidence?"

"Give me a coin."

Robin was taken aback by the almost imperious demand.

"A retainer, Sire," said Terrowin. "Any denomination will do. It will constitute a contractual arrangement between us."

On the castle grounds, Robin never needed money but in his purse he had two coins, the ones that Gerald had given him in Rocky Port. He handed one to Terrowin.

Terrowin bowed and said, "Thank you, Your Majesty. I, Terrowin, am now your Advocate and all communication between us is privileged."

"In that case . . . it's a matter of adultery."

Again, the young man's eyebrows lifted. "Sire, I doubt that Your Majesty needs to concern himself. Adultery is for the most part a female crime, a married woman consorting with a man not her husband. She is, after all, her husband's property and for his support owes him fidelity. Besides, if the illicit union produces fruit there are questions about paternity—"

"I am not the adulterer," Robin said and proceeded to give Terrowin a spare description of the dilemma in which he found himself.

The young man's eyes widened. "This is a complicated matter indeed."

"Because the Queen may have assumed that I was dead?"

Terrowin shook his head. "That may have no bearing. There are some who hold that marriage is between one man and one woman. If adultery is proved there can be separation but not divorce and remarriage would be prohibited. Even if Your Majesty had died, it could be alleged that she was still not free to remarry."

"So, if she should return to us—?"

He frowned. "I think it's too late for that. Your Majesty is certain that the Queen has remarried."

"There were witnesses," Robin replied. Conrad hadn't said that he had actually attended the wedding ceremony, only that he had been told it had taken place, but Zachary . . .

"And she is still married?"

"We would assume so."

"Your Majesty is certain that the Queen does not know you escaped Grimstaff Castle and returned to the Chalklands?"

"We don't know, not for certain." King Ulric's knights may have dunned the Chalklands' subjects for taxes and brought word back to their lord that King Bewilliam ruled once again. Robin had not heard anyone speak of strange knights traveling his kingdom but to be certain he would have to inquire of every soul for miles around.

"It would be good to establish that. If it can be proved that the Queen is aware that you are still alive yet remains with this other king—" Open mouthed, Terrowin looked up and paused. "Adultery and bigamy," he said. "Not just bigamy, polyandry. The Queen is guilty of having multiple husbands. Clearly forbidden.

"The negotiation with which I am now assisting has not quite concluded," said Terrowin. "However I think I can at least get a start on Your Majesty's case without compromising my current involvement. We should have a judge appoint me as proctor. Then I can request that a complaint be made and a letter of citation delivered to the defendants requiring them to appear on an assigned day to hear the charges against them."

"And if they don't?"

Terrowin touched his tongue to his upper lip. "Don't appear? Your Highness means, refuse to comply with a court order?"

Robin chuckled. "Why not? A king and queen? Surely you don't seriously expect them to appear just because some flimsy slip of paper tells them to."

"Flimsy pieces of paper can be quite powerful, depending on who wrote them."

Robin could hardly argue. It was for want of documents that he believed his kingdom to be lost. Finding them had empowered him. He sipped from his mug of ale. "Still, we think we would have a better chance of getting justice if we rode with an army to this land of the Palisades and challenged them."

"A military action? In that case, Your Majesty, you do not need my services. But I believe you would prevail by pursuing the matter through the court and at a lower cost." In a softer voice he said, "No lives need be lost in search of the truth."

Robin opened his mouth to reply, then closed it. He had been picturing this King Ulric at his feet, trembling at the point of Robin's sword, begging forgiveness and begging for mercy, which Robin would grant in the form of a single swift slash of his sword rather than prolonged and excruciating torture. King Ulric dispatched, in his mind's eye Robin turned to Daya—and stopped. He saw her wide pleading eyes, felt a pang in his heart, and wondered if his anger was hot enough to slay the woman who had been his wife. Could he pronounce, much less execute, a death sentence?

He glanced around the great hall. The furnishings were different, but it was the same room in which he and Daya had held many feasts, celebrated happy occasions. He remembered the two of them dancing, her smiling up at him, her eyes alight.

And there was Conrad to consider. He might not want his mother to die at the point of a knight's sword, unshriven and doomed to Hell for all eternity.

"Proceed," he said to Terrowin.

CHAPTER TWENTY-SEVEN

His helmet in the crook of his arm, Sir Kenneth bowed. Robin could see that the man's hair, the color and texture of straw, was thinning on top. No longer a young man, Sir Kenneth nevertheless maintained himself in a lean and fit condition, strong and capable. As true as his allegiance to the kingdom might be, Sir Kenneth's strongest devotion was to his wife. Determined to leave an illustrious legacy, Sir Kenneth dedicated each battle to her, pledging to do his king proud, and his wife even prouder.

The knight straightened and squared his shoulders. "I found Sir Simon, Sire," he said. "Had Your Majesty intended to punish him, someone else has spared Your Highness the trouble. Sir Simon fell in with a band of highwaymen. We were ourselves accosted by these brigands. We bested them and discovered that one of the thieves had some of Sir Simon's possessions. At first we thought that our fellow knight had been robbed. When we pressed the bandits we learned that Sir Simon had actually joined their contemptible ranks. Apparently he was no more deserving of their trust than ours." Sir Kenneth's shoulders slumped. "After they attacked and robbed some other travelers, Sir Simon tried to make away with more than his fair share of the take. The robbers hunted him down and, well, Sire, exacted their own revenge. I regret to inform Your Majesty that Sir Simon is already dead. We have Sir Simon's possessions as well as the highwaymen in custody."

Robin felt hurt and angry. It was bad enough to be betrayed by someone he respected and trusted enough to confer knighthood on him. That Sir Simon had proved himself to be so dastardly made Robin doubt his ability to be an accurate judge of character.

"Take the thieves to the dungeon. We will deal with them. As for Sir Simon, as promised his lands will be given to you."

Sir Kenneth bowed but did not depart. "A question if I may, Sire?"

"Yes, Sir Kenneth?"

"Sir Simon had a wife and two children. He not only deserted you, he deserted them, and they have been suffering in his absence. What is to become of them now?"

"They will be evicted from the land which is now yours." It was unfortunate but Sir Simon's widow would have to find some way to provide for her family.

"I know that we faithful knights were all promised the land of those who betrayed Your Majesty. But Sir Simon's wife is as much a victim of his perfidy as we are. I would find it difficult to contribute to the worsening of her hardship and that of the children. I took an oath not only to serve and guard Your Majesty but also to protect the defenseless, women and children. Might not Sir Simon's wife and children be allowed to stay on the land which will now be mine?"

Robin frowned. The disinherited wife and children of a disgraced knight? "We appreciate your sentiment and your concern which is indeed a principle of the knight's code of service. Allowing them to remain in the kingdom would be like housing a nest of vipers, however. Do you not think that they might come to resent us? Someday turn on you, or us?"

Sir Kenneth pressed his lips together. He nodded. "Of course you are right, Sire. The risk is great." He bowed and turned to leave.

"Sir Kenneth—"

"Yes, Sire?"

"If you wished to give them some of Sir Simon's property, aid them in getting established somewhere else, that might meet your chivalric obligation to protect the weak while guarding our safety."

Sir Kenneth smiled. "Thank you, Your Majesty."

After Sir Kenneth had left, Robin slumped and propped his chin in his hand, his heart heavy. Creeping out from her special seat behind the throne, Meeyoo crawled into his lap, perhaps to snuggle in his warm ermine-trimmed robe. Absentmindedly, he stroked her fur.

Sirs Louis and Simon were dead. That left only Sir Walter to confirm or contradict Sir Henry's recounting of what had transpired at Grimstaff Castle. Meanwhile Sir Henry languished in Bell Castle's dungeon. To all reports he had been a model prisoner, his only request that his king consider Sir Henry's avowals of innocence.

Robin took heart at the speed with which Squire Maxwell's training proceeded. He sent the lad to master tactical skills with Sir Howell and martial arts with Sir Kenneth. Robin soon learned to send Maxwell for training with Sir Alan as a sort of reward for exemplary performance. Sessions with Sir Alan tended to end with drum lessons and ale drinking.

For all his bold words at the renewal of vows, Sir Albert had yet to return. Robin tried not to feel disappointed that Sir Albert had proved himself to be not only a lackluster knight but a faithless one. Even more worrisome was that Sir Albert had found and joined forces with Sir Walter who according to Sir Henry had incited the other knights to accept bribes and desert their king.

At this moment, Sir Walter and Sir Albert could be plotting against him. Sir Albert could have joined Sir Walter and they could be conspiring with King Reynold.

The thought of such a conspiracy left Robin queasy, chilled with fear, and then hot with anger.

He would take action, now. He would dispatch another knight to find the two and bring them both to justice.

He set out across the bailey in search of a servant to convey the charge to Sir Kenneth when the grinding of the portcullis gate caught his attention. The gatekeeper raced toward him. "Sir Albert has arrived, Your Majesty," the man said, bowing. "With Sir Walter."

It was hard to say who was the worse for wear.

Sir Albert's tabard was torn and stained. His shield was split and the dent in his helmet pointed to a swollen left eye encircled by a purpling bruise. But at least Sir Albert was riding.

Sir Walter walked behind bareheaded and towed on a lead, his arms bound tight to his body with ropes. His right cheek was enflamed, the skin split and encrusted with dried blood. His left eye was nearly closed and his lower lip bulged.

Sir Albert dismounted and tugging the lead, dragged Sir Walter forward to approach Robin. Robin watched as the man took in the richness of his surroundings. His gaze then fell on Robin. Though he had doubtless been apprised of Robin's return to power, his one good eye widened.

"Your Majesty," Sir Albert said, got to one knee, and then with obvious difficulty, stood. "I found Sir Walter. He did not agree to come willingly."

Indeed, despite the humiliation of being tethered and bound like a joint of beef trussed up for the roasting spit, besmirched from head to toe with dust and dirt, Sir Walter stood tall and gave Robin the most menacing stare he could manage.

"Well done, Sir Albert," Robin said, dismissing for the moment the fact that Sir Walter had not bowed. "Escort him to the great hall." Matters of consequence were best dealt with in formal settings. "Thank you," Robin said to the gatekeeper and then added, "Tell Prince Con— Brother Thaddeus he is wanted in the great hall."

The gatekeeper bowed and headed for the church.

Robin strode through the hall with long steps that sent his cloak swirling wide and took a seat on his throne facing the two men. While he waited for Conrad he tried to compose his thoughts but they raced and ran in circles and his heart pounded. At last Conrad appeared. He took in the sight of the two

216

bedraggled knights and the hint of a smile crossed his face. He drew close to the throne and bowed.

"Brother Thaddeus, thank you for coming," Robin said. "We hope we did not take you away from an important task."

"None so important as what concerns Your Majesty," Conrad replied.

Unless it's a concern for God, which this may well be, Robin thought. "Sir Albert, thank you for locating Sir Walter whose circumstance was a worry to us." In more ways than one.

Sir Albert bowed. Sir Walter looked like he wanted to spit.

"Sir Walter. We are not dead, as you can see. We are still your king and you still owe us recognition."

Sir Walter gave a barely discernible nod.

"No, we are not dead, and neither are you, although we can think of no other reason you could give for not discharging your responsibilities as you pledged—before God—to do."

Robin glanced at Conrad who blinked once.

"Other than your dismemberment or death, there is no possible excuse for your failure. We are not obliged to ask for an explanation yet we are giving you a chance to proffer one."

For a moment, Sir Walter stood mute. Robin glared at him and Sir Albert scowled but perhaps even more intimidating was Conrad's level unblinking gaze.

"I did what I had to do. I had no choice," Sir Walter said.

"He thought of himself and not his king!" said Sir Albert, his face flushed. "He tried to make excuses to me, Your Majesty," said Sir Albert. "He claimed that the knights of Grimstaff Castle sorely resented their king's enlistment of foreign assistance. They offered our knights bounties to hold back, to leave our king vulnerable, and allow them to vanquish the dragon. That ruse failed as you well know but the die had already been cast. In accepting the bribe, Sir Walter had already transgressed."

Sir Albert frowned. "As long as he believed Your Majesty had died, he thought he was safe. However when the summons went out he knew Your Highness had survived. He must have realized that he was a condemned man and went into hiding—" Sir Albert shrugged.

Sir Walter narrowed his eye and his bruised lip turned down.

"And of Sir Henry," Robin said. "What have you to say?"

"There is nothing I can say, Sire."

Robin sighed. Without an accounting from Sir Walter, testimony about what had transpired between the knights at Grimstaff Castle could come only from King Reynold and his men. Robin wished Sir Walter had spoken in his own defense, had given any reason for Robin to show mercy. "It pains us but we have no recourse but to sentence you to death on the breaking wheel." Out of the corner of his eye he saw Conrad lower his head and close his eyes in assent. His lips moved wordlessly.

"Sir Albert, release Henry from the dungeon. He is stripped of his title and holdings but we grant him the opportunity to earn the right to be called Sir Henry once again. Gather the loyal knights of Bell Castle to carry out the sentence against Sir Walter without delay."

"Without delay" nevertheless bought Sir Walter several days more of life as the remaining knights had to be assembled from their distant manors. To remove any hint of gaiety from this most solemn occasion, Robin directed that they again be housed in the barracks.

On the day of the execution, Robin arose with a heavy heart. Sir Walter's betrayal was a personal affront. Robin would have preferred to exact the punishment in private but the knights were bloodthirsty with their desire for vengeance. He compromised by ordering the wheel to be erected not in the inner bailey but on a small yard behind the barracks.

Sir Albert took it upon himself to escort Sir Walter to the site of his execution. Though Robin had told only the knights and Conrad when the execution would take place, word spread. From the hall, Robin saw Bell Castle's servants drift in from the workshops and stables to line the path from the keep's dungeon. As Sir Walter passed, they jeered and threw clots of dirt, manure, and kitchen trash at his back. Sir Walter maintained a stony expression.

With a sigh, Robin left the hall to attend this wretched and pitiful event. Even the sky seemed dragged down. A layer of clouds hung so low as to scrape the top of Robin's crown. The chill air gave no comfort and the wind was still as if Nature held her breath.

As he cornered the barracks, Robin could hear a strident hubbub. He entered the yard to find servants crowded into the yard, their backs pressed against the curtain wall and the rear of the barracks building. Squire Maxwell stood at the front of the crowd, his face stormy.

At attention, the knights surrounded the wheel, varying degrees of fury and resentment darkening their faces. Sir Albert looked stricken. At Robin's appearance, the assembly fell silent and bowed.

No new evidence that might exonerate Sir Walter having come to light, Robin reiterated the death sentence and commanded the knights to carry out their onerous duty. Sirs Kenneth and Howell lashed Sir Walter to the wheel, stretching his arms and legs over the spaces between the wheel's spokes. Sirs Alan, Ellery, and Albert took up the clubs with which they would pummel Sir Walter. With nothing to support them, the condemned man's bones would break like dry twigs. Were he of strong constitution, it would take days for the convict to die of his injuries.

Conrad's normally pale face was somehow whiter but his voice was steady as he said, "Sir Walter, you have betrayed your King and Your God. Now you must wrestle with your conscience. Out of kindness, your King may forgive you and out of love, the Lord Your God would also but only if you acknowledge your guilt, ask forgiveness for your sin, make amends, and reconcile yourself to those to whom you pledged your loyalty."

When Walter remained mute, Conrad prayed for the salvation of Walter's soul and then with a bow, departed. Robin wished that he too could depart. Death was dealt far too easily by disease, by misfortune, or by one's enemies. To invite it at the hands of one's comrades by one's own misguided actions was a tragic waste.

Sir Michael sent the wheel spinning. Egged on by the crowd, Sirs Alan and Ellery set upon Sir Walter with their clubs. Sir Albert hung back, his club hanging uselessly at his side.

To his credit, the condemned man bore the first few blows in silence and glared at his punishers in reproach but after only a few revolutions of the wheel his tortured screams filled the yard. His voice choked with pain, he cried out, "I am not guilty of the crime of which I've been accused!"

His face pinched, his eyes red and bright with unshed tears, Sir Albert cried, "Stop!" Startled, Sir Michael took his hands off the wheel and its revolution slowed. Sir Albert looked at Robin with eyes pleading to end the man's agony.

Robin could not show weakness but he could show mercy. He nodded.

Henry snatched a club from Sir Alan's hand, raised it high, and brought it down to strike Sir Walter's chest with a fearsome strike that would stop the man's heart and breath. Sir Walter screamed once, then was still.

As if with one breath, the crowd gasped. In the silence, the only sound was the creaking of the wheel as it slowed to a stop. For a long moment, no one moved but stood with eyes wide and mouths agape. Then one by one they lowered their heads and murmuring, filed away from the yard.

The knights looked to Robin.

"Release him," Robin said. "Take him to the woods and bury him." Sir Walter could be left strapped to the wheel for days, food for hawks and rats but enough was enough. Justice had been served. Vengeful fires had been extinguished. An unmarked grave outside the confines of Bell Castle and consignment to the unquenchable fires of hell would be Sir Walter's final condemnation.

That night, Robin tried to rest but sleep eluded him. He flung aside the blankets and sat up. Tired of tossing and turning, he dressed quickly in leggings and a tunic, shoes and a warm cloak. The moon was bright enough to light his path. Work having ceased hours ago the smithy was dark and cold. He lit a lamp, stirred up what embers still glowed in the furnace to take the chill off the room, and took a seat at a workbench. Picking up a whetstone, he set to work sharpening a dagger hoping that soon the absorbing task of bringing out the blade's edge would engross his troubled mind.

After a few strokes, Robin laid down his sharpening stone and sighed. He could not concentrate. Scenes from Sir Walter's execution kept playing themselves out.

Robin couldn't figure out why it bothered him so. The screaming and bloodshed were indeed revolting. They were meant to be. Punishment was as much to warn and discourage those considering breaking the law as it was to penalize a particular lawbreaker. No one privy to that spectacle would want to risk the same excruciating fate.

Robin had witnessed greater anguish on the battlefield and even more disturbing senseless suffering from illness or accidental injury. Death could not be avoided. All one could hope for was to live as long and as well as possible and then pass quietly with honor in a state of grace. No, it was not the punishment dealt Sir Walter that Robin found disquieting. It was the man's final actions.

Conrad had urged Sir Walter to save his soul and absolve himself of his sins. Yet the knight had used his dying words not to admit his guilt and beg forgiveness but to assert his innocence. Why would he imperil himself for all eternity that way?

Was he innocent? If so, why had he waited until the point of death to declare it?

Had Sir Walter's execution been unjust? Had Robin wrongfully taken a life? That would be murder. There would be no atonement for that.

What if Conrad and all the other churchmen were right? What if men's actions during their few short years in the here and now truly determined their fate in the Hereafter forever? Robin shook his head. In his life he had tried to treat people well, be honest and hardworking. He had done much good on Earth, he had!

But if Sir Walter had been wrongfully executed it was a grave mistake, a mortal sin for which Robin would never be forgiven. When he died he would set only one foot in Heaven. The other would forever be ensnared in Hell.

CHAPTER TWENTY-EIGHT

"**A** formal complaint was made," said Terrowin's letter. "The judge drew up a mandate and a messenger has been dispatched to deliver it to the proper authority in the kingdom of the Palisades who in front of two witnesses will present it to the defendants. The mandate summons the defendants to appear at Mathus Abbey in three weeks' time to hear the charges against them."

Robin laid the letter in his lap. Were he King Ulric, the messenger would never get past the gate and the summons would never be delivered. What then, Terrowin? he wondered.

The letter went on to say, "Should it be absolutely impossible to deliver the summons to the defendants a public citation can be declared in the church."

Well, that answered that question.

"Your Majesty had been skeptical about whether the summons would be honored. Should the defendants fail to answer the summons the judge may appoint another day for the hearing. Alternatively the defendants can be declared contumacious. They can be barred from attending church, fined, or even excommunicated."

Robin wouldn't himself find any of those repercussions all that persuasive. He suspected that Ulric and Daya would have to be pried from their castle and dragged hogtied to the abbey.

"We have interviewed many in the kingdom of the Chalklands regarding their contact with knights from the Palisades," Terrowin went on to report. "They have asserted that King Reynold's knights were told of Your Majesty's return to Bell Castle. We next need to ascertain if those knights conveyed this information to their king."

Good luck with that, thought Robin.

In closing, Terrowin had presented his bill to date, a not insubstantial sum. Advocates, Robin grumbled. One day they will rule the world.

Robin set the letter aside on his desk, left his bedchamber, and descended the stairs from the keep headed toward the bailey and the great hall. Meeyoo scampered ahead of him and he noticed how much bigger she had grown. She was fluffier to be sure, her fur thickening in response to the cooler temperatures, but she had also put on weight. He had promised her that she would like being a castle cat and apparently she did. Meeyoo made special friends of the kitchen staff who kept her supplied with rich treats. Robin had learned that she was fond of cakes and apparently could detect the smell of something tasty baking from across the bailey. Not long after dough was put in the oven she would run to the kitchen from wherever she was on the castle grounds and wind herself beseechingly around the baker's ankles.

Meeyoo wasn't the only one at Bell Castle to have put on some weight Robin thought, pressing his hand against the front of his cloak beneath which was a widening waist. Like Meeyoo's thicker fur, maybe his broader girth was in response to the colder weather. Yes, that must be it, he chuckled.

The mornings became darker and frostier with every passing day. Robin would have been happy to stay longer in his cozy bedchamber. Tucked away in the keep at a distance from the bustle of the castle's central ward, his room was quiet and comfortable. He had taken great pains to have it furnished with a wide and pillowed bed outfitted with soft linens and fluffy blankets. Wool rugs spared his bare feet from the chill of the stone floor and a coal brazier warmed the room. Lamps softened the stone walls with their golden glow.

Had anyone suggested that he might have somewhat overcompensated for months of sleeping outdoors on hard surfaces he would not have argued but not a soul begrudged the king a little luxury, at least not aloud.

True, the room still echoed sometimes with Queen Daya's laughter, her cries of delight when Robin would touch just the right spot just the right way, her moans as she gave birth to Conrad and Zachary but the echoes became softer with each passing day.

Seated in a cushioned chair at his sturdy desk by the window overlooking the castle grounds he could work undisturbed while keeping an eye on the surroundings but today he would hold court in the great hall. He was scheduled to have many conferences with the cook, the chamberlain, the steward, the baker, the stable boy, and a half dozen other household servants, all to plan Bell Castle's Christmas feast. Many decisions and compromises would have to be made but Robin looked forward to weighing all the options. He and his subjects deserved this festival, a celebration of all that their efforts had produced and recognition of their accomplishments.

As he strode to the great hall, he imagined how it would look weeks from now, festooned with holly and evergreens, lush with red velvet draperies and cushions, the light of dozens of candles glimmering in tall gold and silver candelabras and glinting off polished and faceted ornaments of precious metals, crystal, and glass. The hall would smell of juniper and sweet spices while the air over the bailey would be filled with the smoke of cook fires, the aromas of roasting meats, baking breads and pastries, and simmering mead and mulled wine. There would be laughter, music, song.

Robin smiled. During the Christmas celebration it would be his pleasure to give his devoted servants gifts. Capping the feast would be his dubbing Maxwell as knight before all of Bell

Castle's subjects. Yes, the lad was still quite young and yes he still had years of training ahead of him but Maxwell had proved himself in battle while still a squire. During the skirmish at the gypsy encampment he had shown himself to be clever, diligent, brave, self-sacrificing, and as worthy of the title as any knight.

And did I mention loyal? Robin silently shot at unseen critics. The matter of loyalty brought to mind Sirs Simon, Louis, and Walter, and Henry. He pushed the troubling thoughts away.

Across the bailey, a feeble light glowed in the window of the church which Conrad had fitted with glass. "It helps keep the interior bright and welcoming with natural light but keeps out the drafts which tend to discourage visitors from lingering," he had explained. Not just visitors but Conrad himself. Conrad put in many long hours at his desk working on concordances, dictionaries, and sermons. Though he no longer slept in the chapel, he didn't sleep in the keep either. Despite Robin's efforts at restoring his son's bedchamber, Conrad refused to take up residence in it, claiming for himself a small room in the upper part of the great hall as though he were but a guest of Bell Castle.

A servant sweeping the floor and preparing the hall for the day's activities bowed and excused himself leaving Robin to settle on his throne. For this long day of conferences, Robin had requested a table so the various tradesman and craftsmen could display and demonstrate samples but there were no chairs for anyone save himself. Having to stand for the length of the negotiation kept presentations and discussions short.

The doors flung open and the gatekeeper rushed in. "Sire!"

Robin forgave the perfunctory bow. The man's breathlessness conveyed a matter of great urgency.

"Forgive the interruption—"

"What is it?"

"A troupe of strange people calls at the gate, Sire. Their leader, Quinn, says Your Majesty will know of them."

Quinn, the leader of the gypsies. Was the entire gypsy band here at Bell Castle? At the site of Marlborough Fair they had threatened Robin with bodily harm. Did they mean now to carry out their threat? "Are we under attack?" Bell Castle under attack by a band of gypsies? The idea was laughable.

"No, Sire. They seek aid for a member of their party who is ill."

Aid? How brazen of them to seek help from someone they had tried to kill. It was a subterfuge, a plot to gain the gates. What a blatant affront—

Zachary! It must be Zachary who was ailing.

Heart pounding, Robin raced ahead of the gatekeeper to the gatehouse where the gypsy band with their donkeys and carts crowded the corridor, their leader Quinn at the head. He was swathed in many brilliantly patterned scarves and shawls but the fabric's bright reds and yellows did nothing for the pallor of his face. Ballooning breeches flopped about his legs and he rushed forward and went to one knee. "Your Majesty."

Robin drew his sword. "What do you mean by this? Gaining entrance by means of a ruse, claiming to be in need of aid. Did you think to catch us unawares and finish what you started at your camp? We want these man arrested," Robin shouted so that the gate guards could hear.

The gypsies pulled back and Quinn cowered at Robin's feet. "Wait, Sire. This is no ruse. I come on behalf of Dale."

"Where is he?"

"In the cart, Sire. Dale is ill."

"Ill? How? With what? And he asked for me?"

Quinn cast his eyes down. "We thought Your Majesty should know. We recalled Bell Castle's magnificence from our previous visit, when we performed here and met Dale. We hoped that here we could find healing resources and skill."

No, Zachary hadn't asked for his father but that mattered not. He grabbed the man's biceps. ""What is wrong with him? An injury? An infection? Tell me!"

Quinn bit his lower lip. "He took a potion."

The chill that Robin felt crawl up his back had nothing to do with the draftiness of the gatehouse. A potion. Magic.

CHAPTER TWENTY-NINE

Pushing the man aside, Robin rushed to one of donkey carts. He didn't hear the gatekeeper send for Maxwell but someone must have summoned the lad. The youth no sooner appeared in the gatehouse than he bowed and said, "Sire, please. As your squire, allow me to see to your needs."

"Sire?" said the gatekeeper.

Robin rubbed his forehead. "Give him your support, do as he says." The pronouncement took some of the weight from his shoulders but did nothing to clear his head.

"Call for some servants," Maxwell told the gatekeeper. "Detain these people." He pointed to the gypsies. "They threatened our king. Take them to the dungeon."

"But I came on an errand of peace," Quinn protested. "Dale is deathly ill. We hoped that here he would find life-saving treatment. We are not the enemy. I swear, we only want what you want: Dale's well-being."

"What's wrong with him?" Maxwell asked.

Robin peered at the blanket-covered body in the cart. Only Dale's face was exposed, his skin pale despite the golden light of the gate's torches. The young man was so still as to appear not to be breathing. "We're told he's taken a potion."

"We should get him inside," Maxwell said.

"Inside?" said the gatekeeper. "Bring an illness into Bell Castle? Perhaps we should send them to the abbey."

Which would be the normal practice but Robin didn't want to explain why this was different. "The keep," Robin said. "There's a spare bedchamber . . ." The one he had outfitted for Conrad which had gone unused.

"Summon servants," Maxwell said to the gatekeeper. "We need a fire lit in the bedchamber's brazier. Tell someone to fetch emetics, bring them to the keep. Maybe we can get the patient to vomit up the potion. And leeches—they can suck out the poison. We'll need pure freshly drawn water. Wine, too, and some juice. Someone alert Brother Thaddeus. We will need his prayers. Take these men to the dungeon—"

"Leave this one," Robin said, pointing to Quinn. "He is coming with us."

"But Your Majesty, this person threatened—"

"You will guard me. Meanwhile we need to question him. We need information about what transpired before Zach— before the patient became ill."

Dazed, Robin trotted beside the cart as Maxwell led the donkey along the path toward the keep. Conrad appeared at his side. "What's this I hear? Someone is ill?"

"Zachary," Robin whispered and pointed helplessly to the silent figure in the cart. Conrad looked at his brother, then at Robin, his face filled with confusion and concern.

"Let's get the invalid into bed." Maxwell said. "Quickly now, but gently."

Conrad supported Zachary's shoulders, Maxwell took his feet, and together they carried him upstairs.

Though kept clean, the bedchamber was musty with disuse. A newly-lit brazier struggled to take the chill off the bedchamber and candles on a bedside table sputtered to life. A servant pulled back the bedclothes and another hurried forward with a nightshirt. Conrad and Maxwell laid Zachary on the bed. The servant removed his shoes and made to unwrap the gypsies' blankets.

"No," said Robin, fearful of what might be exposed. "We don't want to risk a chill. Just get him into the bed and cover him. Brother Thaddeus and Squire Maxwell, stay. The rest of you may take your leave. Say nothing to anyone of this. We . . . do not want any wild rumors spread of any spell or contagion," he said, trying to sound calm and more collected than he felt. "Everything is under control. There is nothing for anyone to fear, so no need to cause worry."

Robin turned to Quinn, grabbed a fistful of the gypsy's wrappings, and pulled him close. "Now tell me! What happened?"

The gypsy cringed. "I don't know exactly, Your Highness. Dale was determined to become more beautiful," Quinn said. "She—"

"Stop that!" Robin cried.

Quinn looked at him, his face contorted in confusion.

"His name is Zachary," Robin hissed through gritted teeth. "HE is a prince. You will accord him respect."

"I will try, Your Majesty. We have known her—him—for so long as Dale. Please forgive me if I err."

"Your Majesty, if I may. Perhaps it would serve for me to conduct this questioning?" said Squire Maxwell.

Robin had to admit, he could barely speak. The inquiry would have little chance of producing any usable information if he kept interrupting and erupting. He threw up his hands.

At the bedside, Conrad clasped his hands, closed his eyes, and murmured prayers for his brother's recovery.

"Go on, please," said Maxwell.

Quinn took a deep breath. "Dale was desperate to leave her—his—" His brow wrinkled and his eyes appealed to Robin. "Your Majesty . . .?"

"Just get on with it!" Robin growled.

"She wanted to leave her painful past behind."

"Painful!" Robin stomped a few angry paces and turned. "Painful? He had everything. He had the best, anything anyone could want. He was fed the best foods, clothed in the most luxurious garments! He lived in a castle, was never too cold or too hot. He had the most entertaining toys, whatever he wanted. The best nurses, the best valets, the best teachers. He had friends, a brother, parents who loved him. His laughter was his family's joy. When he cried he was picked up and comforted, his tears dried. But he rarely cried. He was a happy boy." Robin felt his eyes sting with tears.

"Nevertheless," Quinn said in a soft voice. "There was pain that she wished to forget. Change everything about herself and start life anew. Live the rest of her years as she always thought to live them."

As a woman? Robin felt dizzy. This simply could not be real. Perhaps Quinn was a magician. This was all a scheme to put Robin under a spell, a plot to drive him mad. He would be deposed and then Zachary would take the throne. Or perhaps not Zachary, who might himself be enchanted or insane. The gypsies conspired to take over Bell Castle, rule the Chalklands.

"A beautiful woman," Quinn said with a sad smile. "She tried many treatments and potions."

"She turned away meat so as to become slimmer. She ate mostly barley, beans and lentils, alfalfa, foods she had learned that had properties to promote a curvier figure. She slicked her hair with beaten eggs mixed with oils and twisted the strands in rags to make it curl."

None of that sounded to Robin like something that could leave Zachary near death.

"She remembered being taught as a child that the famous queen Cleopatra bathed in milk and honey to make her skin white and smooth. Dale did that."

Robin too was aware that Cleopatra had used such beauty baths to gain the beauty that enabled her to seduce the great Julius Caesar and powerful Mark Antony. Even Robin's own wife, Queen Daya, had tried it without ill effects.

Quinn's smile softened. "We thought that produced wonderful results but Dale wanted more. At one fair where we performed she learned another secret, a ritual practice in the Far East. There the women soak in red wine to fade blemishes and firm the skin."

Robin couldn't imagine something like that causing injury. Drinking too much wine maybe but certainly not bathing in it.

"All these treatments did her no harm and made her more comely but she was not content." Quinn's face grew grave. "She rubbed charcoal on her eyebrows and around her eyes to enhance them, even though it made her eyes tear. She pinched her cheeks and bit her lips to make them red. She bound her nether parts to shrink them."

Robin felt his jaw drop and even Conrad and Squire Maxwell were agape at this revelation.

"There was a fortune teller at one fair who claimed to have discovered a most powerful beauty secret, one that would give Dale plump lips that everyone would want to kiss."

Robin winced.

"Dale traded her for the treatment and yes, at first Dale was pleased. Her lips became puffy as pillows. But then the potion turned evil. Dale's entire face swelled and reddened. A rash spread across her face, her neck, and chest. She said her lips throbbed and her skin ached. She couldn't catch her breath. She couldn't swallow. She became dizzy and faint, and then she collapsed.

"We tried everything that we knew how to do but could not revive her."

"You tried some gypsy magic! You made him worse!" Robin cried.

Quinn folded his arms across his chest. "We did no such thing. We are not gypsies, Sire, we are itinerant actors. The only magic we make is the imaginary world we create on stage."

"Don't deny it!" Robin cried.

From the bed came a faint moan.

"He's alive! He's coming around!" Robin rushed to Zachary's side and bent down to hear what he said.

Zachary whimpered and turned his head.

"What is this?" Robin asked, pointing to a gleaming drop on Zachary's lip. It looked like water or honey but that should have long since dried or been absorbed.

Conrad peered at the blemish. "Perhaps this is where the witch injected the potion." he said.

Maxwell leaned in for a look. "I think this is the stinger of a bee, with the tiny sac that contains the bee venom." He stood. "I've been stung many times with no more ill effects than burning and irritation that could be eased with juice squeezed from the leaves of the bendable plant. But I've also heard that people can have a severe reaction like this. Their skin swells and turns red, they faint. I've heard that some can die from a bee stings, they're that sensitive."

Had Zachary ever been stung as a child? Robin wondered. How had he reacted? Robin wracked his addled brain to remember but could recall no traumatic incidents. As far as he knew his son was not overly sensitive to injuries, animal, or insect bites. Perhaps this bee venom was empowered with magic. It might contain the potion that kept Zachary entranced. "We should remove it," he said. "Stop the flow of poison into him."

"Sire, if I may. There's a trick to this, to not release any more venom," said Maxwell. Robin watched as Maxwell eased the tiny bead and the barb to which it was attached from Zachary's skin.

"Take it away. Far away. Burn it," Robin said.

"Then leeches, Sire," Maxwell suggested. "To suck out any remaining poison. We can give water with a little charcoal dissolved in it as an emetic." He turned to face Quinn. "When did he last eat or drink?"

"I...I don't know."

"Let's get some liquid into him. Some watered wine. Fruit juice, perhaps."

"Go fetch those items, Squire Maxwell." Robin wanted no one else to attend to Zachary, not until he was better. Meaning, not until the effects of the "beautification" treatments had subsided and Zachary looked more like himself.

Maxwell nodded. "I will make haste."

As he headed for the door," Robin called after him, "Squire Maxwell, how did you know all those things, about the bee venom and the emetic?"

"Some time ago Reggie, the farmer, took ill, much like this. It was so bad it seemed for a time that Reggie might die. When I saw him later, completely recovered, I asked how that had been managed. I was curious."

Despite the desperation of the moment, Robin found himself smiling. "Go." He turned to Quinn. "Your confederates will remain in the dungeon until Zachary recovers, at which time we will deal them. You will stay here, as nurse. You will not leave this room and no one else shall enter but us, Brother Thaddeus, and Squire Maxwell. A guard will be posted at the door every hour of the day and night. If you need something for Zachary you will tell the guard and it will be brought. Meanwhile, you will watch over Zachary. If he moves a muscle, cries, or speaks, we want to know about it.

"With each sign of improvement you will be rewarded with food and drink. Should he fail, you will as well."

CHAPTER THIRTY

Robin spent a restless night dozing in spurts punctuated by many visits to Zachary's bedside to see if his son's condition had improved or worsened. He would find Conrad or Squire Maxwell attending Zachary by turns and Quinn's vigilance was constant. As well, another member had joined the nursing staff. Robin discovered Meeyoo at the foot of the bed watching Zachary with half-closed eyes.

At dawn, Robin stepped into Zachary's bedchamber to find Squire Maxwell already there.

"The patient appears to be on the mend, Sire," said Squire Maxwell.

Robin had to agree. Zachary didn't appear to be quite as swollen or as red. Propped up against pillows, Zachary peered out through eyes that were still puffy and wheezed a faint "Sire, thank you."

"I have been trying to get liquids into him," said Quinn. "He seems to be having trouble swallowing. Perhaps there is still some swelling there, making it hard for him to speak."

At least Zachary was upright and conscious.

"If I may say, Your Majesty, I don't believe he needs twenty-four hour supervision," said Maxwell. "The other servants and I, we can work in shifts and check on him, see to his needs. The gypsy Quinn can be sent to the dungeon with the rest of his band to await judgment and punishment for having threatened our king."

Quinn scowled.

"No," Robin replied. The fewer witnesses to the changes transforming Zachary, the better. "For now only you, Quinn, and Brother Thaddeus may tend the patient."

Maxwell bowed. "As you wish, Sire."

"Come, then. We believe Sir Albert will be arriving soon. You are to work with him today practicing climbing."

"Climbing, Sire?" Squire Maxwell smiled. "I hope Your Majesty and Sir Albert will see that I am already quite good at that. I have been climbing trees since I could walk."

"Of course you have," said Robin. What boy hadn't? "However you will find that climbing a wall isn't as easy. And sometimes, the only way into an enemy castle is to scale a wall."

They met Sir Albert near the barracks.

"You want to hit the wall with a little speed," Sir Albert said, "so you need a running start. Long even strides. Then, take off with your left leg. Put your right foot on the wall and kick out. That will give you some height. Out, not downwards, otherwise you'll fall. Then raise up your left leg. Get that leg as high up on the wall as you can. You want to look up, find a ledge you can grab onto, pull yourself up. Get yourself steady then look for the next landing so you can advance your ascent. All right, give it try," Sir Albert said.

Maxwell launched his first assault on the wall.

Sir Albert turned to Robin. "Begging Your Majesty's pardon . . ."

"Yes, Sir Albert?"

The man drew himself up to his full height. "I know Your Majesty has more important matters to concern himself with than rumors and I'm sure Your Majesty has this matter well in hand . . ."

"What matter would that be?" Robin had sworn to secrecy Maxwell, the gatekeeper and guards, and the few servants who had attended the bedchamber. They had done an admirable job of keeping his confidence. Robin had heard no talk about the patient in the keep other than that in an act of charity Bell Castle had generously taken in a seriously ill invalid to nurse back to health and that strangers had been detained in the dungeon pending the outcome of the sickness.

"Punishment of Queen Daya and King Ulric."

Robin tried not to blush or squirm. He had tried to push the nasty matter aside with little success. Not a day went by that someone or something didn't call to mind his wife's betrayal, as mortifying and problematic as that of the errant knights.

Squire Maxwell fell on his rump with a grunt, the breath knocked out of him in a frosty puff. Rubbing his butt he stepped back from the wall and started another charge.

Squire Maxwell wasn't the only one climbing walls. Robin's complaint had been declared. The hearing date had come and another had been set. Apparently the threat of excommunication and eternal perdition had budged Ulric and Daya from their mute complacency. Declaring themselves innocent, they consented to appear to proffer their defense.

Robin knew he avoided thinking about it because he already knew what action he needed to take. Adultery was a crime against both the state and God, high treason, and mortal sin. The punishment: death. Still haunted by the execution of Sir Walter, Robin found it difficult to frame in his mind the condemnation of his wife. He had loved her. Had laughed and cried with her. Had enjoyed her body and she his. She had born his sons.

"Ow!" cried Maxwell, flat on his back at the foot of the wall. Moaning, he rolled to his side, stood, and shook his bones back into their rightful place.

But Sir Albert was right, Robin thought. The offenders must be reckoned with. To overlook it would not only paint him as weak-willed but would undermine the foundation of right and wrong on which civilization rested. Of more personal concern was the possibility that Daya and her husband had plotted against Robin, and still did.

At considerable expense, Terrowin had interviewed many potential witnesses but had been unable to find anyone from

King Ulric's domain who would support Robin's charge. "We can proceed without that," Terrowin said, "but it would be better to have corroborating testimony."

Robin had given Terrowin his support not to mention many coins, to no avail. The time for action had come.

"You and Squire Maxwell should make yourselves ready to go on a campaign," he said to Sir Albert, "with Sirs Howell, Alan, and Kenneth."

Without further delay, he issued the command to rally the knights. "Get our advocate, Terrowin, as well."

Now for the more difficult task of telling his sons what he planned. Robin sent a servant to summon Conrad to Zachary's bedchamber.

"Your Majesty! Sir Albert!"

Robin looked up towards the sound. Atop the wall, Squire Maxwell stood with his arms crossed over a chest thrust out with pride.

*****

"Zachary is improving," Robin said to Quinn. "We think he is out of immediate danger. Whether there will be lasting effects of the treatments and spells that he has undergone and what they will be remains to be seen. But he will live, no thanks to you and your ilk."

From his bed, Zachary smiled weakly.

Quinn's expression was both apologetic and resentful. "I keep telling Your Majesty that Dale's calamity is not our fault."

"He was in your company when he fell ill. Regardless of what you prefer to believe, he is a Prince of the Chalklands. His life was endangered while he was amongst you. You shall answer for this crime."

"We give thanks for Dale's recovery," Quinn said. "We would hope that Your Majesty would realize that in coming here to seek aid we had only Dale's best interests at heart."

"We have taken that into consideration in making our decision. We need information."

"I have told you everything I know about how Dale came to be ill. Ask any of the others."

"Not about that. About something else. You say you first met Zachary here, at Bell Castle. So you don't perform only at fairs?"

"No, Sire. When the weather is inclement, too cold or too rainy, fairs are small, attendance is poor, and people don't linger. They make their purchases and leave. In those off-seasons we put on private performances at mansions, palaces, and castles. That's how we came to be here."

Robin nodded. "We want you to put on a private performance for another king and queen at a distant domain."

Quinn smiled and squared his shoulders. "With pleasure, Your Majesty. That is a thoughtful gift that I'm sure the recipients will enjoy and will think most highly of the ruler who gave it to them. Our fee—"

"Fee!" Robin stopped himself from throttling the arrogant gypsy and contented himself with grabbing the neck of the man's tunic instead. "You fee is that you get to live. You will put on this play for free. You can explain your generosity however you want—that you wish to introduce yourself to the kingdom, that you are performing a penance. We don't care how you worm your way in. What we do care about is that while you are there you are to acquire certain information."

"Your Majesty wishes us to spy on this other ruler."

Robin shrugged. "Call it whatever you please. Our knights will escort you from the minute you are released and you will be guarded every step of the journey so don't even think about fleeing. We will await the completion of your task at the outskirts of the gate to get your report. Then and only then will we make a final judgment regarding your fate. Now, step outside. We wish to confer with our sons."

Quinn bowed and left the room. Robin bade Conrad to come close.

"Brother Thaddeus, you will have sole charge of the patient here. Squire Maxwell and Quinn will accompany us to the Palisades."

His sons eyes went wide. "Your Majesty, you are not—"

"On a fact-finding mission," Robin said.

"I should go along, Your Majesty," Zachary said.

"No, you should not. This will be a long and taxing march and you are not yet up for it."

"Then wait until I am recovered," Zachary said.

"You want to see your mother, don't you?" Robin asked. He turned to Conrad. "And you? Do you want to see her too?"

Conrad chewed on his lower lip but made no reply.

"You will both see her soon enough. In court."

CHAPTER THIRTY-ONE

They had left the woodlands and meadows at the farthest reaches of the Chalklands behind and had crossed grassy prairies where Robin had never traveled, making discreet and veiled inquiries about the kingdom of the Palisades, its fortifications and their location. It seemed to him that they had ridden, their faces buffed by a chilly breeze, for days across a featureless plain, the horizon unbroken by so much as a tall tree. A virtual sea of dry grass, the plain seemed as limitless as had the ocean from the deck of the Orion. Robin wondered how any traveler found his way as there was not a stone, nor bit of rising ground, nor shrub in evidence to serve as a landmark.

Robin rode at the head of the party with Terrowin, Sir Albert, and Squire Maxwell beside him. Sirs Howell and Kenneth flanked Quinn, followed by the rest of the gypsies. Sir Alan brought up the rear. The wind brought the gypsies' laughter and chatter and the percussion of Sir Alan's drumming to Robin's ears.

He was grateful that they had brought drink for the horses as they found few creeks, brooks, or streams. There was little natural water save for occasional depressions so shallow that the moisture in them was more salt than liquid. The lack of water meant they saw little in the way of wild animals much less people. Now and then a hawk would swoop across the lonely sky or a snake slithering through the grass would startle a horse.

Their nighttime encampments were equally disconcerting, surrounded as they were by the rustling, growling, and chittering of unfamiliar animals. Sir Alan strived to keep spirits light with his singing and drumming. The knights emboldened each other by swapping tales of great combat victories. Not to be outdone, Terrowin recounted fierce courtroom battles he had waged.

When the palisades from which the domain took its name appeared in the distance they were so startlingly unexpected as to seem like an apparition. At first an indistinct blur across the horizon, the palisades came into focus as Robin and his party drew near. Gradual slopes streaked by creeks and rivulets angled sharply at the top to plateaus so level they might have been flattened by the hand of God.

Caprock Fortress stood at the edge, the keep taller than a curtain wall that seemed to Robin superfluous. The difficulty of climbing the natural palisade should be defense enough. The view from the keep would extend for miles. As he considered how they might approach the fortress, Robin wondered if they had already been spotted.

Coming closer to the base of the cliff, they found the terrain less barren. Water flowing down the palisades fed foothill grasses and shrubs and the cliff face itself was whiskered with foliage. Climbing the bluff would not be as impossible as he had thought. What had seemed to be a sheer rock face was tiered into several small cliffs. The top could be gained through a series of switchbacks. The tableland closest to the edge of the cliff had been cleared to make way for the fortress but beyond the fortress walls were woods where he and his party could camp while the gypsies entertained King Ulric and Queen Daya.

Robin breathed a sigh of relief as the horses picked their way over splintered rock toward a stand of trees. So many days spent beneath all that sky had unnerved him just as being on the open water had. He welcomed the cover of trees even if they were scruffy pines and junipers.

Closer to the fortress the foliage was too thin and short to shield them. "We will stop here," he told the knights. He pointed to the fortress and said to Quinn, "There is your target. We will await you here. Gentlemen, time for you to get into costume."

The gypsies had turned uncharacteristically quiet once they had topped the palisade and had the fortress in sight. Now they clustered around their leader. "Traveling Thespians," Quinn addressed them in a bold voice fit for any stage, "prepare to give the performance of your lives."

The gypsies looked one to the other. Murmuring grew to chattering and chortling. From their colorful cart, they pulled scarves and necklaces with which to festoon Terrowin and Sir Alan who remained stalwart despite the ribbing lobbed at them from the other knights.

Once the gypsies had gotten the knight and the advocate suitably garbed, the troupe headed toward the fortress gates, leading their donkey carts, singing and laughing.

To Maxwell Robin said, "Can you climb that tree without being seen? And tell us what transpires at the gate?" Now that they had arrived, Robin had his first doubts about whether the gypsies would even be granted admission. Would they be turned away? Might the arrival of unexpected guests arouse suspicion? Should he and his knights have to retreat they would be easily followed across the open plain.

"Climb? Can I climb?" Maxwell bowed and scrambled up a gnarly pine. "Guards at the first portcullis," he called down. "The gatekeeper is coming out. There is some discussion. No, an argument. Two of the actors are arguing. No, wait. I think it's a little play, they're putting on a little demonstration. The guards seem to be laughing. It's hard to tell with their helmets. Oh, the gatekeeper has been taken ill. Or stabbed!"

Robin felt suddenly sick. Murder at the fortress gate? If violence resulted from a visit from uninvited outsiders, the fortress would redouble its defenses and would be unlikely to let any other strangers in. Robin would be hard-pressed to find a way to get the information that he needed. To flee now he and his knights would have to abandon Terrowin and Sir Alan. The gypsies might reveal who instigated their intrusion. The incident could lead to his men's death and retaliation against his kingdom.

"No, my apologies, Sire," said Maxwell. "He wasn't stabbed. He doubled over with laughter. He is upright again and smiling."

Robin heaved a sigh of relief.

"I can't see . . . no, wait. There is conference with a servant. Perhaps a messenger who will be sent to announce the actors?"

"Keep watching a little longer," Robin said. This could take time. The king or his chamberlain might not be immediately available. Either might want time to consider the gypsies' proposal, might ask them to leave and come at some future date. Might invite them in and offer them hospitality intending to have them perform later, much later. "If nothing has happened by dark—"

"Do not despair, Your Highness. It appears to me that they are being invited in. They are moving into the gateway corridor. I can't see any further from here."

"That's fine, Squire Maxwell. You can come down. All we can do now is wait."

Maxwell launched himself to the ground, landed lightly, and joined the other knights in making camp.

"No fire pit, men," Robin said. "It would be too easily spotted out here from the ramparts. No lamps either." It promised to a cold night. With such skimpy canopy, the ground would be giving up its warmth as soon as the sun set. "Find water for the horses before we lose the light."

Robin heard Sir Albert grumble as he cleared away twigs and brush to make room to sit. "I don't want to wait. I want to go in there and make them both get on their knees for what they did. "

"On their knees," said Sir Kenneth. "Then take off their heads."

"Beheading would be too good for them," said Sir Albert. "They should suffer the way our King did. Know that their lives are in danger and feel that fear. We should drive them from their comfortable castle and make them wander defenseless in the woods. Leave them at the mercy of wild animals."

"Not wander," Sir Kenneth said. "Strip them and tie them to a tree."

"If you could find a decent tree around here," said Sir Howell, earning a couple of snickers. He straightened from the shelter he had been erecting. Looking toward the fortress he tapped his lip with an index finger. "It'd take some planning to storm that stronghold, equipped as we are."

"Unequipped, you mean," said Sir Albert.

"We've got shovels and axes," Sir Howell continued. "We could dig tunnels. Fill them with wood and set them on fire. Make the tunnel cave in and the wall above it collapse."

"No trees, no wood, Howell," said Sir Kenneth.

"Point well taken. We could use the tunnels to get beyond the walls, launch an offense from the inside."

"If we didn't meet their defenders in the tunnel."

"Bring 'em on," said Sir Albert. "Just let me get my hands on them. Then we can drag out that king and his so-called Queen—"

"You'd have to beat me to them," said Squire Maxwell.

"Yeah!"

"Yeah!"

"All right, men. That's enough," said Robin. Every single proposed act of retribution had occurred to him as well but he wasn't finding it pleasant to hear his former queen spoken of in such gory terms. He knew the knights were just trying to keep their nerve battle-ready but he didn't want them becoming a bloodthirsty rabble bent on a massacre. "We stick with the plan."

"How do we know we can trust them, a band of gypsies?" asked Sir Kenneth. "They might strike a deal with King Ulric and Queen Daya. Reveal our wheareabouts for a reward."

"They'll have to get past Sir Alan to do that," said Sir Howell.

"Or get the advocate to shut up long enough to get a word in," Sir Albert said.

Robin and his troop spent a dark and restless night in their encampment. Though Sirs Albert and Kenneth stood watches, Robin found it impossible to sleep. He and Sir Howell passed the night planning strategies should the campaign not go as planned.

The only one who got any rest was Squire Maxwell who slept as soundly as a puppy.

At first light, Squire Maxwell again took his post in the tree. "Nothing, Sire," he reported. "I see lights in the keep. Smoke from workshops. Looks like the kitchen's oven is being stoked for the day. Horses are being watered at the stables. All appears to be quite routine."

"No sign of the gypsies?"

"No, Sire."

Robin sighed with frustration. At least Squire Maxwell didn't detect suggestions that Caprock Fortress was mounting an offense.

The knights tended to their own horses and breakfasts.

At last Squire Maxwell called down, "I see them. I see the gypsies. They are headed for the stables. They're collecting their donkeys. Yes, they're headed for the gate."

"And Sir Alan and Advocate Terrowin? Are they with them?"

"It's hard to tell, Sire, with those costumes. I can say that there are the same number of people going out as went in."

"Men, we need to be on guard," Robin said to the knights. Caprock Fortress's soldiers could be on their way, disguised as gypsies. "Make weapons and defensive positions ready. Maxwell, can you see their faces?"

"Not yet, Sire."

Robin paced in the clearing. If Ulric was sending soldiers masquerading as gypsies at least they would be well matched by Bell Castle's men.

"Sire, I can see Quinn!" Squire Maxwell shouted.

"He's not the vanguard of a band of men who have swords at his back, is he?" Robin asked.

"No, Sire, I don't see any swords, daggers, blades. It all seems very . . . jolly."

Nevertheless, Robin commanded his men to get in formation. The approaching men would be funneled through a gantlet of wary Bell Castle knights bristling with weapons.

The troupe drew near enough that even Robin could recognize the faces of the gypsies as well as Sir Alan and the advocate Terrowin. Quinn approached Robin and bowed. "We Traveling Thespians think that we have a promising future as Peripatetic Plants," he said. "As Ambulant Agents, as Migratory Moles—"

"Enough!" Robin cried. "Your report, if you would be so kind!"

"We actually had very little trouble gaining admittance. We put on a little skit to establish our credentials. Then we told the gatekeeper to remind the King and Queen that we had performed for them before, at Bell Castle."

Robin gulped. Had it been wise for the gypsies to mention their association with the Kingdom of Chalklands?

"The staff was preparing the royal couple's evening meal and there was no specific entertainment planned. We were asked if we could perform that very night, without any further preparation or rehearsal, and we said of course we could. Fortunately we have an extensive repertoire. We would not want to have presented the same drama we did at Bell Castle, which would have been boring—"

"Enough!"

"They so appreciated our performance that they gave us a handsome reward," Quinn said.

"Would you please get to the heart of the matter?" Robin said, his patience wearing.

"After our performance, we were offered refreshments. The King and Queen are very gracious."

Robin scowled.

"Well, we find them to be so. They asked us where else we had performed and we mentioned that we had been at Marlborough Fair in the Chalklands."

"And?" Robin could hardly contain his impatience.

"And that we had thought to call again at Bell Castle, to see if King Ulric and Queen Daya would like a repeat performance."

"And?" Robin thought that he might bite the gypsy if Quinn did not hurry up his recitation.

Quinn waggled his shoulders. "Well, I said, much to our surprise the King and Queen were not in attendance, but King Bewilliam was."

"And?" Robin screamed.

"They were not surprised," said Sir Alan, removing his gypsy costume. "Wary, but not surprised. We were asked ever so casually how Your Highness had fared, given the condition of Bell Castle. I think we were being pumped for information as much as we were trying to ferret it out from them."

Advocate Terrowin bowed. "They know, Your Majesty. In fact, I would say they have known for some time. I got testimony from several of their subjects that they were informed of your return to the Chalklands. It is well established. Sire, your charge is well founded. We can proceed to trial with confidence."

The gypsies hooted, cheered, and stamped out a victory dance.

"He was quite good, I'd have to say." Quinn nodded his head at Terrowin. "Comfortable in front of an audience, knew to project his voice so it could be heard across the room. Used big gestures that everyone in the audience can see." Quinn clapped the advocate on the back. "You'd make a fine actor."

Terrowin grinned and tugged proudly at the lapels of his patchwork gypsy cape, then sobered, swept the garment from his shoulders, and thrust it at Quinn.

"We have done what Your Majesty required of us," said Quinn. "We will go on our merry way."

"Not so fast," replied Robin. "You will return with us to Bell Castle to await the court date. You can relate all that you have told us to the judges. Then you may take your leave."

Quinn grimaced. "Not that we haven't enjoyed Your Majesty's hospitality. We have seen worse than Bell Castle's dungeon, but—"

"We think we can provide more comfortable accommodations this time," Robin said. Until the court date arrived, he would house Quinn and the gypsies in the barracks under the watchful eye of his soldiers. Though he wished to maintain the good faith of his strange new allies, he would keep them on a short leash.

"As you wish, Your Majesty."

CHAPTER THIRTY-TWO

Robin approached the great hall. The officer at arms bowed, turned toward the trumpeter, and signaled the king's approach. The rousing notes of a fanfare reached Robin's ears and he smiled. The day might come when the trumpeter would be called upon to communicate instructions on the battlefield but for now his airs were joyous and celebratory.

Robin flung the folds of his cloak over one hip, the better to display his sword, and strode into the hall. Weighed down with ermine trim, the cloak's hem swept the polished marble floor. Robin held his head steady to support the heft of his new crown, a recreation of the one that he and the Chalklands' kings before him had worn. Ermine-trimmed bejeweled gold encircled the soft bonnet and four gold arches met in the center. Robin felt the burden of leadership as a physical weight on his head as well as figurative burden on his shoulders. Nevertheless a sense of triumph and accomplishment lightened his steps.

To all appearances his hopes and aspirations for the Christmas feast had been met—even exceeded. Plants that had been newly installed about the bailey were still small. Some would not leaf out or bloom until spring. However pots of juniper topiaries lining the path to the hall lent lushness to the grounds. Evergreen garlands tied with big red bows outlined the great hall doors and the light from polished brass sconces gleamed in the wood's fresh varnish.

He stepped inside the doorway and was greeted with the aroma of cinnamon, cloves, and nutmeg. Atop a red-draped console table stood a bowl of mulled wine wrapped in a blanket to keep it warm. Upon entering, guests would be welcomed with small bowls of the beverage. Floating out with the fragrant waft were tunes plucked on dulcimers, strung on lutes, and whistled on flutes.

Directly across the room from the door, Robin's throne sat atop a dais embraced by an alcove set aglow by candelabra. His chair had been garlanded with evergreens. Even Meeyoo's quarter-barrel "throne" had a new cushion.

On the dais a table set for the King and his honored guests gleamed with silver, brass, and gold utensils.

Running perpendicular, long tables had been covered with green cloths overlaid with white linens. Candles in brass candlesticks shone warmly and glowing braziers in the corners of the room kept drafts at bay. Baskets of grapes, bowls of nuts, and stacks of trenchers dotted the tables. Urns of ale and wine stood ready to be poured. New cushions beckoned guests to take comfortable seats on the benches.

The generous menu was to include toasted chestnuts and parsnips, roasted fowl and pig, hare and stag, boiled eggs, gravies and cream sauces, savory and sweet pies, and cheeses. The cook had suggested blackbirds baked in a pie but Robin declined. He found that just too reminiscent of the sparrow Meeyoo had tried to feed him in Lomroddoy Fortress's dungeon.

Every servant and freeman who had contributed to Bell Castle's rebirth had been invited along with their families. The crafts- and tradesmen had been kept especially busy in recent weeks not only with banquet preparations but also with making gifts. Robin would give the smiths' creations to the carpenters, the carpenters' to the cooks, the cooks' to the tailors, and so forth.

Conrad too had invited guests.

"I understand that this is an important celebration for you, Sire," he said, "but—

"Not just for us but for everyone who has worked so hard."

Conrad nodded, his face composed in an expression of forbearance that Robin had come to find annoying. "I don't want us to lose sight of the real reason for this celebration: our Lord."

"Indeed, we will not," Robin said, "You will make certain of that."

Thus the guest list had included the prior of Mathus Abbey who would of course sit at the king's table, several preachers, as well as benefactors from the Chalklands and beyond whose contributions had helped to transform the chapel into a church.

They all now thronged the great hall, the servants, craftsmen, and tradesmen dressed in their finest, gayest clothes while the preachers of Mathus Abbey were easily identified by their plain white habits and black robes. Robin smiled to see husbands and wives dancing and children jigging and skipping to popular ballads. He had to admit that the liturgical chants lent an appropriate seasonal air. Everyone enjoyed the carols, singing and dancing in unison.

He gave a signal to the trumpeter who blew another fanfare, capturing the guests' attention. Robin stepped to the front of the dais. "Merry Christmas, everyone," he said.

His guests bowed, and when they again raised their heads, he was pleased to see not a frown or sign of discontent among them.

"We are delighted to have you join us and we hope that you are enjoying yourselves. It is after all through your efforts and your loyalty that we are able to be here today, savoring this bounty. We have many reasons to celebrate and we wish to recognize them all because each one is precious. However, before we do, we wish to acknowledge—" Robin looked at Conrad, "—the true reason for this gathering. We can think of none better than our own Brother Thaddeus to remind us why we are gathered here today. Brother Thaddeus?"

Conrad looked to the abbot who shook his head. "No, Brother Thaddeus. This is your home, your flock. You should speak."

Conrad dipped his head in acknowledgment, then stepped to the dais beside Robin. He bowed, then pushed his coif from his head. Anyone who didn't already know would have only to look at the two red-headed men to discern the familial relationship.

"Merry Christmas indeed. Thank you, King Bewilliam and you, Father," Conrad said with a nod to his abbot. "Without either of you we would not be together here today." He raised his eyes to the ceiling. "But above all, thank you, Lord.

"Getting to this place was a journey both for me and for our King. Often we were uncertain about our destination and even when we thought we knew where we were bound there never was any guarantee that we would reach our goal. Many times we were met with challenges and opposition that caused us to despair. We were tempted to give up. Yet we had faith and our faith kept us moving forward even in the face of obstacles and doubts.

"Such was the journey of the Wise Men who traveled far to honor and worship their new Lord. They left the comfort of their homes knowing not where they were bound, how long the journey would be, what perils they might meet, or what they would find when they arrived. But they trusted in God and had faith in the promise of a better life.

"We can all take a lesson from them. Even when things look their most bleak, we must fix on that shining star of what we know to be right, and good, and just. That will point the way for us through life, embolden us when we are fearful, strengthen us when we are in doubt, guide us when we are indecisive. In your heart you know what is true."

Robin saw many of the guests gazing at Conrad with rapt attention.

"Keep that before you like the Star of Bethlehem and like the Wise Men you too will find that no challenge is too great for people of faith."

"Well said, Brother Thaddeus." Robin clapped and his guests joined in the acclamation. He saw a number of people look at each other, nod soberly, and smile. He had to admit, there wasn't much fault that he could find with the sermon. In retrospect, there had been many a moment when the only thing that had kept him going was a deep-felt conviction that he pursued his destiny.

"We know in our hearts when we have done what's right, what's expected," he said. "We bring honor to ourselves when we have done our duty, when we fulfill the obligations to which we have committed. Great satisfaction comes when we set goals for ourselves and achieve them.

"Still, a little recognition along the way is like a signpost that tells us we are on the right track. Without further ado, we wish to express our gratitude to those who have contributed to the kingdom of the Chalklands' rebirth." From behind the throne, he dragged forth a large red sack. One by one he presented his gifts to his servants, staff, and subjects, calling each by name and thanking them personally for their service.

"We will not keep you from the celebration much longer but we do have one last announcement. We believe you will not mind the delay." As he had some long weeks ago in the castle's smithy Robin said, "Squire Maxwell, kneel before me."

His eyes wide with concern and dismay, Maxwell looked to his right and his left. Around him, his comrades shrugged and shook their heads. With deliberate dignity, the young man went to one knee and then the other. Robin placed one hand on each of Maxwell's cheeks. "You are to be known henceforth as Sir Maxwell, Knight of Bell Castle." He caught Conrad's narrowed eyes and added, "in the name of God."

Maxwell's expression was sober, his eyes red with unshed tears. "Yes, in the name of God, I, Maxwell, do swear my allegiance to King Bewilliam and to Bell Castle."

Robin drew his sword and tapped the flat of his blade to Maxwell's right shoulder, then lifted it over his head and tapped the left.

The assembly cheered and clapped.

Maxwell stood.

From beside his throne, Robin took a belt with a scabbard and buckled it around the lad's waist, then held out a sword. "Your weapon, Sir Maxwell."

The young man's hand trembled slightly as he accepted the sword. He caught his lower lip between his teeth and for several long moments studied his new acquisition, running his hand along the blade and fingering the edge. He looked up at Robin, eyes sparkling.

"Your father crafted it," Robin said. "He's gotten to be quite good at blade-making."

Maxwell swiveled to find his father in the crowd. Leaning on a crutch, Gregory stretched himself tall and smiled. Maxwell thrust his sword high into the air and twisted it, the better to catch the light in its shiny surface and then with a flourish sheathed it. With a bow, he backed away and into the throng to accept handshakes, backslaps, and hugs.

The formal ceremonial portion of the feast concluded, Robin returned to his throne. His ears sought out the bells that would summon guests to their seats and alert servants to bring out trays of food and drink. Instead he heard a feeble fanfare. The chatter hushed and the crowd parted. Robin followed the motion to see a new arrival.

Framed in the great hall entrance stood a tall female figure. Her rose-colored gown was just a little too short for her height and hung only to the tops of her turnout shoes. Her bodice appeared to have been made from a jacket or tabard with the sleeves cut off and laced to nip in at the waist and flare over the hips. Long dark-red tresses flowed to her shoulders from a half crown woven from twigs and decorated with holly berries and silvery spruce needles. She turned her head and said something to the officer at arms. In an uncertain voice he proclaimed, "The Princess Dale?"

Smiling, Princess Dale made her way down the aisle formed by the guests. She stopped at the dais and curtseyed. Lifting her head she said, "Your Majesty." Rouged cheeks and lips glowed unnaturally red against a face that was pale and drawn from days spent recuperating in a darkened room.

"Zachary, you are . . . well?"

"Perhaps you did not hear the herald. Allow me to present myself, Your Majesty: Princess Dale. Thank you for your concern. I am feeble, but recovered enough to dine with the other noble guests at Your Majesty's table."

Robin wondered if he looked as sick as he felt.

Conrad separated himself from the crowd and came to stand at his brother's side. Robin wondered if any of the guests could see how the brothers resembled each other. Perhaps everyone could.

"Peace be with you, Brother Thaddeus," said Zachary.

"And with you," replied Conrad. His expression was neutral but he looked at Robin as if for guidance.

Robin was about to accede thinking it better for Zachary to sit at the king's table than to circulate among the guests and start rumors.

Henry appeared at Zachary's side and bowed. "Perhaps you would do me the honor of having your company," he said.

"Henry, I would indeed," said Zachary with a winsome smile. He turned and looked at Robin who thought there just might be something chastising in his son's eyes. Before Robin could speak Henry propped a hand on his hip and Zachary took his elbow. Bowing, they turned and merged with the crowd.

CHAPTER THIRTY-THREE

Robin stood in the cloister outside the abbey's hall. His pulse pounded so hard he could not hear the water splashing in the fountain.

Daya and her husband, her co-conspirator, had already gathered in the abbot's hall. In a moment, Robin would enter and reiterate his charges against them. He tried not to clench his hand and rumple the papers he held, and hoped his sweaty palm had not smeared the ink.

He forced his chest out, drew in a deep breath, and pushed open the door.

Across the room and facing the door, the judges sat at a long table in sturdy chairs with tall backs, their expressions as severe as their dark unornamented robes. Silvery winter light from a clerestory window in the wall at their back haloed their tonsured heads and pooled on the table.

Two columns of benches stood to the right and left with a single aisle down the middle. A sizeable party sat on the left. From where he stood at the room's entrance Robin saw the backs of a crowned king and queen, helmeted knights, and coifed retainers and servants, some of whom were likely "oath helpers" who would swear that the witnesses told the truth.

Seated on the right, Robin recognized the figures of the advocate Terrowin, Sirs Maxwell and Albert, as well as Quinn the gypsy and servants who had been part of Bell Castle during Queen Daya's reign. Where, he wondered, were Conrad and Zachary?

Upon Robin's entrance, the judges stood and bowed. Alerted to the arrival of a person of importance, the others rose, turned to face the door, and bowed. As they lifted their heads, Robin got his first glimpse of King Ulric. Swarthy and crowned with thick dark hair, he wore an expression that was equal parts anger and irritation as if the proceedings were an annoying petty nuisance. The jewels set in his massive gold crown glittered and when he moved, the nap in his rich purple robe made the fabric appear to undulate.

Daya's face went pale and her eyes wide. The passage of time had not been unkind to her. Robin still found her features beautiful. Her sons had their father's red hair, not her warm brown locks, but they had her fine nose, full lips, and fair complexion. He held her gaze as he strode to the judges' table.

"I, King Bewilliam, present the libel and request judgment," he said. Terrowin could have done this but Robin hoped that as the words left his mouth, the pain would leave his heart along with them. "King Ulric and Queen Daya are guilty of adultery. Queen Daya is also guilty of bigamy and polyandry." He handed the written statements of the charges to the judges and sat beside Terrowin.

From next to Queen Daya, a man stood. Like Terrowin, his cloak bore the advocate's crest. "We acquiesced to appear out of respect for King Bewilliam and the most holy men of Mathus Abbey but we raise an objection to these proceedings by declinatory exception. We do not live within the court's jurisdiction."

The hell she didn't, Robin thought, and the judges concurred with him. "We have studied the matter and we do not agree. For part of the time during which they are accused of having committed the crime, both defendants were in residence at Bell Castle which is in our jurisdiction," said the presiding judge.

"We also raise an objection by dilatory exception. The libel is redundant."

"Not so," said Terrowin. "We accuse the defendants of erring and then continuing in their erring ways."

"Are there any other challenges to these proceedings?"

No one protested that any of the judges were excommunicate which would have been a bold and offensive accusation, nor did either of the defendants claim to be excommunicate themselves. Had Ulric and Daya not appeared in court today, they very likely would have been declared so.

"Do the defendants wish to admit the libel?"

King Ulric glared at Robin and said, "No, we do not."

"In that case, we will continue with the judgment. All the parties will now swear that they have not brought this case to cause trouble. You state that your position is just and that you will not bring false evidence or witnesses to support it. You vow to tell the truth."

The oaths of calumny taken, the judge asked for Robin to produce proof of the accusation.

"State your positions," the judge instructed.

"There are several positions," Terrowin replied, his voice clear and steady, and pronounced the charges stated in the written summary. "Point One, King Ulric and Queen Daya committed adultery at Bell Castle. Point Two, that they continued to commit adultery at Caprock Fortress. Points Three and Four, that Queen Daya committed bigamy and polyandry at Bell Castle and at Caprock Fortress."

The door at the rear of the room creaked open. Robin turned and breathed a sigh of relief to see Conrad and Zachary.

Daya and Ulric blanched and Robin didn't know if it was in reaction to the young men's garb or if the adulterers had believed the two boys to be well and forever banished. Conrad's habit should have come as no surprise as it was Ulric who had exiled him to Mathus Abbey in the first place but Zachary's appearance and costume could not have been expected. Taller and thinner than he had been when Daya last saw him, Zachary was also still marked from his ordeal with the disastrous beauty potion. His mahogany hair curled past his shoulders and across the back of his light floor-length cape that was roomy enough to disguise his changed form. Had Conrad prevailed on his brother to cover his body or had Zachary come to his senses? Whichever was the case, Robin was grateful.

"We will proceed with terms probatory. Are there witnesses?" the presiding judge asked.

"We have statements of proof and testimonies from witnesses." Terrowin said. Ulric looked enraged and Daya worried.

"We have witnesses too," said King Ulric's advocate. "We need produce only two although there are many more who will attest to the truthfulness of what we avow.

"I, King Ulric, and Queen Daya are innocent of all the positions because we believed King Bewilliam to be dead, leaving Queen Daya a widow free to take another husband," stated King Ulric. "We left Bell Castle with all our belongings and servants and have not since returned. Our domain is far away. We had no knowledge that King Bewilliam was alive and had returned to the Chalklands."

Two of the household witnesses who sat beside them attested to the truth of this.

"Even if the Queen believed her husband to be dead, a case could be made that Her Majesty was still not free to remarry," said Terrowin.

Ulric and Daya looked in dismay at their advocate while the judges put their heads together.

Terrowin waited until they had finished conferring and said, "However, even if the Queen did at first believe her husband to be dead, she soon found out that such was not the case. Our witnesses will testify to that." He named the Bell Castle subjects who would swear to what they knew, relayed what Conrad and Zachary had experienced, and then named the Caprock Fortress knights and servants to whom he had spoken personally. "Our witnesses include King Ulric and Queen Daya who admitted to me personally that they were aware King Bewilliam was alive and not dead as many believed but had returned to Bell Castle."

King Ulric and Queen Daya gaped at Terrowin. Perhaps, Robin thought, they finally recognized the voice as that of one of the gypsies who had performed for them at Caprock Fortress.

Like some verbal chess match there followed move and countermove as the two opposing advocates strived to discredit the veracity of the witnesses while oath-takers swore to the accuracy of the testimony. When it came time for the defendants' advocate to challenge the truthfulness of Robin's witnesses—the Queen's sons, Caprock Fortress's own knights, Queen, and King—he was silent. Of course he was, Robin thought. To do so would have been to call them all liars.

With that, all witnesses had been produced and contravened. The depositions were read. One of the judges sealed a copy of the libel and gave it to King Ulric.

"We will withdraw to consider the positions and the testimonies of witnesses and return a judgment," said the judge. With that, they filed out.

Robin could not have imagined a weightier silence than the one that filled the room. King Ulric did not speak but simply glared at Daya who cowered and avoided looking at either of the men she had called "husband." Ulric's advocate busied himself with his notes and would not raise his head. The Caprock Fortress servants and knights whose honesty had been cast into doubt stared into their laps.

Conrad sat with his eyes closed, his hands folded in prayer. Robin wondered what he prayed for but dared not ask.

Staring at his mother, Zachary looked so pale and dazed that Robin wondered if he was having a relapse.

Robin turned to Terrowin. The advocate sat with his hands folded on his notes and smiled. Robin caught his eye and mouthed, "Now what?"

"We wait," Terrowin whispered.

"How long?"

"As long as it takes."

And so they waited. Robin raised his eyes to the clerestory windows and watched as the clouds scudded by and the light waxed and waned.

When the door creaked opened, the room's occupants jumped as if startled awake.

The judges retook their seats at the table. The presiding judge stood. "We have considered all the evidence and testimonies and here are our findings. King Ulric, you are guilty of adultery. You will perform penance, pay fines, and pay all the court costs, including all those born by the plaintiff."

Which, Robin thought, was a hefty sum.

Ulric balled his fist and pounded his knee. His advocate shook his head and gave Ulric a cautionary glance.

"Queen Daya, much as we wish we could simply give you a penance, your sins are most grievous. You are hereby exiled from the Chalklands and excommunicated."

Daya gasped and sank against Ulric, who slid out from under her and let her collapse on the bench.

"Further, Queen Daya, since you have shown so little regard for it, your marriage to King Bewilliam is annulled. Neither Your Highness nor Your progeny nor heirs shall have any claim to any part of the Kingdom of the Chalklands, now or ever."

Ulric glowered.

"King Bewilliam, as guilty as Her Majesty is, for the sake of her soul and yours, we encourage Your Highness to forgive in your heart. However yes, your marriage to Queen Daya is found null and void."

Daya bit her lower lip and looked fearfully at King Ulric who turned his back to her.

CHAPTER THIRTY-FOUR

Though they followed the same route that they had taken from Bell Castle to Mathus Abbey, the return trip seemed somehow longer. Perhaps it was because in his eagerness to get the trial underway, Robin had set a faster pace. Or maybe it was because now he, Zachary, and Conrad rode in silence, each preoccupied with the proceedings and the judgment.

Robin had expected the sentence to give him a feeling of conclusion: all questions answered, all obligations met, balance restored, and slates wiped clean. He would return to Bell Castle refreshed, renewed, ready to start the rest of his life.

But he wasn't. Terrowin had been wrong. The proceeding had settled nothing, the sentences though harsh didn't abate Robin's anger or salve his wounds. No fine or penance could cause Ulric the pain Robin had endured. The judges had failed to recognize the depth of Robin's suffering. He was angry even with Terrowin for allowing him to believe that the trial would provide closure.

I should have listened to my knights, Robin thought. We should have attacked Caprock Fortress. Just killed every living soul, burned the place to the ground.

He pictured the walls crumbling, the towers crashing, bodies littering the inner ward, blood deluging the ditches. He saw

Ulric's decapitated body slumped on the throne, his head rolling down the steps of his king's dais.

He pictured Daya—"

Robin let out a long sigh as his fury fizzled. More than revenge he had wanted answers. He still didn't know why Daya had betrayed him and now he would never know.

His mount, Hope, plodded along the track with little guidance from Robin who no longer saw the surrounding landscape or heard the crows caw or felt the wind. As if hung on a gallery wall, pictures from his marriage ranged before his eyes. In his mind he strolled through the gallery from one picture to the next, stopped and studied each one, searching for a clue as to when or how he had failed as a husband.

"I loved my wife. I worked hard to make a good life for us both," he protested to an unseen accuser. "If there was an opportunity to provide more for my Queen, I did not flinch."

The Queen had never wanted for food, clothing, or shelter but Robin knew he had contributed more to their life together than security and material comfort. Moments of joy and delight were evident in every painting in the gallery. In this one of their first meeting, a beautiful young woman seated at the banquet table peers around her tablemates to steal a glance at a red-headed young king. In this next one, the young woman stands with her lips parted, breathless with happiness at a proposal of marriage. In this painting, a smiling young couple picnicking in a glade shares affectionate gazes.

Another painting shows the young couple standing at the altar in a chapel. The new bride's face glows brighter than the chapel's candles. Vivid colors enliven a painting of a gala wedding feast; the radiant bliss of the newlyweds creating a veritable halo around them.

Other paintings depict state events and royal caravans in which the king and queen sit or stand side-by-side, confident and content.

Touching are the paintings of the Queen pregnant, then gazing with love at an infant in her arms. In others, handsome young boys at study and play dominate the foreground but in the background stand two parents, affection and pride showing in their faces.

In a formal portrait, the King, Queen, and two Princes all meet the eyes of the onlooker, their faces serene, their postures relaxed and self-assured.

Where in this gallery, Robin wondered, is the painting that shows a mistreated Queen, a neglected Queen, an unhappy Queen? If he could find that painting, he could identify when, how, and maybe why the Queen had become discontented. He could name the cause of her dissatisfaction and discover how he was to blame.

Search as he might he could not ferret out what he had done to provoke the Queen's infidelity. He had learned nothing from the dissolution of his marriage that would help him to be a better mate in the future.

A better mate. Robin shook his head. That simply wasn't going to be a problem. The annulment meant that he could remarry but what chance was there that it would be any more successful? He would never risk his heart again.

The images from Robin's past seemed clear enough. Would that he could move on to another gallery, one that would show his future just as plainly.

He lifted his head, regarded the road, and followed it to the horizon. In the distance the Bell Castle's keep sketched a tall column against the sky. Robin visualized the bailey greening in spring weather, the steamy kitchen crowded with busy cooks, the smoky smithy ablaze with industry, the great hall teeming with contented subjects.

Where in these scenes did Conrad in his habit and Zachary in his gowns fit?

Robin frowned. They were his heirs. Daya's betrayal had left them believing that their status as heirs to the kingdom of the Chalklands invalid, that they would have to set some other life's course. In asserting Robin's sovereignty and revoking any claim Daya and Ulric might have made to the contrary, the verdict had reestablished his sons' succession.

The kingdom was their destiny, just as it had been his. They had been born to rule, as he had. They would see that now. Not just see it, embrace it. He, King Bewilliam, would show them the way.

The towers and curtain walls of the castle came into view. Robin felt his chest swell with pride, his heart beat faster with anticipation, and his mouth tug in a smile. He straightened in the saddle and urged Hope forward.

ABOUT THE AUTHOR

Devorah Fox has written for television, radio, magazines, newspapers, and the Internet and is the author of *The Lost King*, Book One in *The Bewildering Adventures of King Bewilliam* series. Publisher and editor of the *BUMPERTOBUMPER®* books for commercial motor vehicle drivers, she has branched out into developing smartphone apps including the *Easy CDL* apps for the iPhone and iPad. Born in Brooklyn, New York, she now lives in The Barefoot Palace in Port Aransas on the Texas Gulf Coast where she writes the "Dee-Scoveries" blog at http://devorahfox.com.

Connect online:
Email: devorahfox@aol.com
Facebook: http://facebook.com/devorahfox
Twitter: @devorah_fox
Smashwords:
https://www.smashwords.com/profile/view/mbapub.

A melody, strange, yet familiar, whispered in her thoughts. Tangled with her misgivings.

Had she done the right thing? She had been exposed, spotted. That much she knew.

Aya Rose rubbed her temple, brushed her hair back. Didn't matter now. No time for regrets. She'd made the decision, found the information, and had Maury deliver. Trip walking out of the courthouse made the sacrifice worth the effort.

Scrambled vocals twisted with a tune just shy of awareness. Something new...but melancholy. She wished she had the time to write it down. Without pen and paper, the words and notes would continue to be elusive and out of reach. No time now, though in her mind, an acoustic guitar strummed, soft percussion accompanied the masculine words, amplified by the stillness of the night. Aya stopped, tilted her head, and glanced up to the stars above. If only she had her notebook at hand, she'd take the moment. But if it were worthwhile, it'd be there later. Maybe.